AN AMERICAN IN DUKE'S CLOTHING

UNLIKELY MATCH SERIES

MINDY BURBIDGE STRUNK

ACKNOWLEDGMENTS

This book has been a work of love for almost seven years. It is the first story I ever put to paper and has undergone many transformations over the years. I would be remiss if I did not thank my amazing husband. He has supported me all the way. When I've thrown up my hands in defeat, he was there to encourage me to continue. He cheered for me every time I've said I was finished with it, only to discover it wasn't ready yet. I truly could not have done this without him.

To my five great boys who suffered for months with sub-par dinners and picking clothes out of the basket.

Thanks to my many beta readers- Sally Britton Treanor, Jen Johnson, Alyssa Crandall, Jamie Moesser, Kim Ball, Cheryl Johansen, and Patti Knowlton.

To my writers first group- Shantal Sessions, Heidi Thornock, and Heidi Wilde. You guys waded through a lot on this one. Thanks for helping me learn some basics. My Regency Chicks- Michelle Pennington, Jen Geigle Johnson, Heidi Kimball and Sara

Cardon. Thank you for helping me flush out the important parts and calling me out when I tried to fudge over non-historically accurate details.

And thanks to all my readers. Without you, these stories would just stay on my computer. Thanks for all of your support!

CHAPTER 1

LIVERPOOL- LATE SEPTEMBER 1816

"We are clearly not in Pennsylvania anymore." Tad Wentworth rested his elbows on the ship's railing, stretching his shoulders, shaking out the tension lying under the surface. The Liverpool docks looked similar to those of New York and New Orleans. He suspected it was his unique circumstances rather than the location, which intensified his anxiety. Closing his eyes, he tried to calm his breathing. There is nothing to worry about. The phrase went through his mind for the millionth time. It did nothing to relieve his doubts because he knew there was everything to worry about. So many people would be relying on him, their very livelihoods at stake.

The gangplank lowered—people jostled and elbows flew as everyone tried to make their way to the docks below. A large cathedral rose in the distance, its spire rising heavenward, while a smaller church stood next to the dock, dwarfed in comparison. This smaller church brought on a moment of sentimentality for Tad, taking him back to the parish church in Philadelphia. Both were rather simple in design and decoration. Their similarities brought a sense of peace.

The salty breeze blowing through the canals mingled with the stench of rotting fish, tar, and filth from both animal and human, forcing him to cover his mouth and nose with his handkerchief. But the same gust also calmed him, as if it blew away some of the burden weighing him down.

People stood below shoulder to shoulder, pushing and shoving to make their way through the crowds. Crying babes, bellowing animals, and curses flowing from men's lips all converging together to create pandemonium. Releasing a heavy sigh, he ran his fingers through his hair. The stress mounting again. *Did I leave home for this?* He looked to the little church, trying to find the tranquility he'd felt only moments ago.

"Have you regained your senses and decided to return to Pennsylvania?" Dawson leaned on the railing next to him.

Tad removed the cloth from his nose, trying to breathe through his mouth. Cocking a brow at this friend, Tad shook his head. "You have known me since I was three years old. Have you ever seen me quit before a task was completed?" Waving to encompass the chaos around them, he continued. "Besides, the smell is not so bad...once you get used to it." Tears formed in his eyes. Looking at his companion, Tad's lips began to quiver at Dawson's creased brow and half-closed eyes. A laugh pushed its way out. "You are right, the smell is terrible, but we will be away from the docks soon enough."

"You have noticed the crowd down there, have you not?" Dawson sighed, shaking his head in agitation. "I believe you may be too optimistic."

Tad picked up his trunk and bag, joining the throngs on the gangplank, slowly moving toward the chaos below. "Come, Dawson. My uncle's summons did say not to 'dilly-dally.'"

Dawson trudged alongside him. The two began to shoulder and nudge their way through the mass of people. "If you were not so adamant about family honor, we would not be in this mess," Dawson shouted over the crowd.

"But we are in this mess, Dawson, so make the best of it." Tad could barely make out his own words over the clamor surrounding them. "Besides..."

A sudden blow struck him in the eye, pushing him into Dawson. Barely a breath had been taken before a man came hurling at him, laying them both flat on the ground. He grabbed at a mop of hair, pulling it away from him, his brain slowly registered the insults spewing from the attacker's lips.

"You dirty Yank. How dare you show your face on our shores?" A blow landed on Tad's lip. He felt the skin split and the metallic taste of blood filled his mouth. The ache moved up his cheek, making it difficult to decipher where one pain ended and another began.

Tad brought his knee up hard, catching the man off guard, and sent him rolling off. Tad pushed himself up into a crouch. His vision closed in as one eye began to swell shut. His legs wobbled beneath him.

Dawson landed on top of the man with a loud and primal bellow and Tad finally took a breath. Dawson wrapped his arms around the attacker, pushing him back to the ground and striking him repeatedly.

With pain burning in his ribs, Tad hauled himself to his feet, gasping for breath. He looked around frantically for any other potential threats. Unsure what had prompted the attack, he was leery of anyone in close proximity. The crowd around them had moved back, giving room to the brawlers. The people looked on, some bobbing in time to the fight playing out before them. Others moved away, keeping a tight hold of their possessions. It appeared no one else intended to join the skirmish.

Shifting his attention to Tad, the thug shoved Dawson to the side. In a flash, the ruffian's fist flew, but unlike the first time, the punch was anticipated and dodged. Instead, Tad landed one of his own sending the man stumbling into Dawson's waiting arms.

"Break it up." Through his open eye, Tad could see a club glinting in the sunlight, slapping up and down in a man's hand. The watchman stood alert and ready. He was not a large man when compared to Tad or Dawson, but the confident and steely set of his gaze proved intimidating. Tad motioned to the watchman with a flick of his head. Dawson released the man and moved slowly to Tad's side. The attacker jerked away, his fists clenching over and over.

"What seems to be the problem here, gentleman?" There was a hardness in the man's voice.

Tad tentatively stepped forward, hands raised in front of him, palms out. Licking the blood dribbling from his lip, he pushed his anger down; now was not the time for reaction. Before he could utter a word, the brute lunged for another attack.

"He's a dirty yank. I recognize his kind from the war."

The watchman was quicker and reached a hand out, grabbing the man by the collar, but it didn't stop the kicks and insults.

"Control yourself, Connell. Can we not have one day without an incident?" Shaking his captive, the watchman looked from Tad to Dawson with raised brows. "As you can tell, he has a problem with Americans."

Tad took a deep breath, wincing in pain. Speaking flawless King's English, he shrugged. "I figured as much after the second or third punch, sir."

The guard narrowed his gaze at Connell, before turning it

back on them. "Can you tell me what happened?" Suspicion creased his face.

"We were making our way through the crowd when out of nowhere I was struck by this man." Tad motioned with his head to the burly fellow.

Connell closed his gaping mouth several times before shaking his head adamantly. "He didn't sound like no gentleman then."

Tad smiled as if he were talking to a dim-witted child. "The man may have overheard my friend here. We have returned from the war and he finds humor in mocking the American's vulgar tongue." Tad felt Dawson stiffen, knowing his friend in no way wanted to be identified as an Englishman.

Keeping a firm hold on the ruffian, the watchman looked at Tad with appraising eyes. "And whom might you be?"

Tad stuck out his hand, pasting a wide smile on his face. "My name is Thaddeus Wentworth. I have come home at the request of my uncle, the Duke of Shearsby." From the stories his father had told, his uncle's title should help in getting them out of this spot.

The watchman's eyes widened to the size of saucers. "I have heard of His Grace. He is much respected. I hope this man has not caused any permanent harm." Eyes darted back and forth between Tad and Dawson.

Tad smiled slightly until the pain wiped it away. Even if the man thought his uncle the worst kind of scoundrel, it was not as if he would dare give voice to the thoughts. Perhaps there were some benefits to this stifling society.

Clutching the prisoner a little tighter, even though his fight was all but gone, the watchman gave a slight nod. "I will see he is punished for his actions, sir."

"I shall leave him to you." There was an edge to Tad's voice.

He turned to shoulder his trunk, the action nearly bringing him to his knees. Breathing heavily, he tried to smile but it came out as more of a grimace. "Perhaps, there is a punishment that might be beneficial to us both. My uncle was to send a man to meet us, but he does not seem to be here, yet. And it would seem my friend and I are in no shape to carry these trunks, because of Mr. Connell. He is a large man. If he would agree to carry them for us, I believe his sentence would be served. Is that acceptable Mr...?" Tad quirked a brow in question. Gads, even his eyebrows hurt.

The watchman nodded his head vigorously. "The name is Turner, sir." He sketched a brief bow. "Capital idea and no doubt better than he deserves." Mr. Turner leveled a glare at Connell. Then turning his gaze on Tad and Dawson, he cringed. "I am glad I arrived before he inflicted more harm."

"Mr. Turner, would you happen to know the best route to the Mariners Compass? My uncle's man will meet us there to escort us to Morley Park."

"I can do better and take you there myself. Follow me, sir."

True to his word, Mr. Turner led them directly to the inn. Connell stumbled along behind, weighted down with the load of both men's trunks.

Once Mr. Turner and his prisoner had departed, Dawson leaned against the wall, scrutinizing every inch of Tad's face. The longer he stared, the deeper his frown grew. Tad straightened, squaring his shoulders.

"Your mother was right, you know," Dawson growled.

Tad's shoulders dropped back down. He was tired and it hurt like the devil to keep his back ramrod straight. He sighed. "About what, precisely?"

"She said you should speak as your father taught you, for your own protection. You thought she was being a mother hen, but she knew of what she spoke." He looked around suspiciously. "It would seem our kind is not well-received here."

Tad shrugged. "It was one man, Dawson. Do you really think the entire country will act so irrationally?" He tried to grin when he felt his lip split again. "I believe we handled the situation very well."

Dawson shook his head.

Pushing through the door of the inn, Tad's eyes slowly adjusted to the dim interior.

The proprietor narrowed his gaze at them. "What can I help you men with?"

Tad licked his throbbing lip, only now realizing how swollen it was.

Dawson leaned in. "I can barely understand you. Perhaps it is best if I do the talking. We can test your theory here." Dawson smirked before he moved to the counter, addressing the proprietor. "We are in need of some rooms for the night."

"Well, you won't find them here. I don't provide lodging to Americans." The man's lip curled in disgust.

Sighing deeply, Tad pressed his lips together hoping to take some of the swelling down. He spoke as clearly as possible, without a hint of his American origins. "Excuse me, sir. This man is to be a guest at my family's estate. I expected him to be treated better."

The proprietor stepped back in surprise, stumbling over his words. "Excuse me, sir. I, er...that is to say, I did not realize you were a..." His face turned several shades of red as he continued to bluster. Seeing no reason to save him from his embarrassment yet, Tad let him continue until he finally seemed to regain his wits. "How many rooms do you require, Mr....."

"Mr. Thaddeus Wentworth. Two would do us very well. We are in need of some rest."

The innkeeper raised a brow. "Wentworth, you say? I believe I have..." He shuffled papers beneath the counter before standing

7

up and thrusting a folded paper at Tad. "This letter has been here for nigh on half a year."

Tad looked at the paper, noting the layer of dust, his name scrawled across the front in his uncle's hand. It seemed unlikely anyone would be meeting them after all. They would need to hire a carriage and servant to see to the trunks for the remainder of the trip to Morley Park. Something else to add to his list of things needing his attention. A key dangling in his peripheral vision drew his attention away from the missive.

Dawson reached out and grabbed it, a sour expression on his face.

"Up the stairs and to the end of the hall, sir." The man cast a nervous glance in Dawson's direction as they both gingerly shouldered their trunks.

Tad cracked the wax seal on the letter. Hopefully, it would give him some information to help settle his anxiety. His eyes scanned the words as they trudged up the steps. Stopping halfway up he leaned against the wall while he reread the letter. The pain from the attack ceased as the twisting of his stomach pushed to the front. This could not be happening. Did he not have enough to worry about without adding this to the mix? His trunk clattered to the stair in front of him, bringing Dawson to an abrupt stop at the top. "What the devil?"

"What the devil, indeed." Tad looked at his friend. "The old man has negotiated a marriage for me. I am engaged."

CHAPTER 2

KIDSGROVE, CHESHIRE

Violet Allen slowed the gig as she came to the giant willow. She had been passing this tree in her travels for as long as she could remember. The tree was tall—taller than many of the tenant homes on their estate. Its branches fell all the way to the ground, creating a large space beneath, spacious enough for grown adults to stand at full height. Located a short distance down the road from her home, on the way to the village, it held many happy memories. After her mother's death, these branches hid her while she cried. It had been a cove for the pirate ship she captained as a child and a wild jungle waiting to be explored. Today though, she approached it with trepidation, unsure what she would find within.

Parting the limbs, she saw Roger McPhail. He did not look altogether different from the boy who left all those years ago. Could the rumors about him be true? He did not look to be the savage the town's people claimed. Perhaps a bit older, but not markedly changed, which set her slightly at ease. She and Becky, her lady's maid, stepped under the canopy. Violet moved toward the man, while Becky moved to the farthest edge of the branches, hunching as if to make herself invisible.

"Hullo, Violet. I had hoped you would come. You look even lovelier than I remember." He straightened his back, towering over her.

Mr. McPhail smiled as she approached, memories and feelings came flooding back. This was the man on which she had pinned all her hopes of marriage and family. Even after all his years away, hope still bubbled inside.

"Thank you." She smiled politely. "I must admit, you look very much the same." Upon closer scrutiny, she realized he had changed in at least one way. His face was smiling, but his eyes held a vacantness which was new. As a youth, they had been animated and lively.

The change made her wary. A scar starting at his ear and running along his jawline caught her attention, something she had not noticed until he turned to face her head on.

"I thought we were to meet alone." He motioned with his head in the direction of Becky's stooped form.

"Using the under-gardener to pass me your note was far from proper, Mr. McPhail. Becky is here to see propriety is not an issue." Violet smiled up at him, hoping he would understand the difference in their current situation.

"I am to be Mr. McPhail, am I?" His nostrils flared slightly, causing the knot in her stomach to tighten. As a child he had been kind, never raising his voice nor his hand. She was unsure of this different man before her. "I thought we were past the formalities, *Miss Violet*." Contempt colored his voice.

"It has been many years, sir. I have come to an age, where meeting with a man alone would surely cause a scandal. I am sure we have both changed. The formality is appropriate until we have gotten to know each other again." Violet noticed the slight tremor in her voice but hoped he had not.

"So I am to court you, again, am I? You made promises to me before I left. What is to become of them?" His voice was becoming terse and clipped.

"Do you oppose the idea of courting me? Our courtship was never official, nor public knowledge." Violet took a small, involuntary step backward. "As for promises...you made several as well. What of them?" She could not keep the hurt from ringing in her voice. "You have been gone for three years, Mr. McPhail. I only received three letters from you and none in the last year. What was I to expect?" She spoke with a sternness she did not feel.

He stepped forward, closing the distance Violet suddenly craved. "You were supposed to expect I would come home and we would marry, as we planned. It is not always easy to write from a battlefield, Violet. I thought you understood." He reached out to grab her arm, but she stepped out of his reach.

His eyes narrowed.

"For the time being, I would prefer we not use Christian names."

He took in a deep breath, releasing it on a growl.

Raising her chin, Violet pressed on, pushing her growing fear down. "Am I to assume you made your fortune? Have you purchased the estate with a music room and pianoforte you promised?" Violet balled her fists at her side, trying to keep her emotions in check. This meeting was not going the way she dreamed.

"I do not have all of the money, yet. But I will. I have some business dealings, they should get me the blunt soon enough." His smile curled into a sneer. "Really, Violet. I never took you for a fortune hunter."

"Miss Violet," she nearly shouted, stomping her foot in agitation. "I am not a fortune hunter, Mr. McPhail, I am a realist. And the reality is my father's consent is doubtful. He set his sights for me higher than the fourth son of a baronet. The estate would not guarantee his blessing, but without it, I am certain he will refuse."

Mr. McPhail's face suddenly relaxed into a soft smile. "I'm sorry, Violet...Miss Violet. I did not mean to get angry with you. Since the war, I haven't been quite myself. But I know things will go back to the way they were...before I left. You fill the emptiness. And I believe I did the same for you once."

Violet looked into his eyes. His face had calmed, but his eyes still remained cold. She softened her voice to match his. "I understand you want things to be the way they were. But we will never be exactly the same. Things have changed. We need time to become friends again."

Taking hold of her hand, he pleaded. "Let me speak with your father. I am sure I can persuade him to our cause. We could live quite comfortably on the blunt I have coming and your dowry."

Violet flinched, pulling her hand free. He had never made mention of her dowry in the past. She had believed he did not care about it—believed he loved her, not her money. Another thing she had been mistaken about.

"No." Violet did not mean to shout, but panic drove her words. She tried to calm herself until she could leave. "Please do not speak to my father. Not yet. It is not the right time. He is...away on business." The statement was not exactly true, but on this occasion, she did not regret the bouncer. "We need to give it time."

"Time?" he nearly yelled. "More time? It has been three years. What are you afraid of, Violet? Is it my scar you find frightening?"

"No." Her voice rose to match his. "I care nothing about your scar. I am trying to get a glimpse as to the man you have become." Violet could not keep herself from looking in his eyes. The warning she saw there made her voice hitch. "There have been rumors circulating the village since your return. I did not want to believe them. But...but you are making it difficult for me not to consider them, at least in part."

Mr. McPhail stepped toward her again. "And what are these rumors?" he growled.

"Just tales from the war." Her legs began to shake beneath her skirts. "It would not be proper for a lady to repeat them. For now, I believe it is time for me to return home. Good day, Mr. McPhail."

His voice calmed again. "We do not need your father's approval, Violet. We talked once before about eloping. I see no reason why we do not follow through with that plan. I want to marry you." He moved to block her exit. "And let's be honest. Do you really believe anyone else does?"

Violet's head snapped back. She looked to Becky still cowering against the far side of the canopy, hoping for help, but seeing none forthcoming.

His chuckle was deep and menacing. "Or have you forgotten you are nothing more than a by-blow from your mother's little tryst? No gentleman will have you, but I am still willing to marry you. Me. The fourth son of a baronet. I am doing you a favor."

She stepped forward, slapping him across the face in one swift motion. "Never speak of my mother again. We are through here." Violet turned on her heel but was yanked back to face him.

"I will say when we are done, Dragon. You will not cry-off." Even through her spencer, she could feel his fingers dig into her arm. As she tried to pull free, they tightened even more. When a small cry of pain passed her lips, his eyes registered joy and even pleasure. He pushed her up against the tree trunk, leaning close into her. His breath coming hard against her face. She could smell the spirits. The odor made her stomach roil.

"Unhand me, you..."

Mr. McPhail moved one hand to her throat, squeezing until

she could feel her own heartbeat under his fingers. Her breathing became more difficult.

"Stop. You are hurting her." Becky lunged forward but was sent to the ground with a flick of his hand.

Violet looked for Becky but was unable to see her without moving her head. With eyes wide, she searched Mr. McPhail's face for any sign of her former friend and confidante. When she found none, she realized the very true possibility that he was going to kill her.

Her vision filled with pops of light, and then darkness began to fold in from the sides. He released her, letting her fall to the ground. Her huge gulps did not satisfy her need for air.

"You are not worth the trouble. I am done with you." He pushed through the weeping branches, disappearing from sight.

Becky rushed to her side. "Can you breathe, miss?"

Violet nodded her head, her shaking hands gently caressing the skin where his fingers had been. Her voice came out in a raspy whisper. "I will be well, Becky. If you would please help me to the gig, we will return to the house."

CHAPTER 3

A stride a chestnut colored mount, Tad breathed in
deeply, grunting at the pain it caused. Tad and Dawson
were taking a slower pace due to their injuries, but the
pain was ever present. He was grateful they had decided to send
their trunks on the coach but opted for horseback for themselves.
The ruts in the road would surely have been unpleasant and he
would have missed seeing so much of the countryside.

Taking up the reins in one hand, he placed his other lightly on
his thigh, trying to sit taller in the saddle and thus take some pressure off his ribs. He let his mind wander to the letter in his pocket.
Tad had read the note no less than fifty times—the words seared on
his brain.

Nephew,

*Send word upon your arrival in Liverpool. Make haste in
setting out for Morley Park. There is much preparation to finalize
for your upcoming nuptials. I have taken the liberty to secure you a
match.*

Safe travels,

Shearsby P.R.

He could scarcely believe his uncle had arranged a marriage for him. From everything he knew of the man, he was arrogant, proud and at times even mean-spirited. But to be so high handed as to arrange an engagement before Tad had even arrived? He sighed. He did not know his uncle well enough to know if he would or would not do such a thing. The thought left him feeling unsettled and restless.

A smirk graced Dawson's usually gruff face.

"What do you find of such humor, this afternoon, Dawson?"

Dawson's face split into a full-faced grin and a chuckle escaped. "You."

Tad's brow furrowed slightly. "And what have I done to inspire such glee?"

Dawson could not seem to contain his delight. "This whole situation. Not only has your uncle summoned you to *this* country, but now you find he has even found you a wife. Every time I think upon it, I cannot help but grin." His smile widened. "What type of wife do you think the old man has shackled you to, eh Tad?"

The breakfast they had eaten this morning began to curdle in Tad's stomach. Changing the subject, he turned to his traveling companion. "Tell me, Dawson, how do you find England? Is it as terrible as you imagined?"

The grin dropped from the man's face. Looking about, he replied. "I haven't seen anything to impress me. My opinion is unchanged."

The hills surrounding them were covered in golden grass, swaying gently in the breeze. Low lying hedgerows divided the area into half a dozen different sections. Cattle speckled two of the pastures with blacks and browns, while sheep grazed in the others. The sight could have been a painting it was so beautiful. "You do not find this to your liking?"

Dawson turned enough for Tad to see his arched brow. He made an exaggerated point of looking around. "I see nothing grander than I have seen before...in Pennsylvania."

Tad gave a restrained sigh. "If you find this all so distasteful, why did you agree to accompany me on this journey? I will gladly pay your passage back if that is what you desire."

Shaking his head in frustration, Dawson slumped in his saddle. "Return to what? You know I have nothing there. My father saw to that when he gambled it all away. With one turn of a card, he changed my life." He closed his eyes and rubbed angrily at them with his palms. "If I must serve as a secretary," the word was said with great disdain, "then so be it, but I shall not be forced to like it here."

Frustration laced Tad's voice. "Are you never going to give it a chance? Are you determined to be miserable for the rest of your life?"

Dawson's eyes jerked up to meet his. "Give it a chance? I don't understand why you are in such a hurry to love this place and forget your roots. What of your family?" Dawson waved his hand wildly in the air.

Shaking his head, Tad leaned back slightly in the saddle and winced. "You are muttonheaded. Don't you understand? This *is* where my roots are. Pennsylvania has been home to my family for less than thirty years. In Leicestershire, however, we can trace the Wentworth name back over 500 years. As much as it pained me when I received the letter from my uncle, the reality is, this is my family home. Here is where my roots started." Even though he said the words, he still found it difficult to call this place home. His features grew hard. "As for forgetting about my family in Pennsylvania? They are never far from my thoughts. Don't ever make that assumption again."

Dawson leveled a glare at him. "And there it is. Your Duke

look. I must say, Wentworth, you are equal to the task. I shouldn't have doubted you."

Tad clenched the reins tightly in his fists. His horse took several stutter steps. Gritting his teeth, Tad loosened his hold. This man was his best friend, but at times he was infuriating. On the verge of screaming at him, Tad took a few deep breaths. "This is our home now. If you do intend to stay, I suggest you find a way to come to terms with it."

Dawson looked up, anger radiating from him. "How can you forgive them so easily? Do you not remember what they did to us during the war? I can never forget. I have the marks on my back to remind me." His eyes dropped to his hands. Flicking the reins, he increased his pace and moved ahead.

Tad did not have a ready response. It all boiled down to the blasted war. Dawson's reaction was understandable. He had not been treated as well as Tad. Pushing his horse, Tad pulled beside Dawson again. "I have not forgotten. I do not believe it is possible to forget being impressed into a foreign navy. But I have forgiven. I had to, it was killing me." He ran his fingers through his hair. "It takes time, Dugray."

Dawson glared at the use of his Christian name but then nodded, not slowing his pace in the least.

Hoofs beating the dirt sounded in the distance. Quickly, the horse and rider came into sight, racing past them in a cloud of dust. Tad pulled his gelding to a stop next to Dawson.

"What the blazes?" Tad looked around them, assessing if there was danger lurking about.

Dawson shrugged. "Perhaps he was giving the horse his head?"

"Whatever he was doing, it appears he was alone." Tad clicked his tongue and pressed his heels into the horse's flanks, setting him in motion again. Dawson followed suit, the silence descending upon them.

The dust had barely settled when Tad spied a small carriage sitting to the side of the road by a large willow tree. As they approached, he could see the carriage was empty. Pulling his horse to a stop, Tad led the animal in a tight circle but saw no one.

Then he saw a movement in the weeping branches. Pulling the horse around, Tad turned. A hand slowly parted the low hanging branches. Two women stepped out from beneath the canopy. A lady and her maid, if he guessed correctly. The maid had her arm about the lady, offering support. At the sight, Tad leaped from his horse, moving to the women's sides in four long strides.

"Begging your pardon, miss. Are you injured? May I offer some assistance?" He looked between the two, but his words were directed to the young lady.

They both appeared injured. The maid's cheek was red and swollen. The lady showed no obvious signs of injury but was leaning heavily on the girl. The lady's eyes darted between him and Dawson, fear evident in her eyes.

Tad reached a hand forward to help steady her, but the companion moved between them, arms stretched out to her sides, blocking his attempts.

"Be off with you." She shouted, her hands shaking as she balled them into fists. As fierce as she looked, he could hear the tremor in her voice.

Hands raised in front of him, Tad stepped back several paces. Holding very still, afraid he would send the women scampering away, he looked them both over. Something unpleasant had obviously happened to them, for such a reaction to be warranted. He could understand hesitation or apprehension, but the body shaking fear they were exhibiting seemed unusual.

The girl was small and thin. Her light ginger colored hair was coiled into a tight knot at the back of her head.

Tad shifted ever so slightly to his right, trying to catch a better view of the lady behind.

Her head was held high, but her breathing was heavy. Even from his distance, he could see her hands shaking. The gown she wore was made of a light, thin fabric printed with small purple flowers. Her neck craned in a very delicate way as if she were trying to discern his motives without fully looking at him. She wore a shawl tucked about her upper arms and shoulders, which succeeded in drawing attention to her slender frame.

Dawson dismounted and came to stand beside him. The women shuffled back a few steps, the willow branches now at their backs.

Tad talked in quiet tones, as he did when breaking a wild horse. "I apologize for frightening you. That was not my intention." Slowly he dropped his hands to his sides. "You appear to be hurt, miss. Will you let me see you home? We saw a gentleman riding like the devil himself was chasing him. Is he fetching the doctor?"

The servant snorted in derision. "Hardly. He—"

She was cut off by a hand on her shoulder. "Becky, no."

Becky turned her head, casting her gaze quickly at the lady behind her. The girl narrowed her eyes at Tad. "You sound funny. Be you from London?"

Tad sighed, clenching his teeth. After the beating he had received in Liverpool, he had vowed never to speak with his American tongue. Now here he was not two days later, in trouble for it again. He smiled, hoping he looked friendly. "Yes, yes." He tilted his head again, trying to catch a glimpse of the young lady.

Her eyes focused on his face. "I do not believe the man is fetching anyone, sir."

Ah, she spoke. When their eyes met, his heart thumped quickly in his chest.

Her gaze flicked to Dawson, studying him for a moment. She

AN AMERICAN IN DUKE'S CLOTHING

moved out from behind the servant, straightening herself up to her full height. Tad smiled inwardly. This lady had some tenacity. He could see her hands shaking, yet she seemed determined to appear unaffected.

He took a tentative step forward and then another. Her eyes widened at the last step, causing him to halt his forward progression. Red marks covered her neck. Furrowing his brow, he leaned forward slightly, checking his suspicions. A single mark marred one side, while the other showed four distinct discolorations of her skin. A sudden anger reared up inside him. Without thinking he moved quickly to her. Gently cupping her chin in his hand, he tilted her head to one side and then the next. She flinched, stepping out of his reach.

He nodded his head at her, his voice full of anger. "Who did this to you?" Her eyes widened even more.

"It is none of your concern, sir. Now, if you will move aside, Becky and I will be on our way. We have been gone longer than I expected. My father will be very worried." Shooing Becky into the gig, the lady climbed in after her. Taking up the reins, she set the horse into motion.

Standing in the road, Tad could think of nothing to do but watch her as she disappeared down the road.

Dawson, astride his horse, stopped beside him. "Do you think it wise to let her go alone?"

Tad shook his head as he swung into his saddle. "No. We will follow behind to ensure she makes it home safely."

The two pushed their horses until the small conveyance came into sight, then followed behind at a distance. They had not traveled far when the gig turned down a tree-lined lane. Instinct told him to quicken his pace and catch up, but Dawson held him back.

"You will only make her afraid of you. Remember what our mission is right now."

Tad grunted and threw a scowl in Dawson's direction. He knew the man was right.

"Besides, you are not available to pursue her. If you recall, your uncle has taken that task upon himself."

"Did I indicate I wanted to pursue her? I am only concerned for her well-being," Tad snapped.

Dawson nodded his head and smiled. "Of course you are."

Violet could feel the gentleman following behind. She knew it should frighten her, but it did not. On the contrary, she felt safer now than she had since meeting with Mr. McPhail. Using the pretense of coughing into her shoulder, she quickly searched the road behind them. As she suspected, two horses followed them in the distance.

"They are following us, aren't they, miss?"

Surprised her ruse had been so transparent, Violet nodded her head. "Yes, Becky, they are."

"Do you think they mean to harm us?" Fear still lingered in her eyes.

Violet smiled, trying to reassure the girl. "I believe if they were intent on injuring us, they would have done so back at the tree. No, I think they mean to protect."

A smile broke out on Becky's face. "It's a might romantic, don't you think?"

A laugh broke free as Violet shook her head. "Oh, Becky, you are a ninny. They are being gentlemen, nothing more." Heat blossomed on her cheeks, her palms became moist inside her gloves.

"Why did we leave so quickly? Your papa is not even home."

Nor would he be worried if he were. He had not worried about her in a very long time.

"Such a meeting is very improper. We do not even know the gentleman's name." She shifted in her seat, straightening her spine. "And they do not know my father is away."

Becky gave a dreamy sigh. "He was very handsome, was he not, miss?"

Violet tsked the maid, before giving her a pert smile. "And which one did you find so fetching?"

"Well, they were both dashing and very much out of my reach. But for you, I should think the gallant one." She looked over at her through lowered lashes, the dreamy tone returning to her voice. "He seemed very concerned for you, miss." Becky's eyes dropped to Violet neck. "When he saw those marks, he looked quite deadly."

The frivolity of moments ago fled. Violet whispered, "I do not believe you know the gentleman well enough to make such accusations, Becky. Please keep them to yourself."

Becky looked at her hands clasped in her lap. "Yes, miss. I shall try to remember that in the future."

Violet lightly touched her neck, already noticing the pain it evoked. "You must not speak of any of this. Not to a single soul. Do you understand?" She had not intended the sternness in her tone.

Continuing to look at her hands, the girl nodded. Violet lowered her voice. "Do you think we can find a way to hide these marks? If Rose should see them..."

Becky looked up at last. "I think some cleverly placed lace will do the trick, miss." She put a finger to her lips, her brow puckered. "If the lace will not cover it all, we may have to use some beauty paints."

Violet turned wide eyes to the girl. "Do you have beauty paints? Where did you get such things?"

Becky smiled smugly. "I have my secrets. You leave it to me, miss." The gig came to a stop in front of the stables. "For now, we need to get you to your chambers without being seen." Looking around, she shooed Violet toward the house. "I will see to the horses. You hurry on inside."

Violet pulled her shawl higher up around her neck and shoulders, dashing toward the house. As she opened the front door, she glanced over her shoulder. The gentlemen were waiting at the bend in the drive. A warmth settled over her. The gallant one, as Becky called him, tipped his hat to her. She dropped a quick curtsy before closing the door on them.

It was doubtful she would ever see him again, yet the thought that someone, if even for only a moment, had cared about her brought a sting to her eyes.

CHAPTER 4

Darkness engulfed the countryside, the stars hidden by a thick layer of clouds. The last several hours had been quiet between the two men. Dawson undoubtedly was cursing ever coming to this dratted land, while Tad's mind had stayed quite constantly on the young woman they had come upon yesterday.

Her outward beauty was undeniable, but there was something about her that left him wanting to know more. Fear had been evident in her eyes, yet she stood tall and determined. Knowing he would never see her again left him feeling displeased.

It had taken longer than Tad had hoped to reach their destination. He had wanted to speak with his uncle as soon as possible, driving them to press on the previous evening, forgoing the comforts of an inn along the way. Now, in the early morning hours, Morley Park stood before them, looming large and forbidding, save a very faint light in some lower windows.

The inky blackness prohibited any study or evaluation of the edifice. Closing his eyes, he recalled the detailed descriptions given by his father. The images helped calm his racing nerves.

Tad dismounted first, with Dawson following behind.

Dawson's eyes followed the massive walls up to the sky. "Even in the dark of night, she is impressive. I admit to believing your father had embellished his tales of her grandeur."

Tad nodded, his tone laced with awe. "She is beautiful. I cannot wait to see her by morning light. My father used to tell of the early morning rays, striking the pale stones, turning them a soft shade of pink." There was a reverence in his tone. "My sisters used to love that story. They were convinced he had grown up in a fairy castle." He smiled at the memory.

The two made their way to the stables. Finding only one empty stall, they turned the other animal loose in an adjoining paddock. Dawson began the task of unsaddling his mount. "I will brush them down and get them fed." He motioned to the house with his head. "Go ahead. I will be along shortly."

Tad headed for the house, taking the front steps two at a time. The fatigue of moments ago faded as he reached the landing. The heavily patinaed iron knocker—an ancient lion's head with a ring running through its mouth—felt heavy in his hand. He dropped it to the door several times. A deep knock sounded.

As he stood waiting, he took in as much of the surroundings as the darkness would allow. When the door remained closed, he knocked a second time. He jogged back down the stairs and began to circle the home.

A dimly lit window, flanked by a door, glowed on the side of the house. After knocking, he waited only a moment before it cracked open.

A young girl peered out at him. She made no sound, just stared until a voice inside sounded through the crack.

"Well, Agnes, who is it? Don't stand there gawking." The door was thrown open, revealing a stout woman, with graying hair. She wore an apron covered in flour, little bits of dough clinging to her stubby fingers. The smell of warm bread and ham wafted out the door, causing his stomach to growl.

She looked him up and down before leveling a gaze at him. "And who might you be?" Her hand moved to the side, settling back in front of her with a rolling pin firmly in her grasp.

Tad bowed, but kept his eyes on her hand and her weapon. "I beg your pardon for interrupting your breakfast preparation. I have only just arrived, and there was no answer at the front door."

Before he could continue the woman scowled at him, clutching the rolling pin tighter. "That didn't answer my question, sir."

A smile tugged at the corners of his mouth. This cook was formidable. "Again, I beg your pardon. My name is Thaddeus Wentworth. I have come to see my uncle."

The woman's mouth dropped open, the rolling pin clattering to the floor. "Oh no, sir. It is I who should beg your pardon. I had no idea. I should never have presumed to speak to you in such a manner had I known who you were." Her mouth clamped shut. "That is no excuse, sir. It shan't happen again."

Tad smiled even wider. "Please do not concern yourself." He looked past her into the kitchen and his stomach growled again. "Might I come in?"

She scooted to the side, motioning him inside with her hands. "Of course, sir. Let me send someone for Baker. He should be made aware of your arrival." She looked around the kitchen.

Tad waved her down. "Do not disturb Mr. Baker yet."

She nodded, looking a bit worried. "You must be hungry. Agnes, show the master to the breakfast room." She fidgeted with her apron. "I do not have a complete selection yet, but there is enough to hold you over until a proper breakfast is ready."

Holding up a hand to stem the flurry of activity, Tad pulled out a stool from beneath the large counter. "Perhaps I can have a bite here in the kitchen? There is no need to rouse the rest of the staff yet. I presume they will be up before long, anyhow."

She continued to worry the corners of her apron. "I do not believe Mrs. Jeffery or Baker would approve of the master eating in the kitchens."

Leaning forward, Tad whispered. "It will be our little secret." Then he winked.

Color rose in her cheeks, but she nodded and her posture relaxed slightly. She hurried about the room, gathering food.

A soft knock sounded. She threw a look at Tad. Standing he moved to the door in two long steps. "I am sure it is my traveling companion." Pulling the door open, he revealed Dawson, looking drawn and tired.

Tad showed him to the stools and pushed him down into one. "Mrs...? I do not believe I heard your name?"

"Mrs. Bryse, sir." She placed a plate of steaming sliced bread, along with crocks of butter and preserves on the table. Next, to it, she set a platter with two thick slices of warmed ham.

Picking up a slice of bread, Tad closed his eyes as he savored the yeasty, buttery flavor. "If it would assuage your mind, after we have eaten we shall go back to the front door and make our arrival known. No one will be the wiser."

They again climbed the front steps as the first rays of sunshine began to crest the horizon, stopping long enough to admire the edifice. Knocking once, the door was opened promptly. A man, probably not much older than his mother, appeared. Tad recalled cook referencing a man named Baker.

Upon seeing Tad, his eyes widened and he bowed deeply. "You have come home, Your Grace. We have long been expecting you."

Tad liked the man immediately. He was formal, yet not stuffy as he had assumed most English butlers to be, although he was puzzled by the greeting. "I do not believe we have met before."

The butler gave a slight smile. "No, I can say we have not. Although, you are almost a perfect image of your father, except perhaps, your eyes."

Twisting the ring he wore on his little finger Tad nodded. "Yes, I seem to have inherited my mother's eye color."

"I am Mr. Baker. I was your father's valet before he left home. He was a good man." The butler's features slackened. "I was deeply saddened by the news of his untimely death."

Tad's smile dropped away. It had been long ago, but the mention of his father's death never failed to elicit feelings of guilt and regret.

Trying to push the feelings away, Tad focused on the man's greeting. A weight instantly pressed against his shoulders. "What did you call me?"

"Your Grace. That is how you are to be addressed." Tension etched the man's face. "Perhaps you would be more comfortable in the library. You must be chilled from your travels. We can discuss particulars while you and your companion have some tea." Baker looked between the two men. "Or perhaps you would prefer coffee?"

Tad shook his head. "Actually, chocolate is more my preference, but tea will be fine. Mr. Dawson, though, is more partial to coffee."

Baker bowed. "Very good, Your Grace. I will return shortly. Mr. Jones will want to know of your arrival. He is in London, so it may take some time to get him here. If you and your companion," he motioned to Dawson with his head, "will follow me, you can relax in the Red Library."

Baker led them up the grand stairs, giving Tad the first opportunity to notice the entryway. It was swathed in soft pink light coming from two large windows on either side of the oversized door. A staircase flanked both sides of the entryway, dark wood treads with a carpet runner ending at the white marble floor below.

Once at the top, Baker turned down a darkened hallway. A branch of candles in his hand, he led them farther, stopping only once they reached the end. He opened a heavy wooden door and moved inside, pulling the cord in the corner.

Moments later, a young girl entered the room, head down. She curtsied quickly before moving silently to the fireplace. Quicker than Tad had ever seen it done, a small fire burned in the grate. She stood and scurried from the room, stopping only long enough to drop a second curtsy to Tad and Dawson.

"If you will excuse me, Your Grace. I will see what is keeping breakfast." The butler walked properly, if a little urgently, from the room.

Both men looked about the room, neither one speaking. The fireplace was flanked with thick marble columns, intricately carved with the head of a woman on each side, Hera, and Demeter if he was not mistaken. He smiled to himself. Apparently, his father's love of mythology was a family trait.

Above the columns, a marble mantle with more detailed carvings stretched up the wall, telling the story of Jason and the Golden Fleece. On either side of the massive hearth were floor to ceiling windows, currently covered in a heavy fabric. Rugs imported from the Far East covered the inlaid wood floors.

Tad moved around the room taking it all in. He felt the soft texture of the curtains and velvet on the chairs. The nap slid beneath his fingers, smooth then rough as they went back and forth. The motion calming his mind.

Never before had he felt his own family lived a pauper's lifestyle. On the contrary, they were the wealthiest landowners in all Lancaster County. But looking around this room, Tad felt a lowliness in his upbringing. For the first time since leaving the farm, a new doubt crept into his mind. Doubt as to whether he was up to this task before him. Doubt about leaving everything he knew behind him. Doubt about his future here. It was suddenly too much. A heavy, jagged breath escaped his lips. Bending, he placed his hands on his thighs, trying to catch his breath.

A hand rested on his shoulder. Dawson was at his side, concern evident in his eyes. He gave a nod, determination showing in his eyes. "You can do this," he said, his voice barely a whisper

Tad's shoulders sagged. "You heard what he called me. What have I gotten us into?"

Dawson straightened to his full height, his face almost forming into a scowl. "You were raised as an American gentleman, by the son of a duke. Yes, there are some differences," he held up his hand to cut off Tad's protest. "But they will only make you better. Indeed, I would suggest even more than most in your situation, for you were raised knowing how to work and treat people. The combination will prove you to be a remarkable master." Dawson's full scowl returned. "Don't doubt yourself."

The door opened for a maid with a tray, Baker following close behind.

Tad wasted no time before he began his questions. "Am I to assume I have arrived too late? Did I arrive before my uncle passed?"

Baker looked uncomfortable, but slowly bobbed of his head. "I am deeply sorry, Your Grace, but your uncle died five months ago."

Rocking back slightly, Tad let out a long breath. His uncle had not lived long enough for his letter to cross the Atlantic.

Earlier fears came flooding back. It felt as if all the air in the room was gone. When h and Dawson had set out on this adventure, he had been so sure his course was true, but since arriving at Morley, everything had changed. Indeed, he was sorry his uncle was no longer for this world, but it was the knowledge and information he took with him to his grave, which made Tad tense.

What was he to do now? He held little notion of how to run an English estate and everything his new title entailed. He was at a loss. There were surely similarities to running their holdings in Pennsylvania, but the differences were bound to be immense.

"I had hoped to make it in time to meet my uncle. I have heard many accounts of him over the years. I was anxious to reconcile those with my own assessment."

Baker smiled. "Yes, I am sure you did. Your father had many great tales regarding his brothers. He was very entertaining when he shared them." He looked slightly less uncomfortable. "Now that you have arrived, the details of the title and inheritance will be worked out. As I said, I will send word to Mr. Jones, directly. Until then, if you do not mind, might I make a few suggestions?"

Tad nodded slowly. "Please do."

The butler indicated the untouched tray. "Perhaps it would be best to let you recover from your journey for a spell. Then we can discuss what needs your attention first. Your rooms have been readied."

Tad rubbed at his eyes. The grittiness under his lids burned, only adding to a headache already pounding in his temple.

"We can meet after luncheon and get started then. For now, get some sleep, Your Grace." Baker's eyes flicked to Dawson, with only the briefest hesitation. "We have placed Mr..."

"Dawson." Tad motioned Dawson forward. "Mr. Dawson. He will be staying on with us for the time being."

"I will be acting as his...secretary." Dawson bristled.

The tone was not lost on the butler. He dipped his head. "Very good, Your Grace. I will see he is set up in the office next to your study." A fatherly smile crossed the man's lips. "On a personal note..." Tad nodded at the implied question of propriety. "We are very glad to have you home, Your Grace."

"Thank you, Baker."

The butler cleared his throat. "Hopefully you will find things are not so very different from the *West Indies*."

Tad raised a brow. "And what do you know of the West Indies, Baker?" He had almost forgotten his uncle's explicit instructions. He was to keep his nationality a secret, for everyone believed his father had been in the West Indies managing the Shearsby sugar plantation. Tad grinned.

"Not much, Your Grace. I only know it did not hold the same appeal, as say, Pennsylvania. I have heard America is very pretty, in her own right."

Tad chuckled. "You heard right, Baker. It is very pretty. But England has its own kind of beauty."

Dawson snorted next to him.

Baker walked into the hallway. When he returned, a footman followed close behind. "James can show you both to your chambers, Your Grace. Rest well."

CHAPTER 5

Violet lay in bed, her fingers gently smoothing the ointment from cook on her tender neck. The last thing she needed was for Rose to take notice and question her. Rose would not understand. Violet paused in her application. She, herself, did not understand what had happened to Roger... Mr. McPhail—she could no longer think of him so intimately. How could she expect her sister to understand? Rose never had been fond of Mr. McPhail and had questioned Violet's allegiance to him throughout their childhood. She had told Rose of her affections for him, but not of their plans to marry. That had been years ago. After seeing him this morning, Violet knew that dream was not to be.

She continued rubbing the bruises. The action should have brought back the terror she had felt in the moments under the willow, but instead, the image of a tall, handsome man with intense blue eyes, invaded her thoughts.

Violet finished with the ointment and hid the pot underneath her bed. Blowing out the candle, she lay back on her pillow, and closed her eyes, allowing the images of the kind stranger to float about her mind. She knew she was being silly, for she would never lay eyes on the gentleman again.

The warmth and accompanying blush seemed to happen whenever she thought back on him, forcing her to push the thoughts aside until she was in the privacy of her bedchambers. Every mention of him would bring back Becky's wild thoughts on romance and marriage.

His eyes—even with the purple bruising around one—held kindness and concern. When he had seen the marks on her neck, his eyes had turned stormy and angry. At first, it had frightened her, but the anger had dissipated quickly when his eyes returned to her face.

She could not help but compare him to Mr. McPhail. There had been no kindness in his eyes, only a cold aloofness.

Turning onto her side, Violet pushed at her pillow, trying to arrange it into a more comfortable position.

Where was she to go from here? She had no prospects and no hope of finding any. It was not as if their aunt would sponsor her for a London season, nor would some duke request her hand in a somewhat cryptic letter, as had happened for Rose.

Rubbing lightly at her neck, Violet let the images of her dashing hero push the fear and despondency threatening to engulf her to the back of her mind. Dashing...that is how she would remember him. It was terribly juvenile, but she did not care. A smile spread across her face. He was her Mr. Dashing.

Violet returned from her walk, entering through the kitchen. Cook smiled, as Violet snatched a biscuit from the tray on the table.

"I'll be taking that from your tea service, little miss." Cook came over and examined Violet closely. "The fichu hides those bruises well. I would not notice them if I did not already know they were there."

Violet self-consciously put her fingers to the lace at her neck. "Yes, Becky is very helpful in arranging it just so. I believe they have reached their peak of color and should begin to fade soon."

Cook tsked. "Have you told your father of the encounter? He should know, little miss."

Violet shook her head as Cook moved over to stir something on the stove. "He is too busy at present. And it is no matter, I shall not be seeing Mr. McPhail again."

"I always thought that boy was trouble," Cook muttered a string of disparaging remarks about their neighbor.

Violet moved to the stove and kissed the older woman on the cheek. "Thank you for the treat, Cook. And the ointment."

Cook turned from the stove and placed a hand on Violet's cheek. "I worry for you now that he has returned. Please, talk to your father. I know he has not been as attentive as he once was, but he still loves you." Violet nodded. "Off with you then." Cook dropped her hand and shooed Violet out of the kitchen.

Making her way into the morning parlor, Violet was surprised to see her father out of his study. He turned when she entered. "Ah, Violet. I have been waiting for you to return. How was your walk? You look very well."

Violet looked at her older sister, who shrugged as Violet sat down on the settee. "You look lovely this morning, Rose."

Rose smiled. "Thank you. My gown was just delivered this morning. I think the color suits me. Do you not? It makes my eyes appear even bluer." Rose ran her hands down the front of her skirt, smoothing non-existent wrinkles.

Her father walked over, standing before them. "I received word today from your intended," he inclined his head toward Rose.

"He has finally arrived at Morley Park. We have been instructed to set out as soon as arrangements can be made."

Rose clapped her hands together. "Oh, Papa. This is excellent news. I shall finally be a duchess." Rose smiled at Violet. "It seems ages since the offer was made."

Violet grimaced and her stomach burned. She would watch as her sister married a rich and powerful duke, while Violet became an old maid.

"Papa, did this letter give any more information than the first? Do you know why Rose was singled out for such an honor? I still find it strange."

Rose scowled at her. "You find it strange someone should find me a suitable match?"

Violet patted her sister's leg. "No, that is not what I meant. You are admired by all who know you, Rose. But it is not as if we have been about much in society." Violet looked at her father. "The old duke did not know our names or even how many daughters you had. The letter only asked if an alliance could be made between *one* of your daughters. It just seems odd."

Her father harrumphed. "I told you before, the Duke of Shearsby and I were old school chums. We have stayed in contact when I have been in town to attend Parliament. But never you mind. The offer was made and that is enough for me." He moved toward the door. "I shall send off a response immediately. We shall depart within the week."

"But Papa." Rose's whine stopped their father before he made it into the hallway. "What of my wardrobe? I cannot meet the duke in the rags I have now. That will take a fortnight, at least."

"Go into the village. I am sure there are plenty of gowns already made that will serve you very well. We do not want to keep the duke waiting." He turned and disappeared down the corridor.

"He has kept me waiting for nearly a year," Rose grumbled. She looked down at her gown, distaste now evident on her face. "I do not know why we cannot make a trip to London first. There are no suitable dressmakers in Kidsgrove."

Violet stood and moved to the bell pull to summon for tea. "Rose, that would take months. Madame Couture is the best in the county." Violet sat next to her sister and put a hand on her arm. "We shall go into the village together. I am sure we can find plenty of gowns to suit you."

Rose let out one last pout. "I guess you are right. It is not as if he is to be the pinkest of the pinks. Do they even have tailors in the West Indies?"

Violet stifled a laugh. "Yes, I am sure they do."

The door opened and the maid brought in the tea. She set it on the table in front of the ladies. "Thank you, Mary." Violet smiled at the older maid.

Rose leaned forward and began to pour the tea into the cups, her face wrinkled in thought. "Do you really think it odd? That the old duke should seek us out? We are still nobility. Perhaps he heard of me when I was in London. I made quite a debut."

Violet smiled. "So I have heard. But you may be right." Violet put her cup back on the tray. "Now, hurry with your tea and let us get into town before all the desirable gowns are gone."

Rose swallowed her bite and nodded. "Oh, yes. That would be most unfortunate."

CHAPTER 6

Tad sat behind the large desk in his uncle's study staring down at the stacks of parchment in front of him. His study—would it ever feel like his? Running a hand through his hair, he released a heavy sigh. He had been at Morley for more than a week and every day consisted of meetings; with the steward, the master gardener, the stable master, and Dawson— always with Dawson. They had spent hours in this room going over ledgers and letters until Tad's head ached and his eyes burned.

Tad rubbed at the back of his neck. He did not know what he would do without Dawson. Even now he was investigating a questionable expenditure. While he hated the idea of being a secretary, Tad believed Dawson secretly enjoyed the tasks associated with it. Idleness had never been his friend.

They had been very productive since arriving, but it came at the expense of solitude. Even when he went to his chambers, his valet was there waiting. Tad breathed in deeply, enjoying the quiet.

He pushed the papers in front of him away, swiveling his seat until he could gaze out the window. The fields lay barren, only a hint of green covered the surface. From the ledgers he had studied, Tad knew it was the winter barley and wheat.

His mind drifted to home—overseeing the laborers in the fields, at times joining them. It was hard work, but every night Tad had gone to bed with a sense of accomplishment. Last night he had fallen asleep feeling restless and anxious. For the hundredth time, Tad questioned his decision to come here, to take his place as the family's head.

Branches swayed on a nearby tree bringing to mind a different memory. The mystery woman from the willow. Over the last several days his mind had drifted to her often. He wondered if she was well. Had the man come back and hurt her again? There had been times Tad had considered riding back to check, but the notion seemed absurd, especially in the light of day. Instead, he had remained at Morley and speculated on her fate.

"I found something else you will want to look at, Tad." Dawson entered the room, his attention on the book in his hands.

"In a minute." Tad kept his gaze out the window, not wanting to be pulled from his thoughts.

A movement in his periphery drew his attention away from the fields and toward the drive. A carriage pulled by four horses traveled up the gravel lane. Tad watched intently as it stopped in front of the house.

The driver jumped from the box, pulling down the step and opening the coach door. A portly gentleman stepped out first, followed by a woman about the same age as Tad's mother. She looked around the area, her nose turning up slightly.

Tad's spine stiffened at the obvious slight against Morley Park.

Dawson came to stand beside him. "Guests?"

"It appears so." He had no idea who the woman was, but he was disposed to think ill of her.

Another woman was handed out. They looked to be similar in age. In contrast to the first, this one smiled as she looked the house up and down. Her smile only increased the more she studied the surroundings. Tad's shoulders relaxed the more he watched her.

Looking between the two, he could see little resemblance. The first, however, held a look very similar to his father. She had the same fair hair and pert nose as Tad. He grimaced, standing up and leaning closer to the pane. Why must the sour-looking one be his relation?

A young lady stepped down from the carriage onto the drive. She looked to be close in age to the lady from the willow tree. Tad paused at the thought. The girl grasped the arm of the second, kind looking lady. Even from this distance, Tad could see the resemblance between mother and daughter.

The driver began to unload several trunks from the top of the carriage.

"Do you know who they are?" Dawson leaned closer to the glass.

"I believe the one in the lavender is a relation of some sort. She has features similar to my father. I have no idea as to the others." Tad's gaze never left the window, or rather from the group standing on the drive. He watched them as they made their way to the front steps and disappeared from view.

Dawson let out a breath. "Do you suppose they are here to challenge your claim to the title?"

Tad shrugged. "If I do not know who they are, it is doubtful I know what they are about." His smirk reflected in the glass.

Dawson gave his own smirk in reply. "Perhaps the young one is your betrothed."

The smile dropped from Tad's face, causing a chuckle to sound next to him. He was about to refute the possibility when the door opened and Baker entered. "Lord and Lady Mayfield, Lady Rachel Standish and Miss Jessica Standish have arrived, Your Grace. I have placed them in the...."

"Nonsense. That was my father's study. I will not be shut away in some parlor. Move aside, Baker." The lady in lavender pushed her way into the room.

Baker stepped aside. "Yes, Lady Mayfield."

The other women entered behind the butler, with Lord Mayfield shuffling in at the rear.

Both Tad and Dawson turned from the window, staring at the newcomers with raised brows.

Dawson bowed, muttering under his breath. "I believe this is my time to leave. Ring if you need me to fend any of them off, Your Grace."

Lady Mayfield walked to the settee next to the fireplace. She stared at Tad. "Are you not going to ask us to sit and ring for tea?"

Tad moved around his desk. He executed an exaggerated bow to the ladies, earning him a giggle from Miss Standish. "My apologies. Please, do be seated." He walked, without any degree of haste, to the bell pull, summoning tea to his study. "The letter informing me of your imminent arrival must have been lost somewhere along the way."

Lady Mayfield arranged her skirts around her as she seated herself on the settee. Her husband chose the seat in the corner, farthest from his wife. Lady Mayfield gave him a withering look before turning her attention to the butler. "Baker, please see that our rooms are readied. I believe we will be here a fortnight, at least."

The butler bowed. "Very good, my lady."

Lady Rachel and her daughter made their way to the settee, each assessing Tad openly.

"Rachel. Jessica. Stop gawking like a couple of ninnies." Lady Mayfield then turned to him. Her eyes narrowed as she looked him up and down. "You must be my nephew." She squinted at him, her nose raising again. "You look very much like my brother, Edward."

Tad did not know what to say. He knew his father had two sisters, both quite young when he had left for America. Tad did not know much about Lady Mayfield, except she had married a very prominent—and apparently very cowardly—earl. She had corresponded very little with them over the years.

Lady Rachel, however, had written to Tad's mother for years. She seemed the only family member willing to communicate with his Irish mother.

"Are you a mute, boy?" Lady Mayfield's stare bore into him.

"I beg your pardon, no. I did not hear you ask a question. Hence, I did not see the need to speak, Aunt."

She harrumphed. "Lady Mayfield will do, for the time being, nephew."

Tad smiled and gave a deep bow. "Very well, Lady Mayfield. As you wish for formality I believe it proper for you to refer to me as Your Grace."

His aunt gasped. He turned to the other two ladies sitting on the opposite settee. Lady Rachel stifled a laugh, while Miss Standish sat open-mouthed.

He bowed to each in turn. "Lady Rachel, Miss Standish. Welcome to Morley Park. It is a pleasure to finally meet you." His gaze focused on his aunt. "My mother speaks very kindly of you, aunt. She will be most anxious to make your acquaintance when she visits with my sisters come spring."

Lady Rachel smiled brightly. "Your Grace, the pleasure is all mine. This," she motioned to Miss Standish, "is my daughter—your cousin—Jessica."

Although he had only met Lady Rachel a few moments ago,

Tad was already inclined to like her. Apart from the letters she had written over the years, she also had a ready smile and kindness shone in her eyes. The daughter, while shy, seemed to have her mother's propensity for happiness.

Lady Rachel glanced at her sister. "You may call me aunt. I only use the title when I am among the stuffy likes of the ton." A brow arched gracefully. "They apparently need to be reminded of my status, since my marriage." She turned to her daughter. "Jes, say something to His Grace."

Tad colored slightly "Please excuse my earlier attempt at humor. I would be happy if you called me something less formal."

Miss Standish stood and curtsied, caution evident in her eyes. "Cousin?" At Tad's nod, she continued. "It is an honor to finally meet you. We have been anticipating your arrival for many months. When we received word you had come, we set out almost immediately for Leicestershire."

"Where have you traveled from?"

Miss Standish looked at Lady Mayfield and then her mother, who nodded for her to continue.

"Mama and I live in Durham, with my father. He is away on business currently, so we have been visiting Aunt Mayfield at her estate in Nottinghamshire."

Tea and chocolate arrived and Lady Mayfield took the position of hostess, pouring for everyone. Once her own cup was settled in her hand and a cake procured, she stared at Tad. "Now young man, there is much that needs to be done."

Tad opened his mouth to speak but was silenced by the slight shake of her head. He chanced a look at his uncle, pretending to sleep in his chair across the room. One eye squinted open once as if looking to see if the tea service was worth the sacrifice it would be to come and partake. At present, it appeared it was not. Tad envied the man, although the cakes Mrs. Bryce had sent up today were delicious.

Returning his attention back to Lady Mayfield, Tad lifted a brow.

Lady Rachel reached over and placed a hand on her sister's arm. "Lydia, he is the duke now. You need to show some respect."

Lady Mayfield huffed. "When he proves himself worthy of the title, I will do so."

Tad had never met a woman quite like Lady Mayfield. He watched her over his cup.

"A dinner and perhaps even a ball is required. The neighborhood has been talking for months about you. You must show them you are a man of strong character and will be up for the tasks before you." She paused, taking a rather large bite of her cake.

Choking on the chocolate running down his throat, Tad shook his head. "Absolutely not. I am not ready for such an extravagant event. A ball can wait until I return from London in the summer. Or perhaps I could even be persuaded to host one in town. But...."

"Nonsense. Rachel and I are more than capable of seeing to everything. It will be of very little consequence to you. Now Rachel, when should we plan the ball? In a fortnight or will that be rushing things too much?"

Aunt Standish's lips twitched slightly. "A fortnight will be rushing it, but I believe we should consult Shearsby as to his preference. He did mention traveling to town."

Lady Mayfield shrugged. "Very well." She looked at him expectantly. "Well, Shearsby?"

Tad stuttered. "Well, what?"

Shaking her head, she muttered under her breath. Tad could not make out all of her words, but he believed the words daft and heaven help us were among those muttered.

Lady Rachel spoke up. "What are your plans for going to town? When were you intent on leaving?"

Tad set his cup on the table, causing it to clatter. "I do not have my plans finalized yet." His voice came out sounding strained and high pitched. "I arrived here barely a week ago. I have not seen to all the papers cluttering my desk, let alone had time to make my travel plans." He stood, walking behind his chair. He placed his hands on the back, leaning forward slightly.

Lady Mayfield also set her cup down. "I had hoped you would be up to the task before you, but I see my doubts were not unfounded. I should not have expected much from one raised in the colonies." She stood and brushed the wrinkles from her gown. "I am feeling weary after our long journey. I will be in my room. Please send up a tray. I do not foresee being recovered enough to join you for dinner." She swept to the door, stopping just before the threshold. Looking over her shoulder, she eyed her sister. "Rachel? Jessica? Are you coming?"

Aunt Standish shook her head. "No, sister. I believe we shall stay and visit a while longer." She cast a glance in his direction. "Unless Shearsby would prefer some solitude?"

"I would be delighted to have you stay...if that is what you wish."

Lady Mayfield sniffed. "Very well. Come, Mayfield."

Tad tried not to laugh as the portly earl pretended to sleep.

"Mayfield." Lady Mayfield raised her voice. "Come this instant."

The poor man opened his eyes and slowly lifted himself out of his chair. He made it halfway across the room before he stopped. "I believe I will stay also. I would like to speak with the duke, get an idea of how he will vote in the upcoming session." The earl moved to the seat closer to the center of the room.

Lady Mayfield grumbled but left without another audible word.

Tad could feel when she had crossed over the threshold. The tension in the room seemed to leave with her. He scrubbed his fingers through his hair. First, his uncle makes an offer on his behalf and now his aunt is planning balls and dinners and who knows what else?

"You must excuse Lydia, Shearsby."

He waved her aside. "Please, call me Tad."

She smiled. "She has been trained from the time she was in leading strings to be the mistress of a very large household. She takes her duties very seriously. And as there is no mistress presiding at Morley, she sees it as her duty to step into that role—to help guide you through this trying time. She does not intend to be harsh."

The earl guffawed from the settee. Aunt Standish turned in his direction, eyebrows raised in question, or perhaps disapproval?

"You find something funny, Mayfield?"

"Indeed. I believe you are being too kind in regards to my wife. She does indeed intend to be harsh. She knows most people are too afraid or intimidated to stand up to her when she speaks in such a way." He turned to Tad, leaning in closer. "I, for one, would enjoy watching someone stand up to her now and then. Heaven knows I never have."

Jes covered a laugh with her hand.

"Watch yourself, young lady. Lydia has been very good to you. She has even offered to sponsor you for your first season." Aunt's feature softened slightly. "She is not obligated to do so. Additionally, ladies do not laugh uproariously. Especially in front of others."

"But the duke is family."

Lady Rachel silenced her daughter with a look.

Tad found he was having a difficult time keeping a straight

face. He knew he would undermine his aunt's authority with her daughter if he stepped in, but he could not help giving her a small wink when her mother's back was turned. Jes smiled back. Ah, he had found an ally.

A change in subject was in order.

"Aunt, I received a note from my uncle upon my arrival in Liverpool. He wrote to hurry me along and spoke of arranging a marriage on my behalf." He let out a slow breath. "Do you know anything of it?"

His aunt's mouth formed an O. "He did, did he?" Her mouth ticked up on one side. "James always was a bit high handed. Thought himself above everyone. I dare say even the Prince Regent, himself."

The earl shifted. "Here, here."

"Do you know the lady's name?" His aunt poured herself another cup of tea.

Tad shook his head.

"James made the arrangement with Lord Winslow. I believe it is his oldest daughter." All eyes turned to the old man.

"How do you know such things?" Lady Rachel stared at him.

"It caused quite a stir about town last season. The miss did not even come to London for it."

Lady Rachel's face wrinkled. "Lord Winslow? I realize I am not welcome among most of the ton, but I still know of them. Why do I not know him?"

Lord Mayfield scratched at his head. "Let's see. He would have been Mr. Allen before he became a baron. They live in Cheshire, I believe."

"Mr. Charles Allen?"

Lord Mayfield nodded. "Yes, I believe he is one in the same."

"Why did James chose the Allen's? Obviously, they are titled, but are they well connected? He was not when I was about society."

"For that very reason. I asked Shearsby about it. He was very worried about," the earl paused and flicked his gaze to Tad. "His American nephew. He did not have very high hopes in his upbringing. By arranging the marriage to a lesser known family, he believed the new duke would not be about society much and the family secret would be safe. At least for a while. I questioned him, but he made it clear he knew what he was about."

Tad dropped his head back and laughed. All eyes turned to him. "I have never seen so many people with such erroneous ideas about a country."

The earl shrugged. "I confess, I am pleasantly surprised. You even sound like an Englishman."

Jes looked at him with sad eyes. "He has arranged your marriage? That is not very romantic, is it?"

Aunt Standish sighed, shaking her head. "Everything is not romantic or unromantic, Jes. Sometimes practicality must prevail."

"You did not allow practicality to prevail when you married Papa." Jes's chin raised in challenge. Tad had seen that same face on his sister.

"We are not discussing me, Jes. We are discussing your cousin, the new Duke of Shearsby. There are certain expectations and... obligations which come with a title. Especially his title." She turned to include Tad in her conversation. "While I do not agree with my brother's meddling, I can understand why he did such a thing. Especially in light of Mayfield's insight."

Tad was impressed with his aunt. She was kind, yet she also carried herself regally and with grace. Perhaps he had an ally in this woman also. "Do you believe I should marry this stranger?"

"I believe you should consider all options."

He shook his head. "I do not understand."

She patted the seat next to her on the settee.

He moved over to her, sitting down and stretching out his legs in front of him.

"I would guess a missive was dispatched to your intended when word came of your arrival. She will, undoubtedly, be on her way here very soon. I suggest you receive her with an open mind. Perhaps she is the match for you. Do not immediately disregard her as wrong simply because your uncle was the one to pick her."

Tad did not know what answer he had wanted, but this one did not make him feel better. Resting his head on the back of the couch, he closed his eyes, thinking over his aunt's words.

In need of a change of topic, he tilted his head toward his aunt. "What do you remember about my father?"

CHAPTER 7

Tad leaned back in his chair, looking absently out the window. Turning slightly, he reached for the creased paper laying on his desk. He stared at the letter, not reading the words scrawled across the page. He had read it and reread it numerous times since its arrival the previous day.

His eyes drifted to the one important sentence. *We will be departing within the week and expect to arrive at Morley Park on or around the 25th day of October.*

Tad let the paper rest in his lap. That was only a few days away. He thought he had reconciled his feelings on this matter. But the burning, sickening feeling in his stomach told him otherwise. Why must he always give in to duty and honor? What of his wants and desires?

What were his wants and desires? He had not really considered it. There had been too much to learn and do upon arriving. The image of the willow tree girl entered his mind. Perhaps he had been considering it, and just not realized it. Tad shook his head. This line of thought was not productive to anyone. He did not even know the young lady's name. He knew where she lived, but having no idea where they were when they saw her, the information would provide little help in finding her again.

Picking up his book again, Tad forced himself to concentrate on the words in front of him. His gaze drifting to the paper at his hand. Pulling his eyes back to the book, he scanned the page to find his place. This exercise continued for several minutes until a quiet squeak of the hallway floor drew his attention to the doorway. The door slid open and his cousin's head poked in.

"Do come in, cousin, there is no need for you to stand about in the hallway." He laid his book in his lap, glad for the distraction. His head dropped to the side, straining to see her face.

Her eyes darted around the room. "Is my aunt about?"

Tad heaved out a breath. "Thankfully, no. She has not, as yet, invaded my study."

Pushing the door wider, she stepped inside. "Please, call me Jes, cousin...sir. Only Aunt Mayfield's daughters call me cousin and I dislike it immensely." Her mouth turned down in an exaggerated grimace.

Tad could not help but smile. At seventeen, Jes usually acted as a young lady should. However, she did not always speak as one. She spoke whatever thoughts entered her mind, rarely thinking of the consequences until after the words had passed her lips. It was one of the things which endeared her to him.

"Very well, Jes." She smiled brightly at him. He tapped his finger against his chin. "Perhaps it would be fitting for you to call me Tad."

Her eyes went wide. "But...are you sure? I believe Aunt Mayfield would consider it quite improper."

Tad motioned to the chair opposite him. "Then we shall keep it our little secret. Yes?"

She giggled and nodded her head. "But may I tell Mama? I do

not think she would oppose the idea." Her posture relaxed. "Mama is much less concerned with such things."

Tad nodded. "Yes, I have noticed that about her." He looked at the book on the side table. "Do you like to read, Jes?"

She again nodded vigorously. "Papa always brings me a new book when he returns from his travels. What are you reading?"

He picked up the worn leather book, showing her the front cover.

"The Federalist? What type of a book is it?" She asked.

"It is a discussion about government and what responsibilities a government should or should not have. It was my father's." Tad rubbed his hand over the words, now only flecked with gold in the impressions. "I like to read it when I am especially missing him."

The two discussed books for well over an hour. Several novels and a book on mythology now sat at her side. Dawson stepped through the door from his office, a smile curving his usually surly face. Even Dawson was unable to harden himself to her infectious laugh. She would make quite a splash when Lady Mayfield sponsored her for her coming out next season.

Tad tilted his head toward Jes. "It seems I am not the only one hiding from Lady Mayfield. Jes was seeking refuge and I happily granted it to her."

She giggled again.

Dawson nodded. "She is a formidable woman, your aunt. Is she still insisting you marry whomever shows up on your doorstep?"

Tad shrugged. "It would seem so." He glanced out the window. "Is it time for our ride?"

Dawson nodded.

Tad looked over at Jes. She closed the book she was reading, setting it on the table nearby. "I guess I should be leaving." She curtsied to them both. "Thank you for sharing your books with me,

Tad." Her eyes went big as she realized what she had called him. Her glance darted to Dawson, then landed back on Tad.

"I do not believe Mr. Dawson will tell Lady Mayfield of our secret." He winked at her as Dawson put his finger to his lips, pursing them tightly.

Jes rewarded them with a huge grin. "Thank you, Mr. Dawson." Her eyes flitted to the stack of books she had been reading.

Tad stood. "Jes, you may come in and join me any time. And please, feel free to take a book with you."

Reaching out a hand, she snatched the top book from the table, hugging it to her chest. She made her way to the door, turning before sliding through the crack. "Thank you again, Tad." And then she was gone.

Tad and Dawson had fallen into the habit of taking a daily ride, focusing on a different parcel of the estate each time they set out. Tad was pleased with what he had seen. A few tenant cottages were in need of repairs, but from looking at the books, it appeared to be a matter of stinginess on the part of his uncle, rather than neglect from the last six months. Regardless, it was something he intended to rectify as soon as possible.

The two walked to the stables. Henderson already had the horses out and was cinching the saddle of the second one. He straightened at Tad's approach, offering a slight bow. "Your Grace. Mr. Dawson. I noticed you've been riding about the same time each day. I thought I would take a chance and have the horses ready for you." He squinted up at them, his brow wrinkled.

Tad nodded at the man. "Thank you, Henderson." He looked around the building. "This is impressive."

Henderson hung his head in embarrassment. "Thank you, Your Grace. But I can't take all the credit. The late duke made several trips to Tattersall's over the years."

He and Dawson both mounted. "Well, I am impressed with your efforts none the less. I can see everything is well taken care of." Tad tipped his hat to the man as they began to trot the horses out of the stable yard.

"Which way shall we go today?" Dawson asked.

"Perhaps we could make our way into the village. I have a few letters to post and I would like to check on my new boots at the cordwainers." Tad pulled his reins to the side, moving his horse in the opposite direction. Dawson followed suit, pulling up alongside.

"New boots? Was that really necessary?"

Tad scoffed. "Dawson, a man can never have too many pairs of well-made boots."

Dawson's brow rose.

Lowering his voice a touch, Tad added, "I have it on good authority the man has not had enough customers of late." He gave a shrug. "He is Mrs. Bryce's brother."

Dawson looked over, a knowing look in his eyes. "You are a good man, Your Grace."

Tad dipped his head, embarrassed by the sentiment. "Formality, Dawson. Besides, I am only ensuring I will have a bootmaker within easy distance. That is all. Do not make more of it than it is."

Dawson nodded slowly. "I will not tell anyone of your secret, Tad. Although, I am not sure why you feel it necessary for people to think you a tyrant."

Tad looked around the countryside. "It is not my intent for people to think I am a tyrant, but I cannot have them thinking I am weak either. I will be assuming my seat in parliament in the upcoming season. If my fellow Lords do not take me seriously, I shall be an utter failure."

"I was not aware kindness equated to weakness."

Tad turned back to Dawson. "Then you do not know the English aristocracy." Digging his heels into his horse's side, he shot ahead, leaving Dawson to stare after him.

Violet leaned her head against the window pane, watching the countryside slide by. She wondered if Mr. Dashing lived in a place like this. He had only been passing through Kidsgrove when he came upon her, of that she was quite certain. When she had ventured into the village over the past week, she looked for him. On a few occasions even asked if anyone new had moved into the area. The answer was always the same. But she still held out a hope of seeing him again someday.

An excited shudder ran down her back. The purpose of this trip was to finalize her sister's betrothal, but Violet was looking upon it as an adventure. After all, this journey was the farthest she would most likely ever venture from Cheshire. And it would put her three counties away from Mr. McPhail.

The days of traveling had been taxing, but it could not quite extinguish her excitement.

A snort shattered the silence in the carriage. Violet looked over at her sister, huddled in the corner. She was twitching her nose, her hand swiping at it several times. Violet smiled, wishing there was some way to document this unladylike behavior. She thought of the horrified expression on Rose's face if she ever discovered she snored.

The two maids occupying the seats opposite were both sleeping, their heads bobbing back and forth with the swaying of the coach.

Violet let her thoughts wander to Mr. Dashing. His voice echoed through her brain. "Who did that to you?" She thought of him, following behind them and the final tip of his hat. Her heart quickened at the memory.

A ruckus outside drew her attention. The carriage came to an abrupt stop. The other occupants began to stir, still groggy from their sleep.

A deep voice sounded outside. "Stand and Deliver." The door wrenched open, revealing a masked gunman. He moved the weapon from Becky to Mary to Rose, finally ending at Violet. Using the gun, he motioned for her to exit the coach.

Eyes wide, Violet shook her head. Her heart raced, even as a niggling of something familiar hovered at the back of her mind. She burrowed farther into the corner, tossing her reticule out the door and hitting the man in the chest. Surprised, he stumbled backward, his foot tangling in a tree root.

A gunshot rippled through the air and the carriage lurched forward swinging the door shut with a sharp crack, shaking the windows in their casings. The coach began to pick up speed, careening sharply to one side, then to the other as another shot sounded, followed by a heavy thump from the driver's box.

Rose shrieked, her face bleached of all color. Both Mary and Becky held on to one another, as silent tears streaked down their cheeks. Violet placed her feet on the floor, steadying herself with shaking hands. She turned to Rose, placing a hand on·her arm. Her shrieks turned to quiet sobs, shaking her whole body. "Calm yourself. We are unharmed."

Rose pushed her hand away at the same time the carriage began to swerve back and forth. "Perhaps for the moment, but what of the coachman? He is obviously not in control of the horses."

It felt as if the wheels were seeking out every dip and tree root, tossing the occupants about like rag dolls. The coach hit a deep rut, throwing Rose onto the floor, while Violet was flung to the side. Her head struck the window, causing Rose's sobs to echo within her ears.

Before she could right herself, she was tossed to the floor beside her sister, her cheek striking the door handle. Fearing the consequences of pushing herself back up onto the seat, Violet pulled her legs into her chest and huddled on the floor, waiting for whatever fate had in store for her.

A thump banged against the side of the carriage. Raising her head slightly, Violet cautioned a glance at the window. A body was stretched, covering the entire window, hanging from the top of the coach's frame. The body bounced, knocking into the window with every swerve of the carriage.

A yelp escaped her throat before she could silence it. In her panic, she had been unable to look away from the highway man's eyes. She had no idea what clothing he was wearing. This man did not wear a mask, although the features smashed up against the window were difficult to decipher.

He managed to place a foot on something and pushed himself up to standing, his head moving out of view. Slowly his body moved along the coach frame until he passed out of sight. Within moments, the carriage began to slow, finally coming to a stop. The carriage rocked back and forth as people moved about the top.

After what seemed like forever, a deep voice called from outside the carriage. "Ladies, it is safe for you to come out now."

The four ladies looked at each other, fear evident in every eye. Rose broke the silence. "Mary, you must go out first. Once you have determined it safe, we will follow behind."

Mary's eyes widened, looking from Violet to Rose and back again. Violet shook her head, "No Mary, I shall go out first." She moved to stand but was stopped by a hand on her arm.

"No, miss. I shall go and let you know if all is well." Becky moved past her, pushing the door open. Violet felt a tug of gratitude toward the girl, thankful she brought her along.

Becky peeked out of the carriage and then stepped down. Finally, she stuck her head back into the carriage. "It is safe, miss." She gave Violet a knowing smile. "I believe we can trust them." Violet nodded and pushed herself up off the seat. Once again, she was pushed back down.

"I am the eldest. I should precede you out of the carriage." Rose straightened her bonnet, pushing a few loose pins back into place. As she alighted from the carriage, her lips began to move before her first slippered foot touched the ground.

"Thank you, sir. I was afraid we would meet our end in this carriage. We are on our way to Morley Park."

Violet sighed, moving to disembark behind her sister—her voice carrying into the carriage. "I am engaged, you see, to the Duke of Shearsby. He will be most indebted to you for your kindness to us."

Leaving the shade of the carriage, Violet squinted against the afternoon sunlight and stumbled on the step. Two strong hands grasped her by the elbows, keeping her upright and helping her down from the coach at the same time. She registered two men. One was holding the horses, speaking quietly to them. The other stood to her side. Splotches in her vision blacked out their faces.

At last, her vision cleared. She turned, intent on thanking her rescuer and nearly bumped into him. Her eyes lifted to meet his, and the air left her lungs in a strangled gasp.

CHAPTER 8

A smile curled one side of Tad's mouth and a warmth spread from his chest to his extremities. Was it possible he was lucky enough to have encountered this woman a second time? But he did not believe in luck or chance. This was an omen or some kind of divine intervention. Realizing he still held on to her, he dropped his hands to his side, his heart pounding. He flicked a glance at the other women before his eyes came to rest on her again, this time taking in her whole face. The bruising on her neck, while hidden under a lace collar, seemed to have lightened in color. Her face, while still pale, radiated a happiness that previously was not there.

His brow creased as he removed a handkerchief from his pocket, giving it to her. He rubbed at his forehead with his finger. "You seem to be bleeding, miss." He raised his hand, as if to touch the affected area, but seemed to think better of the idea. "Above your brow, there on the left."

She lifted the cloth to her head, her eyes watching him as he retrieved another handkerchief from Dawson and gave it to one of the maids. If he was not mistaken, she had been with this young lady the last time he happened upon them.

Tad stepped back from her, taking in the rest of the group. There were two ladies, along with two maids. The blond one had finally ceased talking, frowning as she watched their exchange. He had not heard anything since his willow tree lady had poked her head out of the carriage. The blond one opened her mouth, ready to resume her incessant chatter but Tad stopped her. Addressing them all, he hoped to stem the flow of words ready to break forth from the young lady.

"Other than these few injuries, is everyone well?"

The chatty one stepped forward. "I will be terribly bruised. I was tossed about that carriage as if I were a rag doll."

Apparently, his willow tree lady was content to let the sister talk. *His* willow tree lady? When had he begun to think of her as his? Tad swallowed.

She continued to look at him; cautious but also curious. He moved to her side. "And you will be all right, miss...?" He drew the last word out.

She opened her mouth to speak, only to be cut off by her sister. "Although we have not been properly introduced, I believe under the circumstances we can skirt propriety."

Tad gave a silent sigh as he turned his attention to the sister.

"My name is Rose Allen and this is my younger sister, Violet. I do not believe we have the pleasure of knowing the name of our rescuer." She took a breath, at last, revealing far too many teeth as she smiled up at him.

Violet. He looked at her with appraising eyes, smiling. Yes, the name was fitting. Her black hair shone with a purple hue in the sunlight and at both of their meetings he had noticed the scent of violets.

"Miss Violet, I am afraid I did not hear your answer. Are you well?" His hands tingled as he waited to hear her voice again. It had drifted across his mind when he was idle. And even sometimes when he wasn't.

She gave a timid smile before ducking her head and settling her gaze on Dawson.

Tad frowned.

"I am quite well, sir. Thank you for your concern. I believe Becky sustained greater injuries than I. Perhaps you could see to her first." Miss Violet's head stayed lowered, but she often looked up at him. His stomach flipped.

Tad saw Becky smiling happily, clutching Dawson's handkerchief tightly in her hand.

With a satisfied nod, he turned to Rose, fearing he had actually heard her correctly. "Did you say your name was Miss Allen? And you are engaged to the Duke of Shearsby?"

Rose nodded vigorously. "Yes. I am on my way there now. I am from Kidsgrove, you see."

He looked at her for several moments, his head shaking slightly. This is what his uncle had secured for him?

She was beautiful. Her golden hair shimmered in the sunlight. Her skin was smooth and fair. But then she opened her mouth and all interest drained from him. Under the right circumstances, Miss Allen would make someone a very proper wife.

He took a step back, rubbing the back of his neck. Must he be that someone? He closed his eyes, taking a breath. Promises had been made. Promises he was expected to keep.

Tad nodded his head. "Yes, so you said earlier. May I ask what exactly put you in your current predicament? Where is your father? Is he not accompanying you?"

Rose shook her head. "No. Papa had business that kept him away longer than expected. He will meet up with us tomorrow before we continue on to Morley Park." She took a rapid breath and continued. "A highwayman forced the carriage to stop and demanded we stand and deliver. Can you believe it? I had thought such things were only done in gothic novels." Miss Allen spoke about the most recent novel she had read that contained a highwayman, but Tad had ceased listening.

His head twitched, perhaps trying to shake the noise from his ears. Could she not tell her story any quicker? The tale continued on with no ending in sight.

"I have never been so scared in all my life. Our coachman, Richard, fired upon the highwayman, but the blackguard fired back." Rose seemed to realize she had no idea the condition of the coachman. She looked around until she saw Dawson attending to the horses. "Is our coachman injured? I heard another shot. What happened to Richard?"

Looking in the direction of the horses, Tad shook his head. "He was knocked unconscious, but does not appear to have sustained any other injuries. The shot missed."

Barely acknowledging the statement, Miss Allen began talking again. "Oh, I am very relieved to hear he will be well. As I was saying, he set the horses going. I do not understand how he became unconscious, but that must have been the reason the carriage bounced around as it did." She took a quick breath.

Tad leaned forward, believing the story was at an end. As her mouth opened, his hopes were crushed. He blinked slowly, leaving his eyes closed long enough to keep his composure as her voice sounded again.

"I am grateful you came upon us when you did, sir. I am well, I assure you. At least as well as can be expected under the circumstances. I am very... Oh." She stopped. "We are much indebted to you."

Ah, she did realize she was not traveling alone.

"And how did you come to be engaged to the duke?" he asked.

"Do you know the family well?" He cast his eyes over to Miss Violet. She quickly looked down at her slippers. He thought he saw a hint of a smile before she lowered her head.

"Only my father is acquainted with the family." Miss Allen narrowed her eyes, flicking her gaze between Miss Violet and him. "My sister and I have never been invited to Morley Park before. The old duke was ill and died before we had a chance to visit. I will admit, the offer came as quite a surprise to all of us. Normally, I would not accept a proposal offered in a letter, but he is a duke." She leaned in as if sharing a secret. "From what I have heard, he has over twenty thousand a year. A lady does not turn down such an offer."

So she was seeking a title and a fortune.

Afraid there was not enough time in the day to hear her answers, Tad tried to avoid asking Miss Allen any more questions. He directed his conversation to Miss Violet. "Are you traveling directly to Morley Park?"

Violet shook her head. "As my sister said, we are to meet our father at the Inn at Shearsby today. We will all travel on to Morley Park tomorrow."

Tad extended his hand toward the carriage. "Then we should get you ladies on your way. We will see you into Shearsby. It is not far from here."

He turned to Rose, his voice lacking in enthusiasm. "May I help you into the carriage, Miss Allen?"

After handing her up, he turned to Miss Violet. Offering his hand, he helped her into the carriage as well, holding on a bit longer than necessary, capturing her gaze in his. "I am relieved you were not seriously injured. But to be safe, you should have a doctor look at those cuts." His chest constricted slightly, feeling genuine concern for her.

Miss Violet lifted her fingers to her brow, running it tentatively over the crusted blood. She gave him a questioning glance, almost as if his concern confused her, but nodded in response. She moved to a seat at the opposite side of the carriage.

Dawson came from behind, ready to help both of the young maids into the coach. When the door was shut and the ladies secure inside, Tad turned to Dawson. "I will drive the carriage into town. You will bring the horses and follow behind?"

Dawson pulled his hat down farther on his brow, shielding the sun from his eyes. "I can manage the carriage. It is not a task a duke should lower himself to do." There was a hint of sarcasm in his tone.

Tad smirked. "As you told me before, I am not an average duke." He grabbed hold of the handrail and swung up into the driver's box. The driver was awake, sitting on the bench but it was obvious he was not yet fit to drive. Tad flicked the reins and the carriage began to move, with Dawson following behind. The coach rambled down the road, not stopping until it pulled up in front of the only inn.

Tad leaped from the box and opened the door, ready to begin handing the ladies out. Once they were safely on the ground, he smiled brightly at Miss Violet, bowing over her hand and placing a kiss on her glove. "It was a pleasure to you see again, Miss Violet. I look forward to our next encounter." His voice was barely more than a whisper. "Although, I hope it shall be under less dramatic circumstances." He turned toward Rose and brushed his lips across her hand as well. Bowing to them all, he mounted his horse and tipped his hat to them.

Becky stepped forward, making a quick curtsy. "I beg your pardon, sir. How shall we return your handkerchief back to you?"

Tad looked to Miss Violet as he spoke. "Keep them for now. I do not believe this is goodbye."

He clicked his tongue, lightly jabbing his heels into his horse's side. The animal began a slow trot down the road. The feeling he was being watched made him want to turn around and look. But he didn't give in to the urge.

"She is still watching you if you were in doubt." Dawson hung back slightly. "The maid is as well. It seems you have made quite an impression on both of them." Dawson glanced over his shoulder again. "The sister has retreated inside the inn. Perhaps she will be as disenchanted about marrying you as you are about her."

"You do not think she liked me, then?" He should not hope for such things. Did it even matter if they got on well? "Unless I lose my title and money before they reach Morley, I doubt I shall be so lucky." His voice sounded as dull as he felt. They rode in silence for several miles, neither of them speaking. Tad replayed the afternoon over and over in his mind.

Dawson urged his horse forward. "You are still intent on marrying her? Even after you have met her?" His voice held wonder. Or was it censure? "I know you, Tad. That woman will drive you mad."

Tad's shoulders sagged. "What am I to do, Dawson? Pledges have been made. It is not Miss Allen's fault my uncle was high handed and made arrangements he was not at liberty to make. Should she suffer because of it?"

"But you should?" Dawson barked.

Tad did not need to have this conversation—again. "I am done speaking of it. They will arrive tomorrow and there is nothing to be done about it."

His neck was tight and his head was beginning to pound. Wishing to delay the stress which was inevitable, he turned his mind to more pleasant thoughts.

He had met Miss Violet a second time. And she was coming to meet him at Morley Park. A picture of her walking the halls of his home brought a warmth into his chest and a smile to his face.

Grudgingly he pushed it aside. If only it could be so...it may not be possible after tomorrow, but until then he was free to imagine whatever he wished.

Dawson moved his horse alongside, but his lips stayed shut. Instead, he watched Tad for several moments.

Finally, unable to stand the silence any longer, Tad turned toward his riding companion. "What, Dawson? You have something on your mind. I can hear you thinking all the way over here."

"There is so much going through my mind, I do not know if I can even put it into words."

"Try," Tad said dryly.

Dawson cocked his head to the side. "I am surprised you are smiling, considering you just met Miss Allen." He leaned forward, looking more closely at Tad. "You do remember her? The chatty one?"

Tad nodded.

"And yet, your smile is so large, it has almost forced your eyes closed. Perhaps you could marry the other one and still fulfill your duty to the family."

Tad shook his head. "From what my aunt has told me if I were to marry the sister it would ruin Miss Allen." Tad shook his head, a sigh escaping his lips. "While I may not enjoy her company, she does not deserve such treatment. No. My course is set. Nothing has changed."

Dawson chuckled. "Oh, I believe many things have changed. For one, the mysterious girl you have been thinking about for nigh unto a fortnight has reappeared and is the sister to your betrothed." He shook his head, pushing his horse a little farther ahead. "Things have changed."

Tad spurred his horse forward, his emotions jumbled. He had been happy to see Miss Violet again, but now? How would he feel when he was married to Miss Allen? Would he be able to think of her as a sister? He twitched. He had never thought of his sisters, Liza and Aisling, the way he thought about Miss Violet.

"I know nothing about her. Perhaps she already has an agreement with a gentleman. Did you think on that, Dawson?" Tad felt slightly better until Dawson chuckled again.

"You know she is courageous. Many have married knowing less. You know Miss Allen even less, but you still seem intent on marrying her." He glanced over at Tad and sighed. "I'm sorry. This cannot be easy on you and I am only making it more difficult."

Tad looked out at the surrounding grounds. They had reached the borders of Morley and all the land in front of them was his. Oh, how his life had changed in less than a year.

"I have put in the order for the cows. They should be weaned from their mothers and arrive just as you return from town. It will take a few years, but I think we should be able to create a sustainable herd." Dawson changed from friend to secretary in the blink of an eye.

The earlier pressures seemed to lift slightly and a small seed of excitement swelled within him at the thought of their plans for this estate. Tad kept his gaze fixed on the road in front of them. "Thank you, Dawson."

He pulled his horse to a stop and sat up straighter in the saddle. Looking out over the land, he could almost see the fields dotted with cows.

Taking a deep breath of the warm afternoon air, he settled back into his seat. Casting a glance at his friend, he shouted, "Race you back to the stables. Loser shines the winner's boots." He dug his heels into his horse's side, shouting "hiya," and shot down the lane, with Dawson only a rod's length behind him.

CHAPTER 9

Tad sat at the head of the table, looking at his relatives seated down the table on either side. He would never have guessed, while on the ship for all those weeks, that he was leaving one family behind only to discover another here in England. It was not the same as having his mother and siblings here, but it was enough to help take the constant ache away. He did not know what he would have done without Dawson as a part of this new family. Even with Lady Mayfield's disagreeable nature, Tad was glad she and Lord Mayfield were here with him.

"We had an interesting morning, did we not Dawson?" Tad glanced down the table. Aunt Standish and Jes stopped eating and looked up at him, while Lady Mayfield continued to tuck away the duck on her plate.

Lady Rachel raised her brows. "And do you intend to share or was it more of a general announcement?"

Tad could not help but laugh at his aunt. She was, in his opinion, almost the perfect lady. She was dignified and graceful, yet knew when the time was right for a little humor and even at times, sarcasm. Her sister, in contrast, was dignified and had some grace, but she lacked something Lady Rachel possessed.

"I shall if you are interested. Some seem more interested in the duck than in any conversation I may put forth." Tad glanced at his aunt and uncle. Neither acknowledged his barb. But seeing Aunt Standish and Jes, still watching him intently, he continued on. "We happened upon a runaway carriage while we were on our morning ride."

Jes gasped. "What happened? Were the passengers harmed?"

Lady Rachel patted the girl's hand. "Now, Jes. If you interrupt the story, we shall never have your questions answered. Let your cousin finish."

"Not to worry, cousin. Everyone was well." He paused. "Except perhaps the driver. He was knocked unconscious, but when we left him at the hotel, he was awake and seemed intact."

Jes set down her fork. "How did it all come to be?"

Tad smiled as Lady Rachel patted her daughter's hand again, looking pointedly at her. Jes closed her mouth and frowned, but did not venture to ask another question. Tad explained about the highwayman and the gunshot. He was surprised when even that part of the story did not draw Lady Mayfield's attention. Her husband did look up when he heard news of the shots but promptly returned to his meal.

Dawson finally cleared his throat, drawing Jes's attention on him. She smiled brightly at him and Tad wondered, not for the first time if his cousin had a tendré for his friend.

"You have neglected to share the most interesting part, Your Grace."

Tad bristled at Dawson's formality, but remembering the lecture from Lady Mayfield about society and expectations, both men had decided to use the title when the lady was around.

When Tad did not immediately share what Dawson was alluding to, Jes turned to Tad, her eyes wide.

"Ah, yes I did neglect to mention the names of the occupants. Dawson and I were fortunate enough to meet Miss Allen and her sister Miss Violet." Tad felt a small victory when Lady Mayfield paused with her fork halfway to her mouth. She set the utensil on her plate and looked at her nephew.

"And what were your thoughts on the girl?"

Tad sighed. His thoughts had been more on Miss Violet than Miss Allen. And the thoughts he had of Miss Allen were not the most complimentary. "The lady seemed to have very healthy lungs."

Dawson choked on his wine. He set the glass down and scowled at Tad. The slight twitching of his lips betrayed his gruff demeanor.

Jes glanced between the two men. "A healthy set of lungs? What does that even mean? Why must you talk in riddles?"

Sitting back in his chair, Tad played with his abandoned fork. "It means she talks a great deal." He smiled at Lady Mayfield sitting next to him. "You should find her very diverting, Aunt."

His aunt huffed. "I am not sure what your uncle was thinking by aligning you with this family. I have been getting reports..." Tad shook his head. He noticed whenever Lady Mayfield approved of something Uncle James had done, it was *my brother*. Whereas when she disapproved of his actions, he was always *your uncle*.

"And what do your reports say, Aunt? Is the marriage to be called off completely?" A hint of hope tingled in Tad's stomach at the prospect of canceling the whole thing.

She shook her head. "I have no details—nothing which could justify such an action." Pushing her plate away from her, she focused her attention fully on Tad. "It is all just vague mentions of a scandal.

One gabster says it is the mother and another claims the sister is to blame. It doesn't rightly matter who is the cause, the whole family is tarnished." Her head began to shake again. "I just cannot imagine that obscurity was more important than a tarnished reputation."

Tad and Dawson exchanged a glance. Perhaps this could be used to break the contract. If there was indeed a contract. They had yet to find any papers linking Tad to the family, save the note he had received in Liverpool.

Aunt Standish put her serviette on the table. "With so little information, it could be there is no scandal at all. Just an unsubstantiated rumor. James knew Lord Winslow. I cannot imagine he would jeopardize the family name or the title by linking Tad to a family such as that."

Tad did not know how he should feel about what his aunts said. Part of him wanted the rumors to be true so the contract could be broken, but another part of him wanted them to be false so Miss Violet was not a part of it. The lady had suffered enough, just in the short time he had known her. He did not want her to be tainted.

Lady Mayfield shrugged. "We may never know the truth of it. But whether it is false or not, the rumor is enough to tarnish the Wentworth name."

Tad leaned forward. "Which will be worse?" He looked between both women. While they were very different in their approach to society, they both knew it very well. One from living in it and the other from being cast out of it.

"It is hard to say. If we knew the extent of the scandal, it would be easier to decide. But without that information..." Lady Rachel looked to Lady Mayfield for her input.

"Normally I would recommend throwing the girl over and breaking all ties to the family. But our nephew is an unknown. His title holds weight in society, but he does not. Not yet."

Tad grunted and ran a hand through his hair. "What shall it be? What do you recommend?"

Lady Mayfield narrowed her eyes at Tad. "I recommend you stay the course until we have a reason to break the contract."

"Very well." Tad's shoulders drooped.

"Disappointment is not an excuse to get indolent. Your American manners will be your undoing." She turned to her sister. "Mark my words, Rachel."

Aunt Standish smiled at Tad. "I believe you are doing it much too brown, sister. Tad will do well."

"You are coddling him." Lady Mayfield motioned for a footman to pull her chair out. "I am ready to remove to the parlor. Come along Jessica."

Staring sadly at her half-eaten ice, Jes set her spoon down and pushed her seat out.

"Jessica." Lady Mayfield did not even turn her head as she walked toward the doorway.

Jes looked at Tad. He shrugged then winked at her, earning him a small smile.

Lady Rachel laid a hand on Tad's shoulder. "Do not let Lydia discourage you, nephew. You are doing well. I am pleased with your effort, as I am sure your father would be also."

"Thank you, Aunt."

The ladies disappeared, leaving the men to their port. Tad hated port and he did not smoke. He did not understand why he should have to stay behind when he could be visiting with his aunt and Jes.

CHAPTER 10

Violet descended the steps and entered the darkened interior of the tap room, feeling the effects of the day. Becky had seen to her cuts and now all she wanted was some food and rest. Feeling as if she could finally take a deep breath, she rubbed lightly at the bandage above her eye.

The room was beginning to fill with people. Between the arrival of the post-chaise and those seeking their evening meal, the public parlor had taken on a rather frenzied feel. Violet slid into a chair, content to retreat into her thoughts.

Her mind still reeled from seeing Mr. Dashing. It seemed he was destined to rescue her from whatever scrapes she managed to get into.

"I thought you were going to secure a private parlor?" Rose asked from halfway across the room.

Waiting until her sister had traveled closer to the table, Violet finally spoke. "Lower your voice. There were no private parlors available. This will have to do. If you cannot abide it, I will have a tray sent to your room, as you requested earlier." Violet knew her voice came out sounding terse, but she was tired. Listening to her sister's chatter after the day's events would only make Violet cross.

A passing servant stopped, asking after their requests.

Rose narrowed her eyes, before turning her mouth into a pout. She pulled out the chair across from her sister. "I am here now, I may as well stay and keep you company."

Violet tried not to let the irritation show. Rose's idea of company was a one-sided conversation about Rose.

"That is very kind of you, Rose. But are you not too fatigued? You did have a harrowing afternoon." Violet tried to look at her sister sympathetically, hoping she would return to her chambers and leave Violet in peace.

Rose patted Violet's hand. "It is kind of you to worry about me, sister. Although I did receive the brunt of the jostles in that carriage, I find I am in need of some society." She turned her nose up. "It would seem *this* is what constitutes society here."

Violet gazed around the room. "I see nothing here so distasteful. You act as if this is so very different than Kidsgrove."

Rose forced a chuckle. "Kidsgrove was equally stifling. I cannot expect you to understand, Violet dear, because I know you have never experienced London. But I can assure you, if you had, you would find this society very lacking." Shaking her head, she turned back to Violet. "It is no matter. I am tired of staring at the filthy walls of my bedchamber so this will have to do."

"Did you not sleep while in your room?"

"The bed is too lumpy. I am sure I will not get a wink of sleep tonight." Sniffing at the food being placed before them, Rose continued on. "When will father arrive? I thought he would be here before us. I still cannot believe he did not travel with us. What if the duke should find out? Such neglect would not look well upon Papa."

Violet ripped a small hunk of bread off the loaf in the center of the table and dipped it into her bowl of stew. This was one of the topics where the sisters actually agreed. Violet was used to her father's lack of interest in them, but sending them on alone had surprised even her. "There was a message waiting for us. His business took longer than he expected. He will be arriving late tonight. I would not plan on seeing him before you retire."

Violet looked around the inn, hoping to see Mr. Dashing standing amongst the other guests or sitting at a table watching her with interest. While he had not specifically said he lived nearby, she believed he did. But he was nowhere to be seen. Chiding herself for her silly fantasies, she took another bite of dinner.

"That gentleman, if he was indeed one, was certainly peculiar." Rose eyed her from across the table.

"Hum? Which gentleman?" Violet feigned ignorance.

"Our rescuer. You do remember him, do you not?"

"Of course I remember him. I am not a dim-wit. What do you mean 'if he is indeed one'?" Violet shook her head. "He dressed like a gentleman. Spoke as one. What would lead you to believe he is not?"

Rose gave a slight shrug. "He certainly did not walk like a gentleman. His cadence was more like that of a farmhand. There was something about him that was different, but I cannot put my finger on what."

"I did not think it overly odd." Violet furrowed her brow, feeling defensive of Mr. Dashing. "His walk was not as stiff and off-putting as many gentlemen I have met, but I did not see it as an indicator of low breeding. He seemed to me to be very comfortable with himself and those around him. I am of the opinion he is indeed a gentleman." Violet looked up to see Rose studying her closely.

"He took a particular interest in you, sister. It was almost as if you had met before." Rose arched a brow and pursed her lips.

The conversation was taking a turn, not to her liking. Desperate, Violet steered it in another direction. "It is of no matter if he is a gentleman or not. After all, it is not as if we will see him again."

Rose shrugged her shoulders. "You are right, the chances are very unlikely, indeed."

"Then we shall not think of him again." Stuffing a large piece of bread in her mouth, Violet hoped Rose would interpret the action correctly and stop talking.

Violet would only admit to herself she was intrigued by him. The more she thought on him, the more curious she became. She had been certain she would never set eyes on him again. Which was precisely why she had allowed herself to think on him. She could give him whatever character she wanted and never be disappointed when he did not live up to it. But now, she was not sure what to think.

Violet sat in a settee near the fireplace at Morley Park, the location offering the best view of the entire room. The butler had called it the Green Parlor, a name well suited. Cream painted panels covered the walls on the lower half, while the upper wall was covered in a light, dusty green damask. The windows were adorned with layers of fabric. A light sheer fabric hung on the inside of the window. Currently, it was pushed open, allowing the full grandeur of the countryside to be seen, but she could imagine the filtered light the sheers afforded in the late afternoon. The chairs were covered in an array of different fabrics, their colors varying in creams and greens.

Her father paced the floor, talking quietly to himself.

Rose walked about looking at the details of the room, before coming and settling herself next to Violet.

"Have you ever seen such a fine room? I have seen none like it, not even in London." Rose smiled, her eyes wide.

Content to live in her own thoughts, Violet shook her head. She could picture Mr. Dashing living in such a place. It was lovely and peaceful here, just as he was. She blushed at the thought of calling him lovely.

The door opened, interrupting Violet's thought. The butler entered, cleared his throat and announced His Grace, the Duke of Shearsby. Rose straightened, running her hands down the front of her gown, before standing up to greet the duke.

Violet stood, even as she tried to recapture her previous thoughts. She was curious about her sister's intended, but not enough to cease her imagining of Mr. Dashing. But her father's hasty movements toward the door captured her attention. His eagerness to meet the duke was obvious and slightly embarrassing. Violet shifted her gaze to her father and the duke. Her breath caught and her mouth dropped open at the same time Rose whispered, "It's him."

It was him. Her Mr. Dashing stood just inside the room, taking it all in with a sweep of his eyes.

Blinking rapidly several times, she clamped her mouth shut. Violet corrected herself mentally. He was not her Mr. Dashing. In fact, he was not Mr. Dashing at all, but rather, His Grace, the Duke of Shearsby and her sister's intended.

When his eyes stopped on her, she felt the heat rise in her cheeks. The folly of her imaginings over the last few days crashed upon her like waves upon a shore.

Mr. Dashing, or rather His Grace, walked with her father toward her. "Lord Winslow, I am honored to welcome you and your daughters to Morley Park."

A fluttering started in her stomach at hearing his deep voice— the voice that had filled her dreams of late.

She pushed the sensation down, casting a guilty glance at Rose as if her sister knew her feelings. Rose stood still next to Violet.

"Your Grace." Her father smiled a bit too widely. "It is indeed a pleasure."

"Please introduce me to your lovely daughters." The duke inclined his head in their direction.

A tightness squeezed in her chest as their eyes met. She could not seem to quell her thumping heart. It beat so wildly, she could feel it pounding in her neck. Convinced everyone could see the reaction, she discreetly moved her fingers over the offending throb, pretending to scratch an imaginary itch.

The duke's gaze studied her, taking an accounting of her.

"Your Grace, this is my youngest daughter, Miss Violet Allen."

Violet curtsied deeply, only able to meet those stormy blue eyes once, before she looked away. "A pleasure, Your Grace."

As she rose, she looked up at him, but Mr. Dashing is whom she saw through lowered lashes. She knew she should not think of him as Mr. Dashing any longer, but looking at him standing before her, she couldn't think of him as anything else. What harm would it do if she thought of him as such? She smiled at her own little secret.

"Ah, but the pleasure is all mine, Miss Violet." He bowed, but not before winking at her.

Her face heated. Nobody had ever winked at her. Who knew it could cause such flutters in her stomach?

It was the first time she had seen him not on a horse or out of doors. The image was as pleasing as before but in a very different way. His hair was neatly styled, save the lock which swished upwards and then back down over his brow. It was most likely the result of a cowlick. Her smiles grew at the thought of him taming the unruly hair each morning. Her eyes dropped to his mouth. A twitch played at the corners, bringing out the dimple in his cheek.

His lips finally curled into a full smile. He knew she was assessing him and that he had earned her approval. Surprised, she flicked her eyes upward, capturing his gaze.

Her father moved Dashing to Rose, breaking the contact. Suddenly, the thought of Rose marrying him made her feel hot and cold at the same time. She would take his title and his money, but would she ever truly love him? He deserved someone who would appreciate him, not what he possessed. He deserved...Violet.

"And this is Miss Rose Allen, my eldest daughter."

Giving a tight smile, the duke dipped his head. "It is a pleasure to see you again, Miss Allen."

She curtsied. "The pleasure is all mine. Although, why you chose to play this little game, I do not understand."

He turned away from them and walked around the coffee table, settling himself into the seat across from her.

Her father took the chair next to the duke's, confusion wrinkling his brow. "Pray, what do you mean, 'It is a pleasure to see you again'? When, exactly have you laid eyes on my daughter before?"

Dashing looked from Violet to Rose and then back to Violet, again.

The door opened and a maid carrying a tea tray entered. A procession of people followed along behind.

Everyone rose again as an older woman with a pinched face walked over and stood in front of them. "Mayfield, go fetch a few more chairs so we might all sit and get acquainted over tea."

The duke moved from his place. "Please take my seat, Aunt Mayfield. I will fetch the chairs." The woman opened her mouth, but the duke gave a slight shake of his head.

A girl about Violet's age followed the duke. "I'll help."

Walking to the far side of the room, he picked up a straight-backed chair in each hand and carried them over. He placed them in the space between the couch and the chair her father occupied. Lady Rachel and her father took these seats and waited while the duke and the girl returned with three more chairs. The duke moved and sat down in the chair next to Violet.

She looked around. Why had they brought over an extra seat? As if in answer to her unasked question, a door on the far side of the room opened and a gentleman walked in. It was the man who had been with Dashing both times she had encountered him. He sat down on the chair next to Lord Winslow, with Miss Standish sitting between them.

Violet took the opportunity to look at the new arrivals as everyone settled into their seats. No one spoke as gazes flicked in all directions.

The pinched-faced woman huffed and looked at the duke expectantly.

His eyes widened and his face pinked slightly. "Oh, yes. I beg your pardon, Aunt. Let me make the introductions."

These ladies were the duke's relatives. Violet looked at them more closely. Now that she knew the connection, she could see the similarities between the duke and Lady Mayfield. It was harder to see them in Lady Rachel, but a few were there—the shape of her mouth and the set of her eyes.

Lady Mayfield poured out the tea in all the cups but one. In it, she poured a dark brown liquid from a second pot. She added a bit of sugar and a splash of cream before handing it to the duke.

"Thank you, Lady Mayfield. It is just how I like it."

"What is it in your cup, Your Grace? It looks different than the coffee I have seen." Rose asked.

Lady Mayfield spoke before the duke was able. "That is because it is chocolate. He grew up drinking it, apparently." There was a touch of disapproval in her voice.

Lady Rachel coughed lightly, eyeing her sister. Returning her attention back to the Allen's, Lady Rachel smiled. "How were your travels? I understand you ran into a bit of trouble?"

The duke leaned toward Violet slightly and whispered. "Surprise?" His eyes held a combination of mirth and vulnerability.

Tilting her head to lessen the distance between them, she nodded. "Yes, indeed."

He quirked a brow at her, his grin slipping back into place. "I hope, at least it is a pleasant one. But from the look on your face, I confess I am not sure." His voice was quiet, the conversation taking place only between the two of them.

She opened her mouth to reply but was interrupted by her father. Thankfully, for she had no idea what she going to say.

"When exactly have you laid eyes on my daughter before?" He asked again.

The duke turned back toward Lord Winslow. "Actually, I have met both of your daughters."

A sharp intake of breath drew his attention back to her once again. *Oh, please do not mention the willow tree.* She pled with her eyes, hoping he could understand what she was telling him.

Dashing never had the chance to mention their first meeting. He never had a chance to say anything else.

"It is him, Papa. The gentleman who stopped the carriage after the horses bolted." There was a look of shock and slight confusion as if she was still reconciling the duke standing in front of her with the rescuer from yesterday.

Lord Winslow looked back to him. "It was you? The gentleman who saved my daughters?"

Dashing turned back toward the baron with a sigh, nodding his head reluctantly. A look of embarrassment crossed his face. Modesty was the last thing Violet expected from a duke, but from Dashing she was not surprised.

Her father set aside his cup and stood up. Crossing in front of the others he stood before the duke. Reluctantly, His Grace stood up. Her father thrust out his hand, and he began to pump the duke's hand vigorously. "Oh, Your Grace. I owe you so much more than gratitude. But I am sure there is nothing I could offer that you do not already have. I am in your debt. You need only ask."

Dashing smiled, what looked to be a genuine one. "It was no more than any gentlemen would have done, Lord Winslow."

"Please, we need not be so formal. After all, we are to be father and son soon enough."

Dashing stiffened.

Rose spoke up. Her earlier look of shock, replaced by one of feigned excitement. "Oh, this will make a delicious tale. It will be all the talk of the upcoming season. I am sure of it."

The duke and her father resumed their seats, but as the duke picked up his cup he turned to Rose. "I would prefer the story not leave this room."

Rose laughed, shooing him with her hand. "You cannot be serious, Your Grace. It is truly a delightful story. Who would ever believe you rescued a runaway carriage only to find it carried your betrothed inside."

Violet's breath hitched as she looked back and forth between the two. She kept forgetting this man was engaged to her sister. Violet needed to quit her fantasies of Mr. Dashing and look upon him as what he was or would soon be—her brother.

The duke gave a stiff smile. "If no one will believe the story, there is no point in relating it." His deep baritone voice resonated with irritation. He straightened, sitting up taller in his chair. "As I said, the story shall not leave this house and that is final."

Rose narrowed her eyes slightly at the insistence, her mouth turning down into a pout.

Violet's eyebrows rose. In all of her imaginings, Mr. Dashing had never spoken in this manner. He had always been kind and gentle. It occurred to her she did not know the duke at all. For the person before her was most assuredly the Duke of Shearsby. It made her look at him in a new light.

He placed his cup back on the tray, then looked from Violet to her father. "The ladies look as if they could use some rest." He turned his gaze back to her. "Mayhap after luncheon, we could take a tour of the formal gardens?" He pulled his gaze away, looking to the group.

Her father nodded his consent. "Capital idea, Your Grace."

Violet moved toward the doorway, falling into place behind Rose. Before moving into the hall she looked back at the duke. He caught her gaze, quirked a brow and gave a half smile, followed by a slight bow. Her heart began its irregular beat. Turning into the hall, she quickened her pace to catch up with the others. It appeared Mr. Dashing had returned and her resolved had all but fallen away.

CHAPTER 11

Violet closed the door to her chambers. Rose exited from the next room, coming to stand next to Violet. Looking at her sister, Violet raised a brow. "I thought you had a headache."

Rose shrugged. "I have decided I shall go on the tour after all. I should get better acquainted with him."

They met the duke and Miss Standish in the entryway. His face showed neither excitement nor disappointment when he saw Rose walking beside Violet. Miss Standish held a small basket in one hand.

"Ah, you have found a fourth for our little party." His voice lowered slightly. "The more the merrier."

Miss Standish led the way as they walked down the stairs of the terrace. Once her foot stepped off the stone step, Violet was surrounded by garden mounds. The centers were filled with tall flower spikes in blues, purples, and pinks, clusters of asters growing among various ornamental grasses. Many of the flowers had lost their bloom, their petals laying on the ground, dried and dulled. Only a few strong plants still bloomed among the beds. Instead of moving along the path through the flowers and trees of the formal gardens, they turned and took the path leading into the wilds beyond.

"There is a river beyond that hedgerow." The duke pointed off into the distance. "I thought we could start there and work our way through the formal gardens back to the house. Do you have any objections?" His beaver kept most of his hair in place, save for the lock in the front, which blew gently.

"I cannot think of even one." It was a lovely day and Violet was happy to spend it outside.

"I can." Rose huffed beside her. "I thought we were going on a tour of the house. I did not dress to go traipsing about the wild countryside. What if I should snag my dress?"

"But I thought..." Tad looked between the two women and then at Miss Standish. She lifted her shoulder and brows. The cousins seemed to almost read one another's minds. Violet felt a tug in her chest. She had never had such a relationship before.

"We could turn back and limit our walk to the formal gardens." Obvious disappointment sounded in his voice.

When no one else replied, Rose grunted, flicking her gaze upward. "Oh, very well. I shall watch my step. But I hope the views will be worth the trouble."

The duke led the way down a path big enough for two to walk side by side. Rose moved up beside him, leaving Violet and Miss Standish to walk together. The duke spoke, but only to point out things around the estate.

They walked mostly in silence, the open fields glowing golden in the sunlight. Autumn was beginning to set in, making the days slightly chilly, in spite of the sun.

"That building over there is where I thought we could lay out the blan..."

Violet shivered, just as the duke turned to point out the little building as it came into view.

"Are you cold?" The duke asked with a touch of concern in his voice. "We can return to the house."

"No. I am well. The beauty gave me gooseflesh. That is all." She looked around her. "These are such lovely grounds. Winter will be here before long; we should enjoy them, while we have the chance."

Tilting her head up, she smiled as the sun's rays kissed her nose and eyelids.

"Very well, we will continue on. But, please tell me if your wishes change." Silence descended again as they walked. Rose turned her head back long enough to purse her lips and widen her eyes at Violet.

"It is very beautiful here." He turned his head to include Violet and Miss Standish in the conversation. "Since coming, I have asked myself many times how my father left this place. Although, I can see why he chose Penn...." His brow furrowed and he looked quickly between each of them. Turning his head forward, he continued. "Er, the islands. There are a few similarities." His voice floated back to her on the breeze. His hand went to the back of his neck, rubbing it several times.

Violet raised her voice so he could hear her. "In what way, Your Grace?"

He came to a stop, forcing Rose to stop also. She folded her arms across her chest. The duke turned back to face Violet and Miss Standish. "There are fields as far as the eye can see. Sugar cane does not look all that different from these grains, at least early in the season. By the end, they are much taller, but the overall look is similar. Although the islands are more mountainous and I am sure the winters are significantly different."

Violet could hear the longing in his voice. She could only

imagine what it would feel like to leave everything familiar and move to a place so far away and vastly different. He must notice even the most insignificant similarities. "You miss it, do you not?" Their gazes met and held for a moment.

"I do, very much. Although, not as much as I assumed I would. I believe it must be because this place feels like home. I feel a sense of history here. My history." He looked around the countryside. "My family has lived here for hundreds of years. My father used to tell us stories about my grandfather and his father before him. So, while I have never been here, I feel as if I have."

He shook his head, a scowl turning down the corners of his mouth. He turned back around and began walking down the path. His voice lowered and Violet had to strain to hear him. "It is something Dawson refuses to understand."

They reached the stream and Violet gawked. What she thought was a stream was most definitely a river. Measuring at least three rods across, it boasted a moderate size waterfall and an arched stone bridge. "I had no idea it was this large. From my window, it appeared much smaller."

The duke looked out over the river and chuckled. "I had the same notion, until Dawson and I explored this area last week. Although I should have known, my father talked of a mill that once operated on the property. I always assumed the flow had decreased because the mill was no longer in use." He nodded to the little building he had pointed out earlier. "That is it, right there."

"This is it? This is what I walked through the wilderness to see?" Rose looked about, her face puckered up.

The duke opened his mouth, but then closed it and frowned. "I am sorry it does not meet with your approval."

Violet stepped between her sister and the duke. Why was Rose behaving like a spoiled little girl? Looking back to the duke, she smiled. "Why did they stop using it... the mill? Is it not used for anything?" The duke glanced at Rose one last time before turning his attention fully to Violet.

"I do not remember being told why they closed it up. According to my father, it was not used while he lived here. From the looks of it, my uncle did not find a use for it either. Perhaps it could lend some shade to place our hamper." He moved toward it, his hands clasped firmly behind his back.

Unable to think of another topic, but needing to be rid of the strained silence, Violet asked, "Your friend came with you from the islands?" The breeze cooled her suddenly warm cheeks. "I beg your pardon."

He shrugged, seemingly unaffected by her forwardness. "Yes. Dawson was..." He put a finger to his lips, his brow puckered. "Persuaded to join me on this adventure."

She frowned slightly. "Why does Mr. Dawson disapprove of all he sees?" She bit her lip. "It seems my family is especially distasteful to him."

Rose swatted a hand at Violet's arm. "Violet, dear. A lady does not discuss such things with a gentleman." A smile curved her lips, but there was no mirth in her eyes.

The duke did not respond, at least not in words. His scowl deepened.

Violet sighed, inwardly berating herself. Why had she discussed such a topic when she barely knew this man? What was it about him that made her speak so freely? And why was she asking so much about Mr. Dawson?

They reached the mill and he removed a blanket from the hamper. Silently he laid the blanket on the ground.

Violet stood in the shadow of the mill and closed her eyes. The river swirled and the leaves fluttered in the breeze. The air smelled of autumn; soil mixed with fresh cut grains. A shiver raced down her body. Whether from the coolness of the shade or the perfection of the moment, she was not sure.

"It would seem it is too cold here in the shade. Perhaps we should put the blanket over in the sun. But will it be too bright?" The duke looked around them, his eyes squinting, before laying the blanket in a sunnier location.

Miss Standish came over, a shaft of wheat twisting in her fingers. She sat next to Violet, looking into the hamper. Pulling it closer, Miss Standish looked to the duke and asked, "May I?" Her hands hovered over the lid.

Rose let out a cough of disbelief. She stared down at the blanket as if the thought of sitting on it was of utmost distaste.

All eyes turned to her before the duke pulled his away and he nodded to his cousin. He sat down, stretching his long legs out in front of him.

Miss Standish began removing several serviette bundles, revealing different biscuits and cakes along with a service of tea.

"Dawson can be hard to figure out." He spoke to no one in particular.

His cousin snorted, then colored as she looked up at them. "I beg your pardon. Mr. Dawson is very kind."

The duke grinned. "I am sure he will be happy to learn of your good opinion, Jes." He turned his gaze back to Violet. "He does not, however, disapprove of you or your family. It is more a disapproval of this place and the circumstances."

"Circumstances?" Rose's voice pitched higher than was necessary. "What circumstances would that be?"

The duke's jaw worked for a moment. "Dawson feels compelled to be unhappy on my behalf. He has never been one to welcome matchmaking in any form. He believes a person should make their own decisions." The duke placed his hands behind him, leaning back slightly. He twisted his head toward her. "It is not you. Please believe me on that account." His voice softened and he genuinely smiled for the first time since departing the house.

Violet stole a peek at his silhouette. There had been several occasions to study him before now, but this was the first she had noticed his long eyelashes. When he glanced down they would fan out over the tops of his cheeks. They were the perfect frame for his beautiful eyes.

Miss Standish coughed, bits of cake flying from her mouth as she sputtered.

Violet's eyes widened and her cheeks warmed, but a small smile crept up. Unable to think of a response, she leaned forward, patting Miss Standish on the back. Her gaze flicked to her sister's face. A scowl wrinkled Rose's forehead and formed little creases around her puckered lips.

Did Rose even understand how fortunate she was? Her intended was not just wealthy and titled, but he was also kind. Violet held no doubts that her sister would be well taken care of and protected.

A burning sensation tightened Violet's stomach as an image of Mr. McPhail entered her mind. What would she give to be in Rose's position? Violet watched as a leaf fell from a nearby tree, landing in the water. It swirled first at one side then was kicked to the other, as it made its way down the river.

The duke finished the last of his cake and brushed the crumbs from his pants. He rocked forward, pushing himself up to standing.

"Who would be willing to investigate this old building with me? Perhaps we can get inside and take a peek."

Violet nodded her head excitedly. Reaching a hand toward her, he helped her up to stand next to him. She was disappointed when he dropped his hand once she was steady on her feet.

"Anyone else? Jes?" He looked to Rose and seemed to take in a breath. "Miss Allen?"

Rose shook her head. "I have already done enough damage to my gown, I do not need to soil it as well." She squinted up at them. "I was not intending to be out in the sun for so long. Please do hurry. I should like to return to the house."

The duke's jaw clenched.

Miss Standish shook her head. "No, thank you, Tad. A damp, musty old mill holds no appeal for me today." She looked over to the building. "We can see you from here. The two of you should go ahead and investigate." The cousins shared a smile.

Violet blushed. "I am sure we will be perfectly safe." Her head tilted to the side as she realized the truth in her statement. She did feel safe with the duke—safer than she had felt in many years.

His Grace moved toward the abandoned building. It consisted of two squares, one slightly smaller than the other, joined by one wall. He lifted the rusty lock and chain, dropping them back in place. "It does not appear this will be an easy way in. Perhaps there is another door." He motioned with his hand to one side of the building. "I will go this way, if you would like to take the other, we can meet back here."

Violet moved in the opposite direction from him. She followed the walls of the building, looking up and down, searching for a door or window they could access. She discovered several windows, but all of them were well out of reach. Coming to the river, she turned around and made her way back to the front.

As she came around the corner of the building, she noticed Rose was no longer on the blanket with Miss Standish. Violet looked around but did not see her sister anywhere. Her toe connected with a rock and she stumbled forward.

In an instant the duke was in front of her, keeping her from falling to the ground. Instead, her hands came up, resting on his chest, stopping her forward propulsion.

He gently grasped her arms, the motion pulling her closer to him.

Mortification burned on her cheeks. "I beg your pardon, Your Grace. I was looking for windows and did not see that large stone in my path." Her palms were splayed across his waistcoat. She yanked them back, stepping away from him. Her heart was pounding in her neck again. Why must she be so obvious with her emotions?

He dropped his hands to his side, then clasped them behind his back.

"Thank you for keeping me upright." The words rushed out on a breath.

His Grace cocked his head to one side, concern in his expression. "Are you sure you are unharmed?"

Violet nodded sheepishly. "More embarrassed than anything." She reached down to rub at her slippered toe. "Although, I am now regretting my decision not to change into my half boots." She looked over to the blanket where Miss Standish sat. "Where is Rose?"

Miss Standish's mouth twitched. "Miss Allen returned to the house. She could feel the freckles forming from the sunlight."

Violet glanced toward the house before returning her gaze back to the smooth rock face of the building. "I only saw windows up high. Did you see any low enough to look into?"

"No, they all seem to be out of reach." He shrugged, motioning to the double doors. "I believe the only way to see inside, is to get that lock."

"Is there a key?"

The duke shook his head. "Not that anyone knows of. I asked the bailiff about it, but he has never seen one." He picked up the lock, turning it from side to side. "Although, with all of this rust, I am not sure a key would help. But I believe I could break this open if I could find a rock or stick."

Miss Standish pointed to the ground in front of him.

His eyes came to rest upon the rock Violet had stumbled on. He bent over, digging about the stone until he could pry it free of the earth. Triumph apparent on his face, he stood, holding the rock in one hand. "This should work."

He removed his tailcoat, placing it on a stump nearby. Strolling back to the doors, he lobbed the heavy rock up and down in the air. Violet could not help but notice the pull of his waistcoat as his muscles stretched with the effort.

She did not realize she was staring until she heard Miss Standish giggle. Her head snapped around, warmth already beginning to color her cheeks.

But Miss Standish was looking at the duke as he began attacking the lock, beating at it until sweat ran down the side of his face. He rubbed the back of his hand across his forehead, leaving several streaks of dirt before he started the assault again.

He stopped and leaned against the door, taking deep ragged gulps of air.

Violet looked over at Miss Standish and the two doubled over in laughter.

He squinted at them as she placed her hand over her mouth, her shoulders still shaking.

With raised eyebrows he set the rock aside and pushed off the door, folding his arms across his chest.

"Is something funny, Miss Violet? Miss Standish?"

A stern look crossed his face, as a bead of sweat rolled between his eyes and down to the tip of his nose.

Another snort sounded from Miss Standish.

The sternness dissolved and a low chuckle escaped. He looked down at them, shaking his head. "Would you like to give it a whack?" He peered at Violet.

She shook her head. "Oh no, Your Grace. I believe you are doing a fine job of it. Please carry on." She then offered him a pert smile and a raised brow.

He stood back, looking at the lock with narrowed eyes. "I think I almost had it on that last strike, a few more wallops should do it. I have little to lose at this point."

After several well placed strikes, the lock tumbled to the ground, dropping on his toe. "Da—" He sucked in a breath, as his gaze caught hers, pride overshadowing any pain.

"Well done, Your Grace." Violet and Miss Standish both clapped their hands.

He stood taller, his new limp seeming to vanish.

The rock was tossed to the side, and he bowed low. "Would you care to investigate, ladies?"

She nodded her head. Looking over to Miss Standish, she waited.

Miss Standish scrunch up her nose but stood.

As Violet smoothed her skirts, the duke retrieved his tailcoat and put it back on. This man was so different from any other gentleman she had ever known. He wore his title with ease, not with the stiffness and superiority she had observed in others.

They reached the doorway and Miss Standish paused. "I believe this is as far as I am going."

The two entered the darkened building, taking a moment for their eyes to adjust. Panels of light, sprinkled with dust particles, slightly illuminated the mid-sized room. A large door stood to the left, while a second, smaller door lay straight ahead. The millstone and all other workings inside had been removed, leaving only the circular base behind. A damp, mustiness mingled with the earthy smell. They walked around the perimeter of the room.

The duke tugged on the handles of each of the doors. Both held firm.

Violet looked over at him, her lips twitching. "Shall I fetch another rock, Your Grace?"

A deep chuckle sounded next to her. "I believe I have slain enough locks for one day." He turned around, looking at the whole of the room. "I am determined to find a use for this old building. I have no notion for what, as yet, but the ideas will come."

They stayed a moment more before she followed him out of the mill and into the blinding sunlight. Trying to find her balance, she reached a hand out to steady herself, grabbing his arm. It flexed at her touch. She shivered, her hand falling quickly way.

"We should not have investigated on such a chilly afternoon. You are ice-cold."

She squeezed her hand into balls, only then feeling the cold within her gloves.

He reached out his hands as if to take hers. Concern creased his brow, but his hands dropped to his side.

Without a thought, Violet took a step forward. Lifting her hand, she ran her thumb along the creases, smoothing them out.

His eyes closed at her touch.

A quiet sigh brushed against her cheek, bringing her back to the present. What have I done? She pulled her hand away as if she had been burned and gave a clumsy curtsy. "My apologies, Your Grace."

Picking up her skirts, she rushed down the path, toward the house, only faintly hearing the cries of Miss Standish behind her.

CHAPTER 12

Tad entered the house after his morning ride with Dawson and handed off his coat and hat to Baker. "Has Dawson come in yet?"

"Yes, Your Grace. I believe he is in his office."

"Thank you, Baker."

The butler bowed. "Of course, Your Grace."

Tad moved through the entryway. He glanced up the stairs, his thoughts turning to Miss Violet. She had stayed to her rooms following her hasty departure from the picnic by the river, even taking a tray for dinner the previous evening. It had made the usually quiet meal even more so.

Tad stopped in the corridor remembering the feel of her finger on his brow. He closed his eyes as a warmth settled into his chest. Breathing slowly through his nose, he let the feeling linger a moment longer before he opened his eyes and headed toward his study. What was he doing allowing himself to linger on that moment? He was engaged to Miss Allen after all.

Before he reached his destination he was stopped by the soft music of a pianoforte. His steps slowed as he approached the door hanging slightly ajar.

Through the crack, he saw Miss Violet seated at the bench. Her eyes were closed, her fingers moving over the keys in a fluid motion.

Leaning against the hallway wall, he listened to the music. While he was not as familiar with composers as either of his sisters, he was fairly confident Miss Violet was playing Beethoven. Tad had been exposed to hours of Beethoven, as his sister played sonata after sonata.

With his head against the wall, he listened with half-closed eyes, his mind jumping from memories of home to thoughts of the woman playing the piece now. She was extremely accomplished on the instrument. While his sisters both played well, neither came close to evoking the feelings and emotions Miss Violet elicited from the instrument. It was as if her soul conducted with her fingers in their tempo, pace and even touch of the keys.

Tad knew he should not be eavesdropping here in the hallway, but neither could he risk interrupting and having her cease.

A door closed quietly somewhere in the room and the music stopped. Tad leaned forward and peered into the room. A small maid entered, a dust cloth in hand. The maid looked at Miss Violet apologetically.

"I didn't mean to disturb you, miss. You can keep playing if you like. I will come back later." The girl bobbed a quick curtsy and moved back toward the door.

"Please do not leave on my account. You may finish your work here. I have squandered too much time as it is." Miss Violet turned, making her way to the corridor.

Afraid of being caught loitering around the hallway, spying on her private moment, Tad hurried down the hall into the library, shutting the door behind him. He moved to his favorite place beside the hearth, picking up the book resting on the table beside him. As he opened it, the door creaked open slowly.

Miss Violet's face peeked in. When their gazes met, she backed into the hallway again.

"There is no need for you to leave." He leaned forward in his seat, craning his neck to observe if she heard him or if not.

The door pushed open again, and she stepped inside, leaving the door open behind her. "Good," he said. "You decided to stay."

Without a word, she walked about the room, looking at shelf after shelf of books. After several ticks of the clock, she reached the fireplace. Looking about, as if she was unsure where to go next, her eyes finally rested on him, though she refused to meet his gaze directly. A smile turned up the corners of her mouth. "How is your book, Your Grace?"

His shoulders relaxed slightly. "It is interesting, thank you."

Her smile only widened.

Tilting his head to the side, he narrowed his gaze, one brow raised in challenge. "Although, it is not a comedy. So I must ask what you find so amusing."

"I was marveling at your great reading ability."

What was she talking about?

"Most people find it difficult to read upside down." She motioned, eyebrows raised, to his book.

He glanced down, surprised to see his book was indeed upside down. Looking sheepish, he grinned. "You will find, I am full of surprises. Reading upside down is only one of many." He closed the book, setting it on the side table.

She looked over to the mantle and the carvings on each side of the great fireplace. "That is a beautiful piece of art. Who are the women depicted?"

Tad followed her gaze, pointing to each woman in turn. "This is Hera and that one is Demeter." He looked over at her. "Are you familiar with Greek mythology?"

She stood in front of the carving of Demeter, running a finger down one of the grooves in the stone. "I have a limited knowledge of the subject. My governess made sure the basics were covered, but she spent no additional time on it. I confess I do not remember much. She preferred languages and numbers to made-up stories."

Tad's brow dropped and his mouth opened to argue.

She held up a hand to cut him off, a smile tempering the action. "Her words, not mine, Your Grace." She shrugged a shoulder looking up to the carving on the mantle. "I gather your family has a great interest in mythology?"

A nostalgic sigh left his lips. "My father loved it. But until arriving here, I had no idea it was a love he inherited from generations before him." Tad pointed to the scepter in Hera's hand. "She was the wife of Zeus and the goddess of marriage and family. The Greeks believed her to be the ideal woman." He looked over at her, noting an interest and amusement in her eyes. "Which I always found interesting because of her vengeful nature. Many women suffered at her hands."

Miss Violet looked closely at the woman's face. "If I remember correctly, she punished them because they..." Her face pinked and she cleared her throat. "I am sure you know why. There is no need for me to explain it further." She kept her eyes focused on the marble.

He chuckled. She turned the loveliest shades of pink when she was embarrassed.

When she did not look over at him, he continued his lesson. "Demeter, as you can see, is the goddess of the harvest. She and Hera are sisters."

"How did you come to know so much about mythology?" Her gaze traveled over to him at last.

Tad moved over to the shelves. He continued to talk as he moved his fingers along the spines. "As I said, my father loved it. He started teaching us the myths through the stars. The stories of the constellations would inevitably lead to other myths and legends."

His hand paused and he closed his eyes as the memories assaulted him. "As long as I can remember when the weather was warm and the chores finished, my father would lay blankets in the back of one of the hay wagons. My brother Phin and I would lie on our backs and look up at the stars as my father pointed out all of the constellations and tell us the myths behind each one. Many nights we would fall asleep in the wagon, listening to stories we had heard over and over. The repetition did not matter."

"It sounds like a wonderful memory. How long has your father been gone?"

Looking over at her, Tad could see Miss Violet knew the pain of loss. It was apparent by the moisture in her eyes, in the way her brow crinkled and her lips curved downward.

"He has been gone for well over a decade. But at times it seems like it was only months ago." Taking a chance, he asked. "When did you lose your mother?"

"How did you know my mother had passed?"

Tad shrugged. "Your look told me you understood what I was speaking of. Since I know your father is alive and well, I assumed it came from the loss of a mother." The connection that began when he found her outside the willow tree grew even more with the sorrow they both understood.

She dropped her head, staring at her toes. "She died when I was eight years old. It was hard on all of us, but especially on my father. He has never fully recovered. I don't believe any of us really did."

Tad nodded in agreement. "After my father passed, I would go and look up into the night sky, hearing him tell those stories all over again in my mind. It may sound silly, but those were the times when I could feel him the strongest."

Miss Violet's eyes brightened. "When I play the harp or the pianoforte, it is as if my mother is sitting next to me. She was a very accomplished musician." Her voice dropped. "She died before she had taught me much. But when I was about nine years old, I was in the music room looking at the instruments—I would do that when I was feeling my mother's loss most keenly. Sitting on her stool I picked at a few strings. In my mind, I could see her plucking them. Even when pulled by an inexperienced child, the sound brought back the feeling of being loved and cherished." Miss Violet shrank back a little, her face pinked. "I believe it is a similar feeling to what you spoke of."

Tad nodded and turned back to the bookcase. Finally, he found what he was looking for and pulled a book down from the shelf. He carried it over to the table by the windows. "When I heard you play just now, I knew there was something deep inside coming out in your music. Do you play more than the pianoforte and the harp?"

She stiffened, the sparkle in her eyes dimming. "I am most proficient at those two instruments, but I am tolerable on the violin and the flute."

He looked at her in amazement. "You play four instruments? That is remarkable. You must be quite sought after for musicale parties."

"I do not play in public, Your Grace." She looked at him through narrowed eyes.

"That is a shame, for I have never seen nor heard anything as beautiful as you at the pianoforte. I am resigned I shall not be satisfied until I have heard you play the other three."

Miss Violet looked up, vulnerability in her eyes. "Even Rose has not heard me play for years. I close my eyes while I play." She nearly whispered as she continued. "I've been told it makes me appear ridiculous."

"Who would ever say such things? It must have been spoken out of jealousy. For no one could hear you play and not be moved." He wished she believed his words, but from her downturned eyes and the way she fiddled with the fringe on her shawl, he did not believe she did.

She looked into his eyes as if trying to read his thoughts. "My father would listen in the beginning, but in recent years his enthusiasm has waned." She paused, obviously trying to muster the courage. "Why did you not make yourself known earlier?"

"I did not want to disturb you. I was afraid you would not continue if you knew I was listening." His voice dropped to match hers. "Was I correct in my assumption?"

Miss Violet bit her lower lip. She cast a guilty glance at him before moving it to her hands. "Yes."

Tad could see she was uncomfortable and it pained him to see her as such. He pointed to his book on the table. "Do you have a favorite myth, Miss Violet?"

She shook her head, coming over to the table. "As I said, I did not learn more than the basics. What about you? Will you share your favorite?" Tad's shoulders relaxed.

"Do you remember the story of Perseus and Andromeda?"

Miss Violet shook her head.

"She was chained to a rock and left to be eaten by a sea monster." The lightness in his chest he used to feel as a boy when he read this story bubbled to the surface. He looked over to Miss Violet and saw the same reaction mirrored in her wide eyes.

"What did she do to deserve such a fate?"

Tad grinned. "It was actually her mother, Cassiopeia's doing. She offended the Nereids by claiming Andromeda was more beautiful. Poseidon sent a sea monster to ravage their country. The only way to save the kingdom was to chain Andromeda to a rock as a sacrifice to the monster."

"The punishment seems a bit harsh, do you not think?"

Tad chuckled. Fascinated, he watched the emotions flit across her face. What would it be like to know her well enough to know her emotions just by the look on her face?

"Perseus was flying by on his way home from slaying Medusa and saw her chained to the rock, crying. He fell in love immediately and saved her when he turned the sea monster to stone by showing it the head of Medusa."

Miss Violet interrupted him. "The snake hair lady?" She cringed as she said the last few words. "I remember her."

Tad's lips twitched slightly. "I take it you have an aversion to snakes?"

Miss Violet smirked back at him. "Yes, especially snake hair. I am more partial to puppies, kittens, and rabbits. You can keep the snakes for yourself." She ducked her head, but not before a blush colored her cheeks. "Please, carry on with your story." She leaned forward studying the picture in the book Tad had opened.

He leaned forward with her, the smell of violets enveloping the air around him. He breathed deeply.

"Because Perseus saved Andromeda, her father gave her to him in marriage." A soft smile played at his lips. What would it be like to feel for a woman as Perseus did for Andromeda? The smile disappeared when Tad realized he did not feel that way for the lady he was to marry.

He looked at Miss Violet. Her lips curled upward. "Why is this your favorite? I would have thought you would be partial to stories where a Cyclopes is slain or something of a similar nature. Isn't that what all boys enjoy?"

Tad laughed. "What is not to love about snake hair and sea

monsters? It is a tale full of things every young boy thinks amusing."

She looked up from the book, a hint of mirth in her eyes. "I do not have brothers, nor know many boys, but I would have thought the love part would ruin it for most of them."

He gave her a sly grin. "When I was a boy, I could overlook the love because there were enough monsters and fighting. But as a man," he caught her gaze and his voice lowered. "I find I enjoy the love story very much."

Her face colored and his heart skipped a beat. They both turned back to the book in front of them.

It was becoming a game, of sorts, for him to bring out that blush. A game he was doing quite well at today.

Silence fell over the room as neither seemed willing to ruin the moment they were having.

"Violet? What are you doing in here?" Miss Allen kept her gaze fixed on her sister. Miss Violet took several steps away from the table, as she hugged her middle. She opened her mouth to speak, but closed it, swallowing several times.

Tad looked up from the book, his face a mask of indifference. "Good day, Miss Allen. I was explaining to Miss Violet the stories behind the carvings here on the fireplace surround. Would you care to join in?"

"I thought we were meeting in your study..." Dawson walked in. He glanced from Tad to Miss Violet and then to Miss Allen.

Miss Allen avoided looking at Miss Violet. She looked at Tad and then to the marble carvings. "I have very little interest in statuary, Your Grace. I prefer paintings and the like." A practiced pout formed on her lips. "I was hoping we could go on a tour of the house. If you are amenable to giving me one today?"

Tad looked to Miss Violet. She did not exactly shrink in her sister's presence, but neither did she shine as she had been only moments ago.

"It would be my honor, Miss Allen." He looked to Miss Violet. "Would you care to join us on a tour of the house?"

Miss Violet looked to her sister, who offered a slight shake of her head.

"I believe I will return to my chambers and do some reading. But thank you for your generous offer, Your Grace."

A sigh escaped as he realized it would just be Miss Allen joining him. "I shall see if Lady Rachel or Lady Mayfield is available. If you should like to wait here, I will return shortly."

Rose moved to the table where the mythology book lay. She turned a few pages before closing it and moving to the couch by the fireplace.

Miss Violet fell into step with him as they both left the library, stopping when they reached the doorway. Tad motioned her through ahead of him. Neither spoke as they walked down the corridor.

When they reached the staircase, he bowed to her. "Enjoy your book, Miss Violet. Shall I see you at dinner tonight?"

She nodded. "Thank you for a very enjoyable morning, Your Grace." She dropped into a curtsy before gracefully making her way up the stairs.

He turned to search for his Aunt, but paused and cast one more look at Miss Violet. She stopped on the first landing, and their gazes met. He had imagined what it would be like to have her in his home, moving freely about—living here and the reality was even better than his imaginings.

Dawson came up from behind. "Am I to assume we are postponing our business? You seem to have other plans at the moment."

CHAPTER 13

Tad found Aunt Standish in the Coffered Drawing Room with his cousin. Jes read while her mother stitched. They both looked up when he walked through the doorway.

"Good afternoon, Tad." Aunt Standish smiled up at him and Tad felt a familiar tug in his chest. He missed his mother immensely, but Aunt Standish had filled a part of that void.

"And to you Aunt. I have come to ask a favor of you. Miss Allen has requested a tour of the house, a task I am ill-suited for. I was hoping you," his gaze traveled over to encompass Jes. "Would be willing to come along and tell us of this great house."

His aunt laid aside her needlework and stood up. "Of course. I would be happy to show you about. I am surprised you have not enlisted either Lydia or myself earlier."

"It was not because I was uninterested. There was just no time. But now..." he trailed off. But now that he had it, he was wishing he was spending his time with someone else. Perhaps it would not be so bad. It was possible Miss Allen had just been nervous in their previous encounters and now that she had spent more time at Morley, she would be at ease.

His aunt interrupted his thoughts. "Very well. Where is Miss Allen?"

"She is waiting for us in the Red Library." He put his arm out for his aunt to take hold.

Jes put her book on the couch next to her and stood up. "May I come along, Tad? I do not believe I have ever had an official tour."

Lady Rachel looked at her daughter. "Come, Jes. Surely I showed you the house when we came last..."

Jes shook her head. "We were not here very long, Mama. And you had other things on your mind." She reached over and patted her mother's arm. "Not to worry."

They reached the library and Tad stood back as his aunt and cousin entered first. Miss Allen stood when she heard them enter.

"Miss Allen, my nephew tells me you are interested in a tour of this beautiful home. If you are ready, let us start here."

Miss Allen nodded with enthusiasm.

Lady Rachel began. "Morley Park was purchased in 1460 by Thomas Wentworth...." Miss Allen interrupted.

"When I was in London, I met Lord Percival's sister, Lady Caroline. She told me their family can be traced back to the 1300's. Can you believe such a thing? I know they are a very distinguished family, but I did not realize they dated even further back than the Wentworth family."

His aunt looked at Miss Allen, waiting to see if she was finished speaking. When she did not begin talking again, Lady Rachel continued. "Thomas was the steward to Robert Penning-ham, the 1st Earl of Thane. As his employer rose in importance, so did Thomas."

"I don't think Lady Caroline's family is descended from a mere a steward." Miss Allen bit her lip and her brow creased. "Perhaps when I show visitors around Morley Park, I shall leave that information out. When did the Wentworth's become dukes? That is where I shall start."

Tad stood at the back of the group. He chuckled as his aunt opened her mouth and then shut it again, her eyes blinking rapidly at Miss Allen. Finally, she regained her voice. "You are correct, Miss Allen. Lord Percival's family descends from a stable master. Not a steward. Thank you for reminding us all of that noble family's heritage." She looked over Miss Allen's shoulder at Tad, her eyes widening.

He offered only a shrug of his shoulders and a grin. Aunt Standish glared back.

She turned her attention back to Miss Allen. "After a victory at the Battle of Ludford Bridge on October 12, 1459, Thomas was knighted. This began a long relationship between the Wentworth's and the Lancaster's. Sir Thomas was elevated to a Marquess, by King Henry VII, in 1487 for his role in the Battle of Bosworth. The original house was destroyed by fire only six years after it was purchased. Construction of this house began immediately. The house was completed in 1479, but over the years others have added their own touch to the house. The majority of the books in this library were acquired by Robert Wentworth, 3rd Marquess of Shearsby, but every marquess and duke have added their own books, making Morley one of the most extensive libraries in the kingdom."

Miss Allen nodded. "Oh, that is something I will share when I give tours. People will be greatly impressed by our library. Although, when I was in London, I was invited to Bromley House. Have you ever been invited to Bromley House? They have a grand library. I would have thought it was a great deal bigger than this one." She laughed. "Obviously, I am mistaken."

Lady Rachel gave a forced laugh. "Obviously." She continued

on, leading the group out of the library and down the corridor toward the Great Hall. They had gone no more than four steps into the hallway when Miss Allen turned to Lady Rachel. "I do not believe you answered my question, my lady. Have you ever been invited to Bromley House? It is the residence..."

"Yes," Aunt Standish cut her off. "I have been to the London home of the Marquess of Kendal. It is a very fine home. You were fortunate to receive an invitation. It seems your season was a great success."

Jes leaned over and whispered to Tad. "I think mama is getting frustrated with Miss Allen. Why does she keep interrupting? Does she not realize mama is the daughter of a duke?" Jes snorted. "Of course she has been invited to Bromley House."

Tad laughed and leaned down so only Jes could hear. "Some people need for others to know they are important." He nudged Jes with his arm. "People of real importance never need to tell others of their consequence. Remember that, cousin."

"Why, do you suppose, does she need people to know she is of importance?"

"I do not know, Jes. I suppose it helps her convince herself that she has worth. If those around her esteem her because of those she knows, she can feel she is important also." Tad straightened. "It should not be whom you know, Jes, but who you are."

Jes smirked. "You are such an American, cousin. In English society, it is whom you know." She eyed Tad. "Perhaps Aunt Mayfield is right. Your American upbringing will be your downfall." Tad's mouth dropped open and Jes snorted again.

Her mother stopped speaking and scowled at them both. "I was under the impression you were both interested in this tour."

Tad schooled his features into a mask of indifference. "I apologize aunt. Do continue." When she turned back around, Jes nudged him and they grinned at each other.

Miss Allen turned and watched them for a moment. As the group moved forward, she paused until she was even with Tad and Jes. Miss Allen looked across him and smiled tightly at Jes, before looping her hand around his arm.

"What were you and Miss Standish speaking of? It seemed to be very humorous." Her face softened as she stared up at him. "I have oft been called a wit."

A grin spread across his face as he tried to imagine anyone calling Miss Allen such a name. In the week since her arrival, he had seen very little wit in her. Not that she did not have other desirable talents and virtues. His brow furrowed as he tried to think of one. She could speak for long periods of time. Someone would surely find that trait charming. And she was beautiful.

"It was not so witty." He smirked at Jes. "Only my cousin found it funny. I am sure someone of your wit would find it rather dull."

"I don't think I would ever find anything you say dull, Your Grace."

Tad almost sighed at the false statement. "Then you have not been listening, Miss Allen. I fear many find me rather uninspiring. Perhaps you should consider yourself fortunate to have missed those conversations."

Jes snorted again. "I have not been so lucky." Her mother narrowed her eyes and shook her head. "My apologies, cousin." She moved forward and walked beside Lady Rachel.

They continued on the tour, with Miss Allen commenting on whose home she thought may have been similar or bigger, or in some cases smaller. She mentioned names Tad had never heard, and from what she said of them, did not care to meet.

Tad found he paid very little attention throughout the tour and still did not know much about the house he owned. It was not that his aunt's information was tedious, but rather when Miss

Allen began to speak, his mind tended to drift. It did not always return when his aunt resumed speaking.

They stood outside of Tad's study door. The tour had finally come to an end and it could not have happened soon enough for Tad. Miss Allen looked expectantly at him. If she wished him to invite her in for tea, she would be disappointed.

"Miss Allen, would you care to join us for tea. We are to meet my sister in the Green Parlor." Aunt Standish met his eyes.

Tad winked and gave a slight bow before turning into his study. Once the door was closed behind him, he rolled his neck and shoulders. His eyes closed and he inhaled deeply. He did not know what it was about Miss Allen which irritated him. He wanted to enjoy her company. After they married, they would be required to spend some time together, would they not?

He sighed. He must search harder for common ground with her. But thus far, he had seen her do nothing he enjoyed. She did not ride, nor read. He had not heard her play, as her sister did. She did seem to do quite well at needlework, but Tad found that particular talent rather boring. Miss Allen did not have an opinion on politics or anything, except the most recent gossip. Most of her conversation centered on her season in London.

Tad grunted.

"Now what is bothering you?" Dawson crossed the room and sat in his usual seat.

"Nothing is bothering me. I just returned from a house tour with Miss Allen." He drew out her name. His nose scrunching up.

Dawson chuckled. "You did not enjoy it? Knowing your connection to your heritage, I am surprised you didn't hang on your aunt's every word." His smile was a little too sweet.

"Normally I would have. But she kept stopping because someone would interrupt. I found it difficult to keep my focus.

Dawson nodded. "So it was not just the excitement from the carriage ride which caused her tongue to be loosed?"

"Unfortunately, no." Tad ran a hand through his hair. How two ladies could be raised in the same house and be so completely different, he did not know.

CHAPTER 14

Violet stepped out of the parlor, leaving Rose to visit with Lady Mayfield. The older woman's pointed stares had not been lost on Violet. Although, what she had done to earn them, she had no idea. Looking down the hall in both directions, her shoulders slumped when she did not see what she had hoped. A restlessness gnawed at her, but she did not know what to do about it. Being a visitor in another's home took away the freedom to go wherever one desired. She did not feel like a prisoner, but rather an intruder. She longed to go outside and walk, as she did so often at home, but she was unfamiliar with the grounds.

She moved to the music room door but stopped short of entering. She had been playing the pianoforte exclusively for the last week because there were no other instruments, but she was not in the mood for it now. She needed exercise and fresh air.

Across the hall a maid opened the doors of the orangery, airing the room out. A cool breeze floated into the hallway. Violet closed her eyes as she breathed in the scent of overturned soil and damp leaves. Without thinking further, she rushed to her chambers to fetch a spencer and bonnet. Practically running down the stairs, her bonnet fluttered from its ribbons behind her. At the landing, she nearly ran into Miss Standish.

"Where are you off to in such a hurry?" Miss Standish raised her brows in question.

Violet smiled, a giddiness jumping about in her stomach. If Miss Standish were with her, Violet would not feel as if she were imposing. "I am in need of fresh air. Would you care to go—?"

Miss Standish did not let her finish the sentence before she ran up the steps. Within minutes, they were pulling the entry doors open. At the bottom, she stopped, closed her eyes and took another deep breath of the heavily scented air.

She opened her eyes and looked about her, pulling Miss Standish in the opposite direction of the river. As they cleared the shadow of the house, fields of amber stubble laid out before them on one side of the low stone wall, while sheep grazed in fields on the other side.

A chorus of bleating could be heard, along with another deep banging sound coming from the distance. It was the sound of a hammer striking wood. Violet looked to Miss Standish, who raised her shoulders.

Violet picked up her skirts and began walking along the narrow path paralleling the low wall, following the sound of the hammer. Miss Standish soon fell into step with her. When they came to the edge of a hill, Violet looked over the countryside laying below. The incline did not appear so great, and her curiosity compelled her down to the valley below.

After a few steps downward, Miss Standish grabbed her by the arm. "This is not a wise decision. It is steeper than it looks."

Violet waved her concern aside. "It does not look so treacherous." She smiled, narrowing her eyes at Miss Standish. "Come along...or are you chicken livered?"

Miss Standish shook her head. "I am using my head. For who shall run for help when you tumble down the hillside?"

Violet shrugged as she ambled her way down the slope. She stopped after a few steps. "Please? It shall be not fun to go on my own."

Miss Standish let out a deep sigh and muttered under her breath. But she slowly followed Violet down the narrow path.

The hillside had been cleared of its vegetation, leaving pointed, razor-sharp stalks protruding only inches from the dusty ground. The two walked down the hillside, neither saying anything as they concentrated on each step they took. Halfway down the path, Violet realized her mistake.

The terrain was much steeper than it had appeared from the top, with stones and divots only adding to the precariousness of the path. The incline made her legs shake. Using the beauty around her as an excuse, Violet rested her weary body. Even in its barren state, the lands around Shearsby emanated a splendor she had never before seen. "It is so beautiful here. It must have been a lovely place to visit while growing up."

Miss Standish's gaze followed the same path. "I would not know. I had never been here until little more than six months ago...for my uncle's funeral."

Violet stared at Miss Standish. "But why?"

Miss Standish shrugged, her eyes focused on the toe of her boot, digging at a rock in the pathway. "My family was not welcome. My grandfather and uncle did not approve of my father."

Violet's chest tightened. She reached out a hand, squeezing Miss Standish lightly on the arm. She hoped the girl would interpret the small gesture correctly.

The hammering rang loudly through the valley, pulling their attention from each other. As Violet scanned the area, she noticed several small houses backed up against a row of trees, nearly hidden in the shadows. From the looks of them, these were the tenant homes.

She took a few more steps down the path. Several men were perched on one of the roofs. Shading her eyes, she strained to make them out. Her legs moved of their own accord further down the slope.

One of the men sitting atop the house seemed familiar. He worked, as he talked with the other men. Even with his back toward her, she could see he wore no tail or waistcoat. Squinting harder, she tried to make out his features. He turned in her direction, hollering down to a man on the ground and she caught a glimpse of his face. The duke.

Violet's eyes dropped from his face to the open neck of his shirt. She knew she should look away, but her eyes seemed to ignore the command. He looked so.... A few shuffled steps moved her down the path and her shaky knees gave out, lurching her forward. She heard Miss Standish yell as her hand grasped unsuccessfully at Violet's arm. The earth came quickly up to meet her— dirt filled her nostrils and mouth as she rolled down the steepest part of the slope. A cry filled the air. Only after coming to a stop did Violet realize it was her own.

She rolled to her back, pain rippling over her body. A whimpered moan escaped her lips. She lay still for what seemed forever, afraid to move. Breathing brought enough pain. Sensing movement around her, she cracked her eyes open, peering up into the faces of a half dozen strangers, worry etched on every brow. Mr. Dawson was the first face she recognized.

"Mr. Dawson?" Violet's voice came out choked and dry. She looked at the rest of the faces staring down at her, just now seeing Miss Standish and the duke looking down on her with worried eyes.

The metallic taste of blood and dirt mingled in her mouth,

causing her to gag. Putting her hands against the ground she moved to push herself up to sitting. Another cry split the air as red-hot pain shot up her arms. Closing her eyes she laid back on the ground. Between the pain and the embarrassment, she was content to stay there forever.

Two strong arms picked her up, one arm wrapping around her back and the other under her knees. She bit back a sob as she felt each footfall. Taking a deep breath she opened her eyes, expecting to see the face of Mr. Dawson.

A startled yowl escaped as she looked into the face of the duke. Heat crept up her neck, mingling with the pain she already felt. She pushed against his chest with her hands. "There is no need to carry me, Your Grace. I can walk." The boldness in her voice sounded fake, even to her own ears.

"I disagree, Miss Violet." His voice was clipped and terse—something she had never heard from him.

Finally, he set her gently on the back of a wagon. Violet sought out Miss Standish among the crowd. Her face was lined and her hands twisting within each other.

Dropping down to his haunches, the duke began to slowly and gently feel her arms and then her legs through her gown.

"What are you doing?" Violet whispered. With wide eyes she searched the faces of the group, looking for shock and disapproval. But she found neither.

Without looking up from his task, he answered curtly. "Assessing if you have broken any bones."

Pulling her legs from his hands, she painfully tucked them up under her. "Thank you for your concern, Your Grace, but I am certain nothing is broken."

He narrowed his eyes at her. "Your hands." When she did not readily present them, his feature softened a fraction. "Please?" It came out as a whisper.

She silently held them out for his examination. He gently inspected one at a time. The scrapes were bloody and caked with dirt and stubble, forming a dark brown paste. There were streaks of blood running up her wrists and onto the back of her hands. The soft fleshy part of her palms was stripped of several layers, bright pink skin showing when the blood was wiped away.

Violet winced as he touched a raw spot, a tear spilling from the corner of each eye, carving a muddy trail down her face. She swiped at it with the hand he had already released. Squeezing her eyes tight, she forced back any other errant tears.

The duke finished his assessment, raising his eyes to hers at last. "You will be sore for days, I dare say." He shook his head, frustration evident. "What the deuce were you doing coming down that hill without watching where you were going? You could have broken your neck."

The vibrato in his voice made Violet cast her eyes down, looking at her bloodied palms. She had made him angry with her. And just when they were becoming friends. If only she would have taken the time to put on her gloves. This would surely prove to be a lesson in propriety from this time forward. "I am sorry, Your Grace. The sun was in my eyes and I was trying to see what was happening. I was distracted and did not even realize I had begun walking until it was too late." She chewed on her bottom lip, her eyes blurred and cloudy.

He lifted her chin with his finger. His voice back to a whisper. "Gads, Violet. You scared me half to death."

She tilted her head. Did he call her Violet?

He ran a hand through his hair, the sweat sticking it to his head. "There was no way for me to get off that roof fast enough to keep you from falling. Instead, I could only watch the scene unfold as I tried to get down the ladder." He sighed, closing his eyes as he did. His voice changed. Not the tone, it was still filled with frustration, but the inflection and pronunciation were different...like the first time they had met. "Please take care and do not ever scare me like that again."

Violet's eyes dried as she replayed the conversation. Never had she felt such concern on her behalf. It nearly brought a new set of tears. Could he genuinely care what happened to her? Not even Mr. McPhail, before he left for the war, had shown the concern Violet felt from this gentleman.

"I will do my best, Your Grace." Violet shifted and looked up at him from under her lashes. The pain undid her and a sob pushed out. "It is not as if I did it on purpose."

Dropping to his knees, the duke scooted closer to her. His brows furrowed. "Please do not cry." He lifted his hand, but then dropped it as if he did not know what to do with it.

She sniffed, wiping the back of her hand across her eyes, the salt burning in the scratches. She blew on them until the pain subsided.

The duke stood up, dusting the dirt from his breeches.

"What had you so distracted you could not pay attention to a rocky pathway?" His voice regained its normal sound.

Her eyes drifted down his face to his exposed neck, and then back up. Heat crept up her checks, warming all the way to her ears.

His eyebrows slowly rose to his hairline, a smile hovering on his lips. His hand moved to his shirt, fingering his buttons. "At least you had a good reason." The mirth dancing in his eyes brought even more heat to her face.

"Tad!" Miss Standish sounded shocked. Her eyes wide and round. Violet had all but forgotten the girl was even there...had forgotten anyone else was there.

She looked down at the mess she had become. Her skirt was torn in a half dozen places. Even her spencer showed several holes and streaks of dirt and blood. She raised her hands to feel the state of her hair. Thankfully, her bonnet had contained most of it, but a few stray locks hung down her back and cheek. Oh, her cheeks! She did not need her hands to feel the grime coating her skin.

Her eyes squeezed shut as the images of her appearance flooded her mind. When she opened them, she focused her attention on Miss Standish. "I really should return to the house. Becky can see to my scrapes. I did not mean to take you away from your work." She gave the duke a quick glance before looking away. "Miss Standish? Are you ready?"

Miss Standish opened her mouth but stopped when the duke placed his hand on Violet's arm. The tenderness in his gaze caused her to take a slight intake of breath.

"Richard, please bring me my horse. Miss Violet needs help returning back to the house." She raised a hand to protest, but he cut her off. "No."

Her head tilted to one side, while her brow creased. "What do you mean, 'no'?" she asked.

"No. No, you cannot walk on your own. No, you are not well. Whatever you were going to say, the answer is no."

She straightened up, ready to argue the point further when she was hoisted again into his strong arms. A squeak fled her throat as she placed one arm around his neck, careful not to get any blood on his collar.

"But what of Miss Standish? How will she get back to the house? She did not even wish to come on this part of the journey. I cannot just abandon her." In truth, she was afraid to be alone with him.

The duke did not reply but over his shoulder, she could see Miss Standish being handed up onto the front of Mr. Dawson's horse. With her one excuse for walking back to the house gone,

Violet fell quiet as they stood waiting. Where was his horse, anyway? Ireland?

A man appeared with a huge chestnut colored horse.

The duke lifted her effortlessly up onto the saddle then swung up behind her. Moving her so he was holding her lightly about the waist, he set the horse into motion.

The first few steps took her breath away. She tried to scoot forward, creating a proper distance, but he pulled her closer, tightening his arm around her.

Unable to stand the silence any longer, Violet leaned away from him and looked up into his face. "What if I had no intention of saying any such things?" she asked.

"Excuse me?"

"Back there" Violet knew she was rambling but was at a loss to stop it. "What if I had no intention of saying any of the things you accused me of?"

He leaned his head in slightly, whispering into her ear. "Please tell me if I am hurting you." She shivered and lost her train of thought. Why did he feel the need to whisper? It was not as if Mr. Dawson was close enough to hear their conversation. He must know what it was doing to her. He continued to keep his arm about her. She tried again for a proper distance between them, but the effort proved too painful.

Relenting, she leaned her head against his chest, her eyes level with his open collar. His heart beat next to her cheek, the tempo picking up its pace with every breath she took.

"Pardon me, Miss Violet. I should not have assumed to know your thoughts. It was presumptuous of me. By all means, tell me what you wished to say earlier. I shall not interrupt you again." There was a mixture of amusement and caution.

Violet pulled her thoughts away from his neck. "Er, what?"

The duke chuckled, the sound reverberating in his chest.

Violet's cheeks heated, but she regained her wits. "If you must know, I was going to say that puppies are delightfully soft and endearing. But apparently, you take exception to that statement." He swallowed and she forgot she had been speaking until the skin along his jaw tightened as he smiled. "I shall not speak of it again, Your Grace." The silliness of the conversation caused her lips to twitch next to his linen shirt.

He heaved a large sigh, lifting her head with his chest. She swallowed hard, keeping her focus on the indent between his Adam's apple and upper chest.

"You assumed correctly, Miss Violet. I do take exception to puppies in general, so please do not let me hear talk of them again."

"What about kittens, Your Grace? Are you opposed to them as well?" With her head resting softly against his chest, she felt his body lightly shake. Violet closed her eyes. She knew this could not be what love felt like, because the duke did not love her. But even still, it was the most pleasant feeling she had felt in a long time.

Violet was disappointed when the duke reigned in his horse in front of the house. The doors flew open and Lady Rachel ran down the steps. The duke gently released his hold on her, climbing down before helping her off the beast. As he bent to pick her up again, she touched his arm. "Really, Your Grace. I am well."

He eyed her suspiciously. "Do I need to reiterate my earlier response?"

Her face warmed at the inference. "I am afraid it will spark all manner of gossip if the servants were to see you carrying me to my bedchamber." Saying the words made her blush deepen. "It is tantamount to a proposal of marriage. And I believe you already have a fiancé."

His smile vanished as he bowed. "Thank you for your foresight, Miss Violet."

"You run along, Tad. Jes and I can see to her from here." Lady

Rachel place a hand around Violet's waist, helping her up the stairs.

His Grace turned and mounted his horse again.

Before he could set his horse in motion she called to him. "Rabbits, Your Grace? What is your opinion of them?"

His eyes danced when he looked down at her. "Intolerable beasts, they are." His mouth quirked into a smile as he dug his heels into the horse's sides.

Miss Standish turned curious eyes to her, but Violet shrugged, limping to the stairs. Her knees felt like potage. Lady Rachel asked questions, while Miss Standish answered them, saving Violet from having to explain.

When they entered the house, Lady Rachel turned her attention to Violet. "I have summoned your maid and sent word for the kitchen to heat water for a bath."

Violet dipped her head. "Thank you, my lady."

Violet sank deeper in the copper tub, being careful to keep her knees and hands above the water. The warmth helped to soothe her sore muscles. She closed her eyes, smiling as she recalled the afternoon. Aside from everything that had happened, it was a rather remarkable day. He had called her by her Christian name, even if he did not realize he had done so.

Now her mind raced. Was it possible he thought of her in a more intimate way? The thought made her smile and then laugh, a nervous, giddy laugh.

Her hand slipped into the water, sending a sharp pain up her hand and arm, reminding her of everything that had happened. A fresh wave of embarrassment washed over her. Why did he always find her after some sort of incident? First, he had rescued her after the confrontation with Mr. McPhail. Then there was the carriage mishap. Since being here, she had tripped on a rock and now thrown herself down a hillside. What must he think of her?

A new thought struck her. What if it was not her the duke found appealing, but rather the role he played? There was no doubt he played the knight in shining armor very well. Perhaps that was his interest. It certainly explained a great deal. What else could someone like him find appealing about her? She had very little to recommend herself. She had been told as much on many occasions by several young ladies and even a few gentlemen.

Becky came in to help wash her hair, turning the water a murky brown. Scrunching up her nose in disgust, Violet quickly left the now tepid water behind. After helping her into a dressing gown, Becky led her to small writing desk so she could comb out Violet's wet tangles.

A smile split the maid's face. "I heard talk, miss, below stairs. Several servants witnessed His Grace bringing you back to the house on his horse. Many are saying he...."

"You should not be listening to gossip, Becky." Violet cut her off.

The girl sighed dramatically. "But it is all so romantic. A gentleman rescuing a damsel."

Violet's brow creased as her suspicions were confirmed. "He was being a gentleman. Nothing more. Now, please put a stop to the gossip circulating below stairs."

"But miss...."

Part of her rejected the rumor's validity, as another part yearned for them to be true—hoped he could feel that way toward her. Which could not happen. Violet closed her eyes. He was to marry Rose, not her.

Placing a stern look upon her face, she stared at Becky in the mirror. "You had best not listen to the rumors anymore. It will only get you into trouble. We are guests in this house and will only be here a short time. Let's not cause the duke any more problems than he already has." She hoped her voice did not quiver, as the rest of her did.

It is the rumors of servants, she told herself. *What did they know?*

CHAPTER 15

Violet limped about the formal gardens. The breeze blew the last remaining leaves off the trees and lifted the curls off her cheeks. The low cut hedges made it an easy path to follow as it wound around, ending with a large pool in the middle. At present, the rose bushes and other plants boasted pale, dried flowers and leaves, which soon would be gone with the breeze.

She wrapped her pelisse a little tighter around her. The sunshine from yesterday was nowhere in sight. A shiver ran down the length of her body. Closing her eyes, Violet took several slow, shallow breaths. As much as she wished to spend her morning out of doors, she was not sure she could endure many more shudders.

She followed the path toward the outer edge of the garden. The orangery was just ahead. It was not out of doors but did have a similar feel. It would have to do for today. She rounded a large, sculptured tree at the entrance to the garden and was nearly knocked off her feet.

Mr. Dawson quickly reached out and grabbed hold of her arms, keeping her upright.

"Ooph." she moaned. It was unknown to her if the sound was more from the surprise of running into the gentleman or from the pain of his tight grip on her arms.

Mr. Dawson dropped his hands immediately. "I am sorry if I hurt you. It may have been less painful if I had let you fall." His face held its usual scowl.

"Really?" Violet's face wrinkled. "You would have let me fall?"

His frown seemed to deepen. "Obviously not or you would be seated on the ground right now."

Violet nodded, unsure how to respond. "Thank you? For not letting me fall?" She sounded as if she were asking him if she were grateful. Why was it so difficult speaking with this gentleman? It was not this difficult with His Grace.

A gust of wind pushed her skirts around her legs and she closed her eyes as the fabric rubbed painfully at her scraped legs.

"You should not be out in this weather."

Violet opened her eyes when the pain subsided and looked at him with one arched brow. "I was just making my way into the orangery, but I was detained."

A rare smile curved his lips. "Yes, it seems you were. May I see you inside? I would hate for you to be detained again."

Placing her hand on the arm he offered, Violet walked beside him on the path leading to the back side of the house. "Do you like it here, Mr. Dawson?"

He tilted his head to one side. "Yes, when compared to some places I have been."

"And when compared with others?"

He remained quiet for a moment. "Compared to others? No. I do not like it here. I should like to return home, but His Grace is very stubborn. For him, it is all about family honor and to return home would mean...I am not sure, exactly. Therefore, it is not an option."

"Is that why he will marry my sister? Out of duty only?" Why was she asking such personal questions about the duke? Surely, Mr. Dawson knew the direction of her questions.

He cleared his throat. "That would be a question for His Grace, Miss Violet." They were both silent, reaching the doors to the orangery without another word. Would Mr. Dawson tell the duke of this conversation when next he saw him? Violet wished the questions back. Now when she looked on him she would wonder if he knew.

They stepped inside. Immediately Violet felt warmer and her muscles relaxed. The smell of oranges and other flowers filled her senses.

Mr. Dawson turned to her. "Do I think he loves your sister? No. I don't." He studied her closer. "But do I think he will still marry her? Yes, I do. To not marry her would tarnish the family name, and that is not something he is willing to do. His happiness will not be considered." Mr. Dawson's scowl returned. "I beg your pardon. I should not have spoken so freely, especially about your sister."

Violet placed a hand on his arm. "Not to worry. Your remarks shall not leave this room, Mr. Dawson. Thank you for being so candid."

A rustle at the far end drew their attention. The duke stood next to a potted lime tree. He looked at the two of them, then smiled. "Dawson, I have looked everywhere for you. Are you ready for our ride?"

Mr. Dawson nodded. "Indeed, Your Grace. I was on my way to the stables when I ran into Miss Violet outside."

The duke studied her. "How are you feeling this morning?"

Violet straightened her dress and pulled her pelisse closer to her body. "I was a little sore, but I have walked most of it off. Otherwise, I am no worse for the wear." It was a bit of a Canterbury tale, but she was not about to confess how much pain she had awoken to this morning. It would only add to the already humiliating events of yesterday.

Mr. Dawson coughed and the duke glanced at him. He looked at the foliage around them, but Violet saw the slight shake of Mr. Dawson's head.

The duke turned to her, his eyes narrowed even more now. "It appears most of your injuries are in discreet locations. If not for your split lip, there would be no visible evidence of your tumble." He held out his arm. "I am glad you are well. I was concerned about you. Would you care to take a turn about the room?" He smiled, but there was a challenge in his gaze.

"I thought you were just leaving for a ride." Why was he delaying? She didn't wish to have him see her hobble and limp about like an old woman. While she may have exaggerated her healing, she was confident that now she was in the warmth of the house, she could do just as she had said and walk out any of the tightness lingering in her muscles.

"I am sure Dawson would not mind if we delayed for a moment. Would you, Dawson?" The duke and Mr. Dawson exchanged a glance. She knew they had spoken volumes to each other in that one small look. What would it be like to know someone so well as to be able to communicate with only a look or a gesture?

Mr. Dawson proved to be no help. "Not at all, Your Grace. I am at your leisure." He then processed to the nearest bench and sat down.

Realizing this was all a ploy for the duke to see how badly she was injured, Violet let out a quiet huff and placed her hand on his arm. "A walk would be lovely, Your Grace. Thank you for accompanying me." Her voice lacked any kind of warmth or true gratefulness.

A low chuckle sounded next to her and she turned to look at the duke. The skin at the side of his eyes was creased. Even his dimple made an appearance.

Normally seeing him looking so handsome would have been her undoing. But she was too unhappy about his ploys to feel inclined to reciprocate. "Is there something funny, Your Grace?" Her gaze challenging. "Please do share. I find I am in need of a good laugh today."

His smile dropped, and he assumed a contrite expression. "I do not believe you would see the humor just now. Perhaps in a day or two, we can revisit this conversation and both get a good laugh." He motioned to the walkway ahead. "But for now I will be content with a walk."

They took the first few steps. Violet limped heavily.

Without saying a word, the duke removed her hand and slid his arm about her waist. She should have pushed him away, and she would have if she had not needed his support. Her time outside had served to only stiffen her already tight muscles more.

They stopped in front of a beautiful purple orchid. Several other plants of yellows, reds, and oranges surrounded the flower, creating a dazzling display of color. The duke kept his focus on the plants in front of them. He smiled. "Your earlier declarations of health and wellness appear to be slightly exaggerated. Why not just tell me the truth?" He looked at her from the corner of his eyes. "We could have avoided this charade."

Violet sighed. "I was hoping to avoid any further mortification. But it seems you are determined to see me at my worst." Would he ever see her at her best? Without bruises, cuts or a limp? Did it matter if he did? As it stood, she could console herself with the notion that it was the injuries which made her undesirable.

His eyes crinkled again. "I find your worst quite lovely. Now that I think on it, I am quite glad you exaggerated and forced me to call you out." He looked around at the other plants. "I do not believe we have any violets here. I shall set the master gardener to work on that, immediately." Finally, he looked her in the eyes. "Now, shall we stretch out those muscles a bit more and try to not make a liar of you?"

All she could muster was a nod. Her soreness melted away and all she could think was that he thought her lovely. How could that be possible? No one had ever called her lovely that she could recall, except possibly her mother. But that had been when she was a child and all children are lovely.

They walked around the room several times. With each round, her gait evened out and the soreness lessened. Gradually, she leaned less on the duke and relied more on her own strength. She reluctantly allowed him to pull his arm from around her waist. When they reached the bench where Mr. Dawson sat, his legs stretched out in front of him and his back leaned against the wall, Violet stopped. "You have kept Mr. Dawson waiting far too long, Your Grace. I thank you for your kindness in helping me, but as you can see I am much recovered."

He tilted his head. "This is not another faradiddle, is it Miss Violet?"

Violet grinned and walked several paces out and back. "As you can see, I am well." She turned in the direction of the house, calling over her shoulder. "Enjoy your ride, Mr. Dawson. And thank you for your patience."

A lightness carried her out of the orangery. Never had a walk had a more healing effect. Although, she suspected it had more to do with the companion than the actual exercise.

CHAPTER 16

T ad and Dawson turned onto the drive after an especially hard ride.

"Well, did it work? Have you excised the demons putting you in such a pensive mood?" Dawson's mount pushed slightly ahead. "It is obvious you are not convinced of your decision to go through with the marriage contract."

Tad leaned over, putting his forearms on the horn of the saddle. "I know it is the right thing to do. But..."

Dawson looked at him with sympathy in his eyes. "But you prefer Miss Violet to Miss Allen."

Tad remained silent. He had only just admitted to himself the extent of his feelings for Miss Violet. Her little tumble down the hill had helped him realize this. But Dawson would not understand why Tad could do nothing about them.

Dawson slowed his horse. "I don't blame you. I cannot stand to be in the same room with her. The lady is never at a loss for words. If we were home..."

Tad pulled even and held his hand up. "We are not in America, making whatever would happen there irrelevant. It matters not my feeling for Miss Violet. There is an agreement and I need to honor it." He looked Dawson in the eye. "I need your support, not your lectures, Dawson." Tad shook his head. "I just wish that Miss Allen was not so..."

"Contrived and false?" Dawson cocked a brow. "Then why not expand your options? Wouldn't Miss Violet still fulfill the agreement?"

Tad shrugged. "I do not know. We still have found no contract specifying Miss Allen as my intended. But if I abandoned her in favor of her sister, what would it do to Miss Allen and her reputation?"

Dawson sighed. "Forget about Miss Allen and Lord Winslow, for a moment. Do you love Miss Violet? Could you be happy with her?"

The corners of Tad's mouth drooped. "Love her? How should I know if I love her? I have only known her a week."

Dawson grunted in irritation. "I see how you look at her—saw your reaction when she fell down the hillside. You have not been that scared since...."

"Yes, Dawson? Since what?" Tad snapped.

Dawson rubbed at his earlobe. "Since you watched your father fall from the hayloft. You wore the same look yesterday."

Both men fell silent.

Finally, Dawson broke the stillness, his voice quiet. "It is obvious you have feelings for the lady."

"I was merely concerned..."

Dawson held up his hand, cutting off Tad's denial. "It may not be love or genuine affection, yet. But there is interest. Your brain is not the only thing you should be using, Tad. This is a matter for the heart as well."

A grin broke out on Tad's face. "Watch out, my friend. Someone might actually believe you have one."

Dawson's face colored slightly, his normal scowl deepening, but he made no more comments.

They rode into the stable yard. "Can I take him for you, Your Grace?"

One of the stable hands took the reins, leading the horse in the opposite direction. Tad and Dawson entered the house and each went their own direction—Dawson to his office and Tad to the ante-library.

He stopped in the doorway, struck by the scene in front of him. Miss Violet sat in the corner of the couch, her feet tucked up under her dress. A book was balanced on the arm of the couch. One hand held the book in place and turned the pages, while the other twisted a small tendril of hair at the back of her neck.

This is what he wanted to come home to. This was the picture in his mind of how his life would be. The room darkened as a cloud passed over the sunlight.

He stepped inside the room, walking over and standing in front of her. "Are you enjoying your book?"

She lifted her eyes and a smile immediately formed. "Very much so. I hope you do not mind, I believe this is your book? Miss Standish recommended it."

Tad looked down to see *The Federalist* opened up in front of Miss Violet. "A brave choice for your first venture into American politics." He was impressed. The essays were not read by many American ladies, let alone an English one. His estimation of her increased.

She shrugged. "It is interesting. I had always assumed all Americans wanted the Constitution from the very beginning. But in reading the articles, the men writing them paint a different picture."

"It was a new concept. Many found it frightening and not worth the risk."

Her gaze drifted to the shelves next to the window where he had placed all of his personal books. "Why do you have so many American books in your library?" She flicked a worried glance at him. "I am sorry, Your Grace. That was terribly impertinent of me."

He was quiet for a moment. How was he to answer? His conscience would not allow an outright lie, but could he trust her with his secret? He could act affronted and intimidate her from ever speaking of it again. Or he could share everything.

It was an uncertain course of action. From his conversations with his aunts, Tad had learned there were several distant cousins waiting, anxious to assume the title. If word of his nationality made its way to one of them, there could be a challenge for the dukedom. The recent turmoil with America would certainly not help the outcome, should his cousins fight his claim. The thought of being forced from this land made his stomach twist. Without totally recognizing when it happened, he had come to love his new home.

Did he trust this lady enough to risk so much? As he looked over at her from the corner of his eye, his mind calmed and his muscles relaxed. He sat down on the couch next to her, twisting his body so he faced her.

"You need not apologize, Miss Violet. Your directness is one aspect of your character I find refreshing. I am learning most people tell me what they think I want to hear. It gets a bit tiresome." He glanced over to her. "But before I answer your question, I have one for you."

She looked at him with curiosity but nodded in agreement.

"What are your feelings on Americans? I have encountered several people who are less than...cordial."

Miss Violet tilted her head, her face scrunching up in thought.

"I am sure there are many fine Americans. I would guess there are some scoundrels, but England is not devoid of them." She paused and her hand moved to her throat, rubbing it several times. "What has it to do with my question?"

"I have been keeping a secret from you—from everyone. It started as my uncle's idea, but I had not been here long before I saw his wisdom."

Violet furrowed her brow. "A secret?"

"Everyone has one, do they not?" Tad asked.

Her body stiffened and she pushed further into the corner. "I suppose you are correct. Most people have something to hide."

Breathing deeply, he plunged ahead. "I am not what I appear to be."

"Who are you, exactly, if you are not the Duke of Shearsby?" Looking more scared than shocked, her eyes flicked to the open door.

"I am the Duke of Shearsby. I have papers to confirm it." Why had he not planned this better? He was muddling this whole thing. Why could he not just tell her? "I am not saying this correctly." His heart pounded as the words tumbled from his mouth. "I was not raised in England."

Miss Violet's face relaxed and she nodded. "Oh, that is no secret. Everyone knows you were living in the West Indies."

Tad took in a deep breath, his shoulder dropping slightly. "That is what my grandfather wanted people to believe." He dropped the King's English he had been using since his arrival, this time speaking as he would in Pennsylvania. "I was actually born and raised in Chester, Pennsylvania—in America." He flicked his gaze away, unable to bare her scrutiny. What would she think? Had he made a colossal mistake?

Her eyes widened, her mouth opened and shut. But no words came out.

Tad sighed in frustration, raking his fingers through his hair. "Let me tell you about my family. Perhaps it will clear everything up."

Her fear faded but was replaced by cautiousness.

"My father was the youngest of three sons born to the Seventh Duke of Shearsby. When my father reached his majority he decided there was very little for him in England. Neither the military nor the church held any appeal. He was given the inheritance he would receive upon my grandfather's death and left for America."

Understanding and interest smoothed out the features on Miss Violet's face.

Perhaps this would not be the disaster he had originally believed. "While he was on the ship crossing the Atlantic, he met and fell in love with a feisty Irish lady. When they reached America, they married, bought a large piece of land in Pennsylvania and started a farm. Eventually, it grew into a plantation. It is not as vast as Morley, but by American standards, it is very large."

Tad hesitated to add the last part but pressed on. "I lived in Pennsylvania until the war broke out."

Miss Violet's head slowly began to bob up and down, her mouth forming an O. "You are an American." Then her brows rose. "And you fought for America."

Tad nodded his head. "I had not been back long when we received the letter from my uncle."

She started twisting a button on her spencer. Her brow furrowed. "Within a year, England went from being your enemy to your home. I can scarcely conceive the feelings you have experienced." Wonder filled her face, followed by a sympathetic smile. "I can only imagine your shock when you arrived and found your uncle had arranged for you to marry a stranger." A chuckle escaped. "Your reaction when we met on the roadside makes much more sense."

Tad laughed, feeling lighter than he had in days. "May I ask one more question, Your Grace? Why must you change your speech? Why not speak as you always have?"

"My uncle insisted on it and my mother agreed. I thought it silly until I reached Liverpool. I was quickly convinced of its necessity." He explained about the fight at the docks and the reaction of the innkeeper. "My uncle also worried someone may challenge my right to the title if it became known. He would turn in his grave if one of the distant cousins took the title. It has been in the Wentworth family for more than three hundred years."

She was no longer pushed so tightly into the corner of the couch. Her feet peeked out from under the edge of her dress. The book dropped to the floor and they both leaned down to retrieve it. He picked it up, kneeling in front of her. They both paused and he stared into her eyes. Black flecks broke off the pupil, adding intensity to the green of her iris. He had never seen eyes like hers before.

Her tongue ran over her lips, moistening them and drawing his attention. She was close, but not close enough. He wanted to hold her, to feel her lips on his. He leaned closer, his heart beating painfully hard in his chest. Just a little more and he could close the distance, but he hesitated. Maybe Dawson was right. Maybe he could choose her. But how would she respond?

She leaned back on the couch and his breath pushed out of his lungs. His chance was gone.

"You can trust me to keep your secret, Your Grace." Her voice was a hoarse whisper. "People would try to use it against you. Many have done worse to achieve less. A dukedom is a great motivation. Do many know of this secret?"

He sat back on the couch. The lump in his throat and the haze clouding his brain made it difficult to answer. "My aunts and cousin. Dawson. And now you." He knew he should move to a chair or the far side of the couch, but was rooted where he knelt on the floor.

Her eyes lit. "Mr. Dawson is an American also." It was a statement, rather than a question.

Tad stepped back, confusion wrinkling his brow. Dawson?

"Did he serve in the war also? Is that the reason he dislikes it here? I can understand why he may feel ill at ease."

Why was she asking about Dawson? Realization crashed down on him like a cold wave. Miss Violet had set her sights on his best friend. How had he not seen this before? The image of them walking together in the orangery surfaced. It had been Dawson she cried out for after she fell. The signs had been there, but Tad had not seen them. Or maybe he had ignored them.

He sat back on his heels, heat creeping up his neck as he considered what he had almost done. Kissing her would have been tantamount to a marriage proposal, which in this new light would surely have been unwelcome.

A bigger stupe there was not, believing her to be open to an engagement with him. He cleared his throat, trying to get his bearing. "There is...business which needs my attention. If you will excuse me." He stood up, unable to leave the room fast enough.

Her brow furrowed, her body slumped, but all he could think about was getting away from her—from her enchanting green eyes, and her intoxicating smell.

As he turned toward the door, Miss Allen walked through it. "Oh. Here you are. Together." She eyed her sister.

Miss Violet looked only at her sister. "We were not together. I was reading when His Grace came in from his ride. The book I was reading confounded me and the duke was kind enough to explain it." Miss Violet stood and curtsied to him. "Thank you,

Your Grace. I believe I am in need of a rest." She left Tad standing alone with Miss Allen.

Tad scowled. He did not know who he was more unhappy with right now. But there were plenty of options to choose from.

Miss Allen looked up at him. "I was considering a walk and would not mind the company."

Tad plastered a smile on his lips as he extended his arm to her. "It would be my pleasure, Miss Allen."

As they stepped onto the gravel drive, Miss Allen shivered.

"Is it too cold for a walk? We can return if you wish."

She shook her head fiercely. "No." Then lowering her voice to less of a shout she added, "I have scarcely seen you these past few days. If I did not know better, I would think you were avoiding me." A forced giggle sounded next to him.

Tad looked down at her but was unable to meet her eyes. His stomach burned. "I have been busy. That is all. I apologize if you have felt neglected."

He had let feelings for Miss Violet develop and cloud his judgment. But now that he knew her heart, he could focus on Miss Allen and his duty toward her. Tad turned them to the right. "The village is just more than a mile. Would you care to see what our lovely little town has to offer? I hear the confectioner's shop is well stocked."

Miss Allen nodded her head. "Oh, that sounds lovely. I do hope they have some butterscotch candy. Papa brought some back from a business trip he took to Yorkshire. It was divine."

Tad opened his mouth to respond, but he never had the chance. Miss Allen scarce took a breath. Tad had no idea there was so much to say about sweets. Nor did he understand how the subject turned to bonnets. Miss Allen carried the whole of the conversation until they arrived at the candy shop, only stopping just long enough to taste a few of the confections available.

When she had made her selections, they turned back toward Morley.

"Thank you for the candy, Your Grace."

Tad looked at her with surprised eyes, when she waited for him to answer. He smiled at her, placing his hands behind his back as they walked. "You are quite welcome, Miss Allen."

Those would be the only words he spoke. What she talked of on the way back, Tad could not say. The only thing he had learned in his time with Miss Allen was to interject an *umm-hmm* from time to time. She managed the rest of the conversation without him.

Unfortunately, it gave him time to think. He tried to decipher how he had missed the clues as to Miss Violet's preference for Dawson. Tad had seen them returning from a walk the day before but had not thought much of it.

He looked to Miss Allen. Did he dare share his secret with her? The knots in his stomach answered the question for him. But she was to be his wife. Should that not be enough to trust her? He thought about the peace and calm he had felt before telling Miss Violet. What made it easy for him to speak openly to her but not her sister? What was the difference?

He was brought from his thoughts when she stopped in the middle of the lane. He looked at her blankly.

"Do you not think, Your Grace?"

He tried to think if he had heard any of what she was saying, but when he turned up nothing he stood there, staring at her. He could lie and say he was distracted by her beauty. Tad dismissed that idea almost as soon as he thought it.

"I apologize Miss Allen. I let my mind wander to another matter which has been plaguing me. It was most rude of me. Would you mind repeating the question?"

Her annoyance softened when she saw she had his full attention. "I was asking if we will be going to London for the season? I do love London. There is so much to do and see. And I will be the most sought-after lady. I shall be privy to every bit of gossip."

There was the difference. Miss Allen could not wait to be the center of the gabsters in London, while Miss Violet appeared hesitant to even leave the country.

As it turned out, Tad was never required to answer the question. When he finally bid Miss Allen good afternoon, he escaped to his study. Tad sat down behind his desk, putting his elbows on the top and his face in his hands. Contrary to his hopes, his walk with Miss Allen had only made him think of her soft-spoken sister more.

Why had he insisted they stay on for a fortnight? He still had a week remaining. It would be torturous if he didn't do something to protect his heart. The best course of action was to avoid the lady as much as possible, only making conversation when necessary. He would instruct Mrs. Jeffery to seat Miss Violet farther down the table for all meals. Additionally, he would need to spend more time with Miss Allen. Surely there were things about her he would admire. He just needed to look harder.

Rubbing his hands over his face several times, he growled low in his throat.

"Tad?"

He jerked his head up, only then noticing Jes curled up in the window seat. He let out a deep sigh.

"Is something wrong?" She put her book to the side, looking at him expectantly.

He shook his head. "No. Everything is fine. Nothing to concern yourself with." Then to change the subject, he stood and walked over to her. "What is that you are reading?"

Jes held up the book. "It is called *Pride and Prejudice*. Have you read it?" Her eyes danced with excitement.

"I have not. Who wrote it?" Tad picked up the book from Jes's outstretched hand. "It only says by the author of *Sense and Sensibility*. Am I to know who that is?"

Jes smiled wickedly at him. "I have that book also, so I shall tell you. It was written 'By a Lady.'"

Tad looked at her, waiting for her to finish. When she did not, he shook his head. "That only gives me a very small clue. Why will you not just tell me her name?"

Jes laughed as if they shared a joke. "I do not know the lady's name. It was published anonymously. 'By a Lady' is all we know. I very much liked *Sense and Sensibility*, but this one," she snatched the book out of Tad's hands. "This one is my favorite."

Tad sat down on the settee next to his cousin, pushing his earlier disappointments to the back of his mind. "Will you tell me about it?" Stretching out his legs in front of him, he leaned his head back, listening to Jes's animated retelling of the story. Just as Tad was about to doze off, Dawson entered the room. Without thinking, Tad glared at him.

"Whoa, what put you in such a foul mood? I thought you were over whatever was troubling you."

Tad relaxed his face, understanding Dawson was not at fault but still finding it difficult to not scowl. "It is nothing." He motioned him to come closer. "What is it you needed?"

Dawson looked over at Jes. She smiled at him, but then stood and moved from the room.

"What is so important and secretive my cousin needed to be forced from the room? I was enjoying her storytelling."

"I found the item you had me inquire about. It was in Wales and should be delivered within the next few days."

Tad sat up. "So soon? I expected it to take longer."

Dawson moved to his usual seat across from Tad's desk and adjusted it so he was facing Tad. "I expressed the need to have it here as soon as possible." He raised a brow. "I may have indicated there would be a financial reward should it get here quickly. The note I just received indicated he would see it delivered immediately. We were lucky he had one already made."

Little fingers tickled inside his stomach as he thought about her reaction. Seeing it would be rewarding, but he suspected hearing it is what would make the whole expense worthwhile.

CHAPTER 17

Violet walked down the front steps on her father's arm. They stopped at the carriage waiting in the drive. "Must you go, Papa? Can your business not wait until next week?"

"No, I am afraid it cannot. But I shall only be gone a few days, Poppet." Violet stilled at her father's words. He had not called her Poppet in years. "I am to meet our bailiff in Rutland. His associate returned from Germany, where he learned new ways to increase seed production. It may be what we need to make the estate profitable." He patted her arm, as he would an obedient puppy. "But not to worry, Lady Rachel insisted it was no trouble for you and your sister to stay on as planned." He moved toward the carriage, turning back slightly as he reached for the door. "Leaving from this location will save me several days travel. A happy coincidence, don't you think, Violet?"

The front doors opened and the duke bounded down the stairs, coming up short when he reached the bottom. He looked from Violet to Lord Winslow. "You are sure you must go?"

Her father shook his head, chuckling. "Yes, yes. Your Grace. And thank you for allowing my daughters to stay on in my absence. After their harrowing journey here, I find myself ill at ease with them traveling alone." He chuckled. "And I am sure they would be most disappointed to miss the grand ball."

He stepped up into the coach, settling himself in the far corner. Waving a dismissive hand, he knocked on the rooftop, summoning the coachman to proceed.

Violet stood, watching the carriage amble down the drive. Her mouth pulled down in a frown.

His Grace remained standing next to her. "Are you sure you would not prefer to return home? I can arrange an escort if that is your wish." His brows pulled down, obvious displeasure on his face.

Violet felt her face heat. He wished them far away from here. Was there any other explanation?

"I am sorry for my father's presumption, Your Grace. My sister and I will be packed up before the day is done. We shall trespass on your hospitality no longer." She moved toward the stairs, trying to hide the tears pricking at the back of her eyes.

The duke had been noticeably absent over the past few days. She had been moved farther down the table at any meal they were together, giving her little chance to talk with him. And when he had been present, his conversation was clipped and curt. Whatever friendship she had believed was developing, was now gone and she had no idea why. She thought this time was going to be different, but it seemed it was not.

A hand reached out, stopping her. "Don't leave." He grimaced as if it pained him to say the words. "I was not a gracious host just now. Please accept my apology. It was not my intention to drive you back to Cheshire."

Violet had yet to turn around, keeping her back to him. "You need not feel any obligation, Your Grace."

"It is not an obligation. I truly wish you to stay." His stance was rigid, his voice filled with agony.

She blinked several times. "Very well. But if you should change your mind, you need only say the word." She looked over her shoulder, swallowing the lump in her throat. She needed to get out of his presence, go somewhere to gain some sense of decorum. "Now, if you will excuse me, I was not intending on staying out in the cold so long." She dipped a quick curtsy and practically fled up the steps.

There was only one place in this house Violet knew she could compose herself while thinking over her warring emotions. Moving through the entryway she made her way to the music room.

The door stood open wide. She stopped when she saw two footmen standing in the middle of the room looking down at a large wooden crate. They glanced around then back at the box, brows furrowed. One mumbled something to the other before turning to leave, nearly bumping into her in the hallway.

"I beg your pardon, miss." The footman bowed slightly, before hurrying off. Peering through the doorway, she saw the remaining footman standing alone staring at the box as if his intense gaze could pry it open. Violet did not want to enter the room and play while they were completing their task, but neither did she want to leave. Curiosity about the contents of the crate held her in place. She looked in the direction the footman had gone, seeing no sign of him.

Her foot tapped with impatience. When she thought she might burst with inquisitiveness, the footman rounded the corner carrying a crowbar. His brows furrowed as he passed her again.

Turning back he asked, "Is there something I can help you with, miss?"

Violet stammered. "No, no. I was waiting to use the music room."

The footman nodded, taking the few remaining steps, he thrust his head into the room. "Benny, the miss would like to use the pianoforte. Let's move the box to the side. We can come back later to unpack it."

Eyes large, her brow wrinkled, Violet moved forward. "Oh, no. Please do not stop your work on my account." She could hear the desperation in her voice. "I can wait until you are finished." Clutching her hands together, she held her breath in anticipation.

"Very well. If you are sure you do not mind. We will make haste, so as not to keep you waiting any longer than necessary." He motioned her into the room. "There is a couch there in the corner if you wish to sit."

Her breath came out as a quiet whoosh of relief. She entered the room but did not make her way over to the couch. Instead, she stood to the side, allowing for a better view. The footman wrinkled his brow but said nothing more to her.

After prying off the lid, the two men removed large bundles of loosely bound grasses. Bits and pieces fell to the floor around them. A coarsely woven fabric was then removed and placed to the side. The men bent simultaneously, reaching down into the crate. When they straightened, each held an end of a harp. Violet's squeak was acknowledged by the closest footman with the quirk of a brow. The men gently placed the harp out of the way of the debris cluttering the floor. They then removed a small stool.

Violet used every ounce of restraint to keep herself from racing over to the instrument and examining it thoroughly. She strained to see it but was unable to get a good view. Her jumble of emotions, mixed with anticipation, made her fingers twitch, her body shaking beneath her gown.

The men moved at a snail's pace, sweeping and cleaning up the little bits of grass. *Why must they move so slowly?* A footman cast a glance in her direction and she wondered if perhaps she had actually shouted the question. An edgy sigh crossed her lips.

Finally, after what seemed hours, the footmen picked up the empty crate, leaving her alone in the room. Taking deliberately slow steps, fearing it might still be a dream, she neared the instrument. Interwoven Celtic knots were carved down the column and body. The deep walnut stain bringing out every shape and whittle. She had never seen such workmanship. The column was wider and more angular than her harp at home, but it was every bit as beautiful.

Reaching it, she lightly ran her fingers over its curves. Levers followed the arch of the harmonic curve. This harp had no pedals. She had never played a lever harp before, but right now she did not care. Thrill and longing surged through her body.

She raised trembling fingers to the strings, at first only caressing them. Then her fingers curved, plucking out a note. Violet closed her eyes, letting the sound vibrating through the instrument wash away the tension in her shoulders and neck.

Lifting the seat of the stool, she found several sheets of music and the tuning wrench. She pressed a key on the pianoforte, then began to tighten each string until each one was perfectly in tune.

"It is a beautiful instrument. I am eager to hear you play it."

Violet's head whipped around. She snatched her hand away. The tautness returned to her body. Her throat went dry and her heartbeat sped up. Keeping her attention on the harp, she attempted a normal tone. "Yes, it is beautiful. I have never seen anything like it."

The duke took several steps into the room. His face was

unreadable, leaving her emotions teetering. One moment he was cold, hardly able to stand her company and then in the next he was contrite and apologetic. Gone was the humor they had shared over the past week.

"Forgive me for intruding. Baker told me it had arrived. I was anxious to see how it looked in the room." He motioned to the harp with a nod of his head. "A music room cannot possibly be complete without a harp. Will you allow an audience for this performance?"

Her stomach constricted at the thought of him listening, but a thrill also burned inside her at the thought of him wanting to hear. No one had taken an interest in her or her music in so long. "If it would please you to attend, Your Grace, I would be honored to play for you." She hated the shake in her voice. "I would, however, ask for some time to practice first."

He had been slowly coming closer to her as if he was afraid she would bolt at any sudden movement. Perhaps she would have. Her emotions were jumping in every direction of late.

"Has it been so long since you played that you require practice?" He was only a small step away now. The warmth from his body seemed to seep through her lightweight morning dress, or perhaps she was imagining it.

She stared up at him, finding it difficult to speak. "It is not that I am out of practice, per se, but rather I am unfamiliar with this harp." She swallowed hard. Every part of him seemed rigid, making her tense in response. Her voice came out in a strained whisper as if her throat was being squeezed. "I have never played a lever harp before."

The duke's eyes flicked to the harp, then back to her. His brow puckered, disappointment registered in his face. "I purchased the wrong one? I did not even know there were different kinds." He shook his head. "I should have known better than to undertake such a thing without assistance." His shoulders dropped a fraction, as a deep sigh sounded. His normal composed manner seemed to waver.

"No, please do not apologize. It is a remarkable instrument."

A look of hope flickered across his face.

"It is not that I cannot play it. The strings are the same, I will need to practice using these levers, as opposed to peddles, of which I am accustomed to."

"I should have known there was a hitch when I was told it would be here within the week." His Grace ran his fingers through his hair, a sign of frustration she had seen before. Too many times of late. He must be ready to be rid of her and her whole family. "I believe it came from Wales. To get one from London would have taken a month. I had wanted you to have the chance to play before you left." He cleared his throat, his voice lowering. "I hoped it would help you feel more at home...that is to say when you come to visit."

Violet looked at him in confusion. Could he find her so distasteful if he had taken such pains as this to make her feel welcome? But only moments ago he had all but asked her to leave. *Oh, this man was confusing.* She had very little experience with men, but from what she had observed, most did not appear to be this difficult.

She looked at the harp. He claimed to have bought it to complete the music room, but he had also bought it with her in mind and that was what she was going to focus on for now. "Indeed, it is the kindest thing anyone has ever done for me."

He tilted his head, studying her, evaluating the truthfulness of her words. "Truly, you like it? I can send for a different...one with pedals?"

Violet smiled. "There is no need. I would not wish for a different one. This will do very well."

The duke moved toward the harp. "How is it dissimilar? Could you show me?"

Coming up next to him, she pulled a string, the note resonating in the column. Taking hold of the lever, she pulled the string again, a different tone sounded. "These levers allow me to change the key, without re-tuning. The harp in our music room at home has pedals to do the same thing." She sat down on the stool sitting next to the instrument. Pointing to her toes she explained. "Normally I would sit like this and push the pedals to change the key." Her feet moved up and down mimicking the movement. "But with this harp, I use these levers here at the top."

He looked at the strings, confusion evident in his eyes. "How do you move these, if your fingers are busy pulling the strings?"

Violet released a small chuckle. "You do it very fast with one hand while the other hand continues to play. It can be a little tricky."

She stood up and lifted the seat of the stool she had been sitting on, shuffling through a few pages, she pulled out a piece. She held the sheet in front of her, turning back and forth, looking for a stand, but found nothing. Thrusting the paper at him, she asked. "Would you mind holding this?"

He shook his head, holding the music out in front of him.

Sitting back on the stool, she leaned the harp into her shoulder and began to pluck at the strings. The music would stutter every time she raised her hand to move a lever. It sounded terrible to her trained ear. After a few lines, she pushed the harp back to standing. Heat rose in her cheeks when she saw him watching her intently. "As I said, I will need some practice. I am not fast, which makes it difficult for my other hand to keep playing." She was surprised at how easy it had been to play with him in the room. Indeed, she had not even thought about it until she saw him watching her.

"I disagree. I heard only beautiful music. You are very good."

Her eyes held his steady gaze. She swallowed hard, her heartbeat throbbing in her neck.

His Grace handed her back the sheet music. As he walked away, disappointment crashed down on her. While she could not blame him for leaving, she had already told him she did not allow an audience, she was crestfallen he had not chosen to stay.

She stretched out her fingers, bending them and then straightening them several times. She intended to play out all of her frustrations until she heard a scraping on the parquet floor. Following the direction of the noise, she saw the duke dragging the settee from the corner of the room, over to a position next to the harp. Sitting at the end closest to the instrument, he retrieved the music from the stool where she had set it.

He held it up in front of him. At her look of dismay, he lifted a brow. "I neglected to order a stand. You cannot practice without something holding your music." A slight smile turned the corners of his mouth. "I will volunteer to be that something."

Tipping her head to the side, she smiled. He may only be staying because he neglected to order a stand, but she did not care. He was sitting here now, holding music so she could play. She was still confused about him. Confused about her feelings for him. But he was interested in her music and for now, that was enough.

She lifted up the seat on the stool again and removed all of the music from within. Sitting down, she pulled the instrument into place, playing the music the duke held in front of her. At first, she was nervous, constantly glancing at him when she made a mistake. He seemed to hardly notice the false notes.

After one time through the music, she found herself paying more attention to the strings and levers than to the man holding the papers. Slowly, her hands began to find the rhythm, the plucking and lever turning becoming more fluid.

She played for some time, barely remembering His Grace was there with her, but then the paper slowly dropped until it rested on his thighs. Unable to see the music any longer, she stopped playing and looked at him. His eyes were closed, the lines normally creasing his eyes and forehead lay smooth and relaxed.

Violet felt her heart flutter. She removed the paper from his hands, placing all of the music back into the stool. Careful not to awaken him, she sat on the couch, scooting as close as she dared.

An urge to run her finger across his stubbled cheek made her hold her hands tightly together. That action would surely awaken him and then what would she say? *My apologies, Your Grace. I needed to feel your skin beneath my fingers.* Ugh, that would never be acceptable.

A small, giddy giggle escaped as she thought about saying such a thing to a man of his position and status. The sound caused him to shift positions. Violet leaned away from him, ready to launch herself to standing. But he did not awaken, so she continued to sit and stare.

The longer she watched him, the harder it was for her to breathe properly and the more she wanted to touch him. Only his hair or his face, nothing so very untoward.

She leaned forward slightly, building up the courage to follow through. If she touched very lightly, surely he would not awaken. Reaching out a shaking hand, she moved it toward his slightly parted lips.

A cough from the doorway brought her hand jerking back to her lap at the same time her face turned a deep crimson.

Turning her head toward the sound, she saw Mr. Dawson standing in the doorway, his eyes narrowed, mouth twisted into what? A smile? Or perhaps a sneer? He began to walk across the room.

She stood, moving to the side of the couch, hoping to put a small buffer between them. He stopped short of the settee.

"Did I interrupt...something?" His eyes held mirth.

Violet did not think it possible for her blush to deepen any more than it already was, but she was wrong. "I was, um." She stammered guiltily. Taking a steadying breath, she squared her shoulders. She had done nothing wrong. Yet. "I was practicing on the new harp His Grace had delivered. There was no music stand so he was holding the music for me."

Mr. Dawson's lips twitched. "I would think it difficult to play the harp while sitting all the way over here."

Her breath hitched slightly, her eyes widening. Mr. Dawson barked out a laugh.

The duke jerked up, his body rigid as his eyes searched the room. His posture began to relax until his gaze rested on her and then Mr. Dawson. Like a shot, he came to a standing position.

"Dawson." A look passed between the two men, causing Mr. Dawson's brow to pucker. The duke turned to her, "Miss Violet. I apologize for falling asleep. Please do not interpret the action as boredom and believe me when I say the opposite to be true." His gaze flicked back to Mr. Dawson, his scowl from outside returning. "Now, if you will excuse me." He bowed, then turned on his heel and left the room with his secretary following behind.

CHAPTER 18

Violet did not know why she continued to read the book. After the duke had all but dismissed her yesterday, she found she could not stop reading it. She hoped it might provide some insight into him, but she had learned nothing except about the American government. Although, in a strange way it made her feel closer to him, as if they shared something no one else did. She had even sneaked back into the library and borrowed the book she had seen on Pennsylvania.

When she looked at the pictures, she could almost imagine the duke in them; managing their plantation, working alongside his servants. Violet sighed. Why was she doing this to herself? Why could she not accept that he was going to marry her sister? Why did she keep hoping the circumstances would change when she knew they would not? Mr. Dawson had told her the duke would follow through with the arrangement.

A knock on the door of her chambers brought her eyes upward. Rose swung the door open and stepped into the room.

Violet put the book in her lap, while her sister stood just inside the doorway. She said nothing as she watched Violet closely.

"Hello, Rose. Were you in need of something?" Her sister looked at Violet with narrowed eyes, openly appraising her. When Rose finally spoke, Violet wished for the silence back.

"Do you love him?"

Violet's eyes went wide. "Please shut the door, Rose. I don't think this is a conversation for all to hear."

Rose took several steps forward and pushed the door closed behind her. "There now. You have your privacy. Now, will you answer my question?"

Violet smoothed her dress, surprised her hands were not shaking. "To whom are you referring? I cannot tell you of my feeling for someone when I know not of whom you are speaking."

Her sister moved to the bed, sitting down on the edge, fingering the coverlet trim. "Do I really need to say his name, Violet? Surely you know I am speaking of His Grace." She took a deep breath and repeated her question. "Do you love him?"

Violet let out a shaky laugh. "I hardly know the man. How could I love him?" Violet paced the length of the room, crossing her arms around her middle. "Why would you ask such a question? You are the one marrying him."

Rose stood and stepped in front of Violet, halting her steps. "I have seen the way you look at him, the way you smile whenever he looks in your direction."

"I do no such thing." Violet protested. "And even if I did, what am I to do when he looks at me? Would you wish me to scowl or frown at him?" Violet's stomach dropped. If Rose thought such things, what must the duke be thinking of her?

Rose shook her head. "I did not begin to worry until I saw the two of you in the library the other day. Then after you flung yourself down the hillside, it seems he cannot keep from watching you."

Violet pushed back the surge of hope. "Don't be a ninny, Rose. He is merely making sure I do not do myself another injury while under his care. It is nothing more, nothing less. Besides, he has hardly spoken ten words to me since your walk into the village."

Rose seemed to be evaluating Violet words. "And yet, he still watches you when he thinks no one is paying him mind." Violet opened her mouth, but Rose stopped her. "Are you trying to ruin this for me? I am his betrothed. I am the one to be the duchess. How could you develop feelings for him? How could you try to win him away from me?" The hurt in Rose's eyes twisted Violet's already queasy stomach.

"I do not love him, Rose. If I have given him the impression I do, I am sorry. I wish only for your felicity." Violet held her sister's gaze, even as she lied until it was too much. Turning away, Violet thought about her time with His Grace in the library. It had been days since she had thought on him as Mr. Dashing. It had been the duke who carried her after her fall and the duke who had been with her in the music room. And it had most definitely been the duke who dismissed her after their conversation in the library yesterday.

But there had been a moment—she pushed the memory away. Gah! This had to end. She could not torture herself with believing he cared for her more than he would a sister. She turned and faced Rose. "I have no intention..."

Rose reached out a hand, patting Violet on the arm and smiling sweetly. "I know you would not willfully hurt me, Violet. I just needed you to know how your behavior was being perceived."

Violet jerked back as if she had been slapped. Her sister believed Violet was purposely trying to win the duke? Violet paused. Was she right?

Rose moved toward the door but stopped when her hand touched the handle. She turned back to Violet. "I would advise against being alone with him, Violet. Even if the door is open. You have brought enough scandal to the family. We do not need anymore." There was kindness in her tone, but the accusation shouted louder.

Rose slipped out the door, closing it behind her. The urge to escape seized hold of Violet. She needed to be away, to walk and to think. What was she to do? She had fallen in love with the man her sister was to marry. The air around her suddenly thickened.

Gathering her pelisse and muffler, Violet tied the string of her bonnet under her chin as she rushed down the stairs. She had been staring at the hedge maze for days. In the center was a very lovely fountain. Sure she could find the much needed solitude within the high hedgerow, she rushed outside and to the entrance of the maze.

Pushing aside the thoughts crowding her mind, Violet focused her attention on the path before her. She closed her eyes and envisioned the maze as she viewed it from her window. Stepping through the entrance, the walls rose up around her, reaching several feet above her head. Her muscles relaxed and her breathing slowed.

Only a few steps inside, she was faced with her first decision. Continue straight or turn to either side? Violet turned to her left, trying to remember each turn she needed to make to get her to the middle. With little trouble, she turned through the last break in the hedge and came to the center of the maze. A small fountain filled the space. A path wide enough for two people to comfortably walk side by side wound around the fountain and led to several breaks in the hedge. Violet pulled a piece of string from her pocket and wrapped it loosely around the end of a branch. The last thing she needed was to exit through the wrong gap and find herself lost.

The trickle of the water spilling from the maiden's pot filled the silence. Violet sighed. If only it could drown out the thoughts running through her mind.

CHAPTER 19

Tad sat at his desk, studying the plans for the south fields. Most of them were already planted with winter wheat and barley. It was the beginning of his objective for the estate and his excitement bubbled up in his stomach. For the first time since arriving, he actually felt up to the task of managing this estate.

A knock sounded at his door. "Come."

Lady Rachel opened the door, not quite closing it all the way behind her. "Do you have a moment, Tad?"

Rolling the map up, he placed it on a table to the side. "Of course, aunt. Please come in."

She stood in front of his desk, scrutinizing him. Finally, she shook her head. "I feel like I am being called to task by my father. Could we please move to the couches by the fire?"

Tad chuckled softly, as he stood. "As you wish, my lady." He made a great show of bowing, then swept his arm in the direction of the fireplace.

The bland expression she gave him indicated she was unimpressed with his grand gesture. She glided over to the bell cord and rang for tea, before settling into the corner of the settee.

From the serious look on her face, Tad doubted this conversation was one of their typical 'memories of your father' talks. He hesitantly sat down.

She wasted no time in getting to the point. "You have been out of sorts of late."

Tad raised a brow. "Oh?"

"Don't be impertinent with me, young man, or I shall have to send Lydia in to speak with you." She leveled her gaze at him, daring him to test her. "And I do not believe either of us wants that to happen."

Tad let out a breath, irritation creeping into his voice. "What is your question, Aunt Standish?"

She scowled. "I want to know why you are in high dudgeons."

"Really, Aunt. It is nothing to concern yourself with." First Dawson and now her? Why could people not leave him well enough alone? Why must they all take such an interest in his affairs?

"I am concerned. Even Jes has mentioned your shifting moods. That is worrisome in and of itself. We both know she is not the most observant girl. If she has noticed your behavior, there must be a problem."

"I think you are mistaken, Aunt. I have found Jes to be quite observant. I suspect there is very little going on in this house of which she is unaware."

"Really? I had not noticed." His aunt looked at him with a knowing gleam in her eye. "But we were not discussing Jes. That conversation can wait for another time." She gave him a coy smile. "Her observations have led her to believe you are angry with Mr. Dawson. But she has no idea why."

Tad scowled at her. His aunt was a clever woman, and every

bit as determined as Lady Mayfield when she wanted to be. While he refused to tell her everything, he could tell her enough to hopefully satisfy her.

"Very well. If you must pry..." He was surprisingly satisfied with her intake of breath. "Mr. Dawson is not convinced I am making the right decision by marrying Miss Allen. He believes I am forgoing a chance at happiness out of a misguided sense of duty." While not the whole truth, there was enough truth to words to hopefully satisfy his aunt.

"I see." She looked at him closely. "So have you reconsidered?"

He shrugged. "No. I have not changed my mind, but I do find myself thinking on it more oft than I should." He picked up a nearby book, running his thumb across the pages. "Would I really ruin Miss Allen's chance for making a suitable match if I choose another?"

His aunt nodded slowly. "There are many who will see her as less desirable. Although, it is not as damaging as if formal contracts had been drawn up. If this had occurred in town, the harm would be irreparable. Unless they have told everyone of their acquaintance, they should be able to cover it up. It is the advantage of country living."

"And if they have? Told everyone, I mean. I believe Miss Allen to have made the announcement far and wide. She told me of the engagement upon our first setting eyes on each other."

"Then there will be some scandal attached to her name." Aunt Standish thought. "And where there is already some questions concerning the family? They may be unable to recover, socially."

A maid brought the tea into the room, placing it on the table between them. Aunt began to pour, while Tad grabbed several cakes.

"What if I married Miss Violet, instead? What would it do to Miss Allen?"

Lady Rachel looked at him, a slight smile on her lips. "Miss Allen would be completely ruined. It is doubtful she would ever make a suitable match." She took a sip of her tea.

"Even if someone of great social prominence sponsored her?" There would be no way to remove the stain?"

"It would have to be someone very great, indeed. The problem would be in finding this someone. There are not many within the ton who would take on such a challenge."

Tad sat staring into his teacup. "What if Miss Violet married someone else? A gentleman of some sort, but I did not marry Miss Allen?"

Her brow furrowed in confusion, which gave him a sense of satisfaction. She thought she knew what he was about, but now she was unsure. Perhaps next time she came to invade his personal rooms with questions that did not concern her, she would think twice.

His aunt put her teacup down on the tray. "If that were to happen, Miss Allen would still be ruined, but Miss Violet would stay relatively respectable." She was quiet.

Tad looked up to make sure she had not quietly slipped from the room or fallen asleep. When their gazes met, she held his. His mother did a similar thing when she wanted him to really listen to her.

"Tad, I cannot tell you to ignore your heart and marry someone you do not love, for I did not follow that advice, myself." There was no regret or remorse in her words. "Nor will I tell you to abandon family honor and marry for love. For some, honor will govern every decision and for others, it will be their heart. One is not right, while the other is wrong. They are different. You need to decide for yourself what governs your decision. It is you that will have to live with the consequences for the rest of your life. Do not let anyone make your decisions for you."

Tad leaned forward, placing his elbows on his thighs. He rubbed his hands over his face several times. Perhaps she was not as confused as he believed her to be.

She stood, placing a hand on his shoulder. "Think on my words, and know I am here. If you would ever like to talk, about anything, I am a willing ear." Bending over, she placed a motherly kiss on the crown of his head.

He assumed she had left the room, but when he finally stood and stretched, he saw her sitting quietly in the window seat, reading. Tad smiled at the similarities between mother and daughter. It left him with a pang of longing for his own mother and sisters.

A quick knock sounded seconds before Dawson's office door opened. Tad scowled at his friend before he schooled his features.

"What has you in the doldrums lately?" Dawson stood with his arms crossed over his chest, his scowl firmly in place.

"I don't know what you are talking about," Tad lied. Even thinking on the sight he had awakened to in the music room made his chest hurt. He was supposed to be distancing himself from her, not falling in love with her. Not that he was in love with her, he reminded himself.

"Your scowl would indicate the falseness of that statement."

"It is not the responsibility of the help to evaluate their master's motives."

Aunt Standish's breath caught.

As soon as the words left his mouth, Tad wished them back. He had never considered Dawson a servant, but his words, spoken in anger, belied that notion.

Dawson's head snapped back. "Correct you are, *Your Grace*. My apologies." He turned toward the door, calling over his shoulder, "I'll be in my office if you need me, sir." Before Tad could utter an explanation or apology, Dawson was gone.

Tad ran a frustrated hand through his hair. He needed air. He needed to clear his head and figure out how he was going to fix the messes he had created. Not only was he in the briars with Dawson, but he was also quickly losing the tenuous friendship he had with Miss Violet. He retrieved his great coat from Baker and headed to the maze. Perhaps if he walked for a time a solution would present itself.

Entering the high hedge walls, he moved in the direction of the fountain located in the center. The root of this whole mess was Miss Violet and his growing attachment to her.

His plans to avoid her were not working as well as he had hoped. For such a large house, he was amazed by how often they met in one place or another. It seemed all of his favorite places were hers as well. The library, the stables, the gardens, and the music room. He shrugged, correcting himself. The music room had not become a favorite until the first time he heard her playing the pianoforte.

There had been a risk of seeing her on his last visit there, but he had felt compelled to learn if she had discovered the harp. He had not been disappointed. Not in the beginning, at least.

Breathing deeply in the crisp fall air, he tried to order his thoughts. First on his list? He needed to apologize to Dawson. After all, it was not his fault Miss Violet was attracted to him. Tad sighed, shame washing over him at his treatment of his longtime friend. The two had never let anything come between them. Not war or financial ruin, yet here Tad was letting a lady jeopardize their friendship. He had to make things right between them. A thought entered his mind, making his stomach clench and his throat tighten.

Trying to order his thoughts, Tad passed through the large hole in the hedge, entering the heart of the maze, where he spotted Miss Violet sitting on the edge of the fountain.

She turned at hearing his footsteps on the dry leaves. Tad

backed up a few steps. "Pardon me. I did not expect to find anyone here. I will leave you to your solitude."

Walking back to the gap in the hedge, she stopped him. "I wish you wouldn't. Seclusion is not always desired. Sometimes it is simply what we are given."

He walked slowly toward the small fountain. "I am surprised you were able to find the fountain so quickly. It took me almost a week of solid searching before I was able to reach the middle. And another full day to find my way back out."

Disbelief wrinkled her brow. "Why did it take you a day to find your way out? Did you not remember the turns from your journey inward?"

He cringed. "That would have been the more intelligent approach, but no. I had given up on remembering the turns several days before. I happened upon this spot while stumbling around the maze one day. I had no idea how I got here, nor how to return back to the outside." Taking a seat on the edge facing her, he removed his glove and cupped his hand beneath the maiden's vessel. The biting cold water forced him to spread his finger apart, letting it run out. "Tell me, how did you find it so quickly?"

A timid smile curved her lips. "I saw the maze from my window and found the middle. Then I memorized the turns."

He gasped, mouth gaping open. "Why, that is cheating." He put his hand to his heart. The action left a damp handprint on his great coat.

"And how did you find the middle—the second time? You said yourself you did not memorize the turns. What type of strategy did you use?"

Tad averted his eyes, unable to meet her gaze. "Actually, I found the same window you did, and memorized the turns."

A huff, accompanied by a smack on his upper arm, pushed his laugh out.

"It would seem I am also a cheat. I had hoped to keep that character flaw hidden a while longer."

A full smile broke out on her lips, her whole face alight.

The sight took Tad's breath away. Unable to speak, he sat staring and smiling like an idiot.

Miss Violet twisted, pulling a small red leaf out of the water. The moisture left spots on her white gloves.

He shifted and their knees touched, sending heat rushing through him. Miss Violet scooted back, smoothing her dress over her legs.

Rubbing his hands together, trying to warm the one he had run through the water, he looked about the inner room of the maze. Silence filled the small space, neither seeming to know what to say. His mind suddenly hit upon something she had said earlier.

"Are you lonely here?" He blurted.

Caught by surprise at the obvious change in conversation, she opened her mouth and then shut it again. Tilting her head to one side, she seemed to think about the question. After a moment, she shook her head. "No. In truth, it's the opposite, Your Grace. Why do you ask?"

"Your comment when I was going to leave, made me think perhaps you are lonesome."

Her gaze dropped to her hands, working feverishly at a button on her pelisse. "I spend a great deal of time alone and have since I was a young girl. I am quite used to it. However, sometimes it would be nice to have some company—someone to talk to." There was no whining or self-pity in her voice; she was merely stating a fact. A fact Tad found difficult to understand.

"What about your sister? I do not know her well, but surely you spend time together."

What could only be described as a smirk turned Miss Violet's lips upward. "You are correct. You do not know my sister well. For if you did, you would realize she is not always the best company." Her face pinked slightly. "Forgive me. I spoke too freely." She dropped her head and mumbled quietly. "It is something I do too often when I am with you." Straightening she met his eyes. "Rose is not at home much. She is always out visiting this person or that."

"Why do you not go on visits with your sister? Both my sisters would accompany my mother on such errands." Perhaps this was another custom that differed from America.

She looked up to the sky as if trying to formulate her thoughts. "It was rare for me to be invited along. Rose and I would both make visits when I was younger, however, after an initial introduction most would be unavailable to me when I called." Violet shrugged her shoulders.

Tad sensed she was trying to appear unaffected, but the hurt was not totally absent from her expression. She forced a laugh. "After four or five attempts, I began to understand they were not eager for my company. It was the same with gentlemen I met at the assemblies. I would dance with them once and then never again. I would hear them talking behind their fans and gloved hands."

She sat up straighter. "I found I did not need people. Mozart, Bach, and Beethoven—they all made very good company." An edge entered her voice.

Anger surged through him, and a feeling of protectiveness propelled him to his feet. He would like nothing better than to get a list of every one of those young ladies who snubbed her. Unsure of what he would do to them, he did know it would not be pleasant.

"Did you never find out what caused this ostracism?" It was asked through clenched teeth, his breath sounding more like the snort of an angry bull.

Miss Violet stood, moving a few paces away from him. Her

posture tensed, her brows rising slightly. "I have ideas, but nothing factual. It more likely than not is something lacking in my character." She swallowed hard as if admitting it out loud made it the truth.

Her expression held a degree of uncertainty. Was she worried this would change their friendship? He took a calming breath, mentally making his hands relax. "What a crock." He shook his head in disgust.

Her eyebrows rose almost into her hairline. "Crock? I am afraid I do not know what that means."

He stared at her, confused. "Crock...nonsense...balderdash. It means I don't believe it."

"It is an American term, then." She nodded in acceptance.

Tad continued. "I know enough of your character to assure you it is not the reason people treated you poorly." He did not know what expression he expected to see, but disappointment or perhaps defeat were not on the list.

Her shoulders dropped. "I figured it was not the whole of it. Part, perhaps, but not the reason entirely."

"Then what is it?" Tad wanted to know what was so horrible about this girl, people felt compelled to avoid her company.

She hesitated, taking another step back.

"Well?" Somewhere in the recesses of his mind he registered her reaction and knew he should stop the questions. He pushed it aside, curiosity and anger pushing him on.

Her face turned ashen which only increased his need to know.

Violet took a deep breath, squaring her shoulders, and held his gaze. "My mother was compromised, in a most brutal way, while my father was away on business." Her voice took on a cold detached tone. "The man left her, beaten and bleeding, in our stable."

All at once Tad realized his mistake. It was not his place to make her tell this story, but he was too late to take the demanding questions back. What had he done? Running his hand over his face, he knew his father, who was certainly looking down on him, was beyond disappointed. Tad was disgusted with himself.

"Please, you do not need to continue. I had no right to ask this of you." There was a pleading in his voice.

"You asked to know, Your Grace. You would now deprive me of telling you the whole story? Not allow me to repair my mother's reputation?" Her voice dropped to a whisper. "That is cruelty, indeed."

His voice came out in a croak. "I do not wish to be cruel." Shaking his head, he cursed himself over and over.

Miss Violet released a breath. "Several months later, my mother discovered she was with child. My parents had a love match, which made my pedigree unknown. They kept it from me at first, but on my mother's deathbed, she confessed everything. My father, who insists I have his father's chin, was adamant I was his and has raised me as such."

Staring at the woman in front of him, trying to be strong and unyielding, his heart ached for what she had lived with all these years.

Not sure how to handle a lady in these circumstances, he thought about what he would do if it were one of his sisters. Stepping forward, he reached for her hand. When his fingers touched hers, she flinched, backing away from him. "I am so sorry." He was sorry for demanding she repeat the tale. But mostly he was sorry for what she had endured all these years.

Her already ramrod straight posture, straightened even more. "I do not need your pity, Your Grace."

Tad detected a slight tremor in her voice.

"You do not have my pity, Miss Violet. You have my deepest respect. You are truly a lady in every sense of the word." The words seemed inadequate for describing how he saw her. "Thank you for trusting me enough to tell me. I promise I will never betray it."

Her shoulders lowered a fraction and her chin dipped slightly. If it were one of his sisters, he would wrap her in a hug. But she was not one of his sisters and he did not believe a hug would feel the same with her as it did with Liza or Aisling.

"Thank you, Your Grace. Pity is a terrible burden."

Tad frowned. "I cannot imagine people would forgo your friendship over such a thing if they did, indeed, know about it. Surely it wasn't common knowledge."

Miss Violet twisted at her button again. "You are new to the English ton, Your Grace. People are despised for much less. And while it was not to be common knowledge, somehow it got out. I overheard conversations, saw the looks of disdain."

Tad took a step closer, unsure if she would retreat again. While this had begun as a terrible folly on his part, he felt as if it was now drawing them together. Perhaps he had not totally muddled their friendship after all. His heartbeat picked up its pace, but his brain pushed it back down, regaining control once again. Dawson and Rose. He had to keep them in mind.

CHAPTER 20

Violet and Miss Standish walked through the hedgerow soaking in the last rays of fall. The weather had been cooling off more each day. Violet pulled her shawl a little tighter as a breeze lightly picked up her hem.

"Do you think your father will return before the ball?" Miss Standish asked as she stooped to pluck a lonely stalk of wheat, twirling it in her fingers.

"Oh, yes. His business was only to take a day or two, at most. I expect him to return at any time."

"Do you think there shall be anyone interesting attending? It shall be my first ball and I fear there will only be boring old men with which to dance." Miss Standish gave a disgruntled huff. "All the eligible gentlemen are in London."

Violet smiled. "I am glad you will be attending, Miss Standish."

"Please, call me Jes. We are dearest friends now." When Violet nodded, Jes continued. "My Aunt Mayfield agreed because I will have my official coming out in just a few months time." Jes pinched up her face. "And it is only a country ball, after all. They are of little consequence."

Violet laughed at the girl's imitation of Lady Mayfield. "I do not think you will be disappointed. Your cousin and Mr. Dawson will be in attendance. They are not old." Violet suspected Jes might have a bit of an affinity for Mr. Dawson.

Jes sighed. "You are right, Mr. Dawson will likely be there. He is very handsome, do you not agree?"

Violet smiled. Jes was young and in love with the idea of love. Violet had no doubt she would develop affections for no less than a handful of men before her first season was done.

"Yes, he is indeed handsome."

Jes sighed. "But that is only two gentlemen. I cannot dance every dance with only two men."

A twig broke behind them, causing Violet to turn around. Her stomach dropped and her heart raced. Standing before them was Mr. McPhail.

"Hullo, Violet." He tipped his hat to her. "You are a difficult person to find."

"Mr. McPhail. What are you doing here?" The strangled tone of her voice made her wince. She knew how much he enjoyed her fear. Pushing her chin up higher, she straightened her back. "I was not aware I needed to inform you of my whereabouts, sir." She took a small step back, wanting as much distance as she could get between them. "Nor was I aware of your acquaintance with the Duke of Shearsby."

Jes came up behind her, giving her the support she desperately needed.

"I did not come here to see the duke, Violet. I came here for you."

"I have asked you not to use my Christian name. Now, if you

will excuse me. We must return to the house." She tried to move around him, but he blocked her path.

"Your friend may return, but I am not finished speaking with you, Miss Violet."

Glancing to the side, Violet could see Jes's wide eyes. The hair at the nape of Violet's neck lifted. What if Mr. McPhail hurt Jes? There was no doubt in Violet's mind he would do anything to get what he wanted. "Yes, Jes. Please return to the house. I will be fine." The shake in her voice belied her words.

"But Violet, it would not be proper for me to leave you alone." Jes stepped closer, linking her arm with Violet's. "Mr. McPhail, why don't you come and join us for tea. I am sure my cousin would like to meet you." Jes swallowed hard.

Violet moved Jes to the side, motioning her to move around them. "Perhaps if you stood off a bit, you could provide a watchful eye, while still giving Mr. McPhail and I a little privacy." Slowly Jes walked toward the house. She stopped far enough away she would not be able to hear much of the conversation, but still close enough to watch.

Mr. McPhail snorted. "You never worried about a chaperone before." He cast a leering glance over his shoulder at Jes before turning his gaze on Violet. "Although, she is a pretty little thing. Perhaps she could stay."

Violet's stomach lurched. "I have not been alone with you since I was a girl. Do not make such insinuations. I do not know why you came all this way. There is nothing to talk about, Mr. McPhail. I believe I made my feelings clear before I left Cheshire. Now, if you will let me pass." She moved to walk around him, but he reached out and grabbed her, his fingers digging into the scratches on her arms. She swallowed the cry of pain, unwilling to give him the joy from it.

"You may have said all you wished, but I am not finished..."

"If I recall," she interrupted him. "You said you were finished with me. And I am finished with you. Now, please unhand me and let me return to the house." She wrenched her arm from his grasp, quickly moving around him. "Miss Standish," she called, relieved when Jes moved a few steps in her direction.

Walking faster, Violet caught up to her friend and they both walked quickly to the house. Tears formed at the bottom of Violet's eyelids, blurring the steps as they ran up them. Entering through the terrace doors, Jes looked at Violet with a creased brow. "Did he harm you?"

Violet shook her head, raising shaking hands to wipe at her eyes. "No, just frightened me a little."

Jes took one of her hands. "You are shaking like a leaf. Who was that man? Why did he come for you? I think we should make my cousin aware of this matter."

Violet felt her face blanch. "No. Please. I believe Mr. McPhail will go away. He knows we have nothing more to discuss." She pulled her hand free, trying to regain some composure. "His Grace has plenty of things to worry about. There is no need to add another burden to his list."

Jes's eyes narrowed. "I do not agree, but I shall honor your wishes for now."

"Thank you, Jes. You are a true friend."

Violet sat at the harp, trying to regain some peace after her encounter with Mr. McPhail. She heard footsteps padding across the floor and looked up to see the duke standing a short distance away. She smiled at him, hoping it would encourage him to come closer, perhaps even stay and listen for a time. When he did not, she stopped playing. "Would you like to pull a chair over and listen? I do not mind." Why did her voice have to wobble when she asked? She felt like a child again, asking her father for a book.

He stepped closer. "I would enjoy nothing more." His words said one thing, but his face told a different story. "But I am come to fetch you."

Violet smiled. He wanted to see her? Spend time with her? She put the harp up and placed the music in the stool. "Of course. Where did you wish to go, Your Grace?"

"You have a visitor." He frowned when her smile dropped.

Of course, he did not want to spend time with me. I am cotton-brained for thinking as much. "Oh? A visitor, Your Grace? I cannot guess who it would be."

"He said you were friends from Cheshire."

Violet stopped in her tracks. "He, Your Grace?"

The duke halted with her, frowning still. "Yes, I believe his name was McPhail? Perhaps I have his name wrong. He did not have a card."

Violet put a hand out, reaching for a support that was not there. Her breath came in short bursts as her mind raced. *No, no, no.* Why would he not leave her be? What could he possibly have to say? And in the duke's presence?

The duke led her to a nearby chair. "What is the matter, Miss Violet? You seem quite unwell. Do you know this gentleman?"

"I do not believe Mr. McPhail can be considered a gentleman, Your Grace."

The duke kneeled before her, peering up into her face. "I shall return directly." He stood and walked out of the room. Violet watched him go, not sure if she was more disappointed he had left her alone or scared to face Mr. McPhail.

The duke returned moments later. "I have asked Baker to send for tea. He will also have a tray delivered to Mr. McPhail and your sister with regrets that we have not located you as yet."

Violet looked up into his stormy blue eyes. Why did gentlemen like His Grace—kind, gentle, and compassionate— never find her interesting? Then something struck her.

"You said my sister was with him?"

"Yes, when she heard he was here, she came to welcome him. She said he was a dear family friend."

Violet's brain worked to reconcile why Rose would be in the same room with Mr. McPhail. She had never cared for the man and without remorse would dismiss him or ignore him completely. Why was she now claiming an acquaintance?

A knock sounded at the door and a footman, along with Lady Rachel, entered with the tea. She directed the servant to the table in the corner, dismissing him immediately.

"Aunt, I hope Baker did not pull you away from anything critical." He smiled kindly at the older lady. Violet found it hard to believe he had known Lady Rachel only slightly longer than herself.

"Nothing that cannot wait a few hours." Her eyes dropped to Violet's shaking hands. "Would you care for some tea, Miss Violet?"

Violet nodded, not sure she could trust her voice.

The duke waved aside the offered cup. "Now, would you mind telling me who the gentleman is in my drawing room? And why you are so afraid of him?"

Violet left her tea on the table, afraid she would spill it down the front of her dress. Perhaps that could delay her seeing Mr. McPhail. She took a deep breath, knowing he would not be deterred so easily. And her nerves would only increase the longer she waited. At least this time there would be others about.

"I believe you have witnessed Mr. McPhail's...gentlemanly behavior," her fingers drifted to her neck, rubbing absently. "When first we met."

The duke's face crinkled in confusion before understanding

dawned. His eyes widened. "That was his doing?" He shot to his feet, pacing about the Oriental rug.

"Oh, my." Lady Rachel whispered.

Violet knew she should feel humiliated that his aunt knew of her encounter, but she didn't. Instead, she felt relieved and safe. It was something she had not felt since she was a child, but it gave her strength.

Picking up her saucer, hardly shaking it at all, she sipped slowly at the brown liquid. She looked at His Grace over the cup. His normally stormy eyes raged. It was for Mr. McPhail she worried this time.

"Take your time with your tea, Violet. You will not be visiting with your friend today. But I find I am very anxious to hear what Mr. McPhail has to say." He paced a few more times before rushing to the door.

Violet looked to Lady Rachel, who patted her kindly on the leg. Putting her cup back on the tray she turned to Violet with raised brows. "Are you ready, dear?"

Violet looked at her with wide eyes. "Ready, my lady?"

"You do not intend to sit in here while that man slanders you to my nephew, do you? For you know he is spinning some sort of tale. That is what men like him do." Lady Rachel smoothed her dress. "Let us wait in the hallway outside the sitting room, in case there is a need for our presence."

"Eavesdrop, my lady?" Violet was not sure which shocked her more, listening at the doorway or confronting Mr. McPhail and hearing what he had to say face to face.

They made their way to the sitting room, grateful the door was cracked enough for them to hear the voices inside.

"Thank you for the introductions, Miss Allen. Now sir, if you will tell me what business you have with Miss Violet Allen, I will see she is informed as soon as she is located." The duke's back was to her, but she recognized the steel in his voice.

He continued. "Pray, Mr. McPhail, what brings you all the way to Leicestershire? It must be very important indeed, to make such a trip."

Mr. McPhail leaned carelessly against the fireplace, a reptilian smile distorting his face. Violet looked between the two men. The contrast was almost laughable.

Mr. McPhail finally pushed off the mantle, walking toward the duke. "I have come to collect my wife and return with her to Cheshire."

Silence permeated the room until it was at last broken by His Grace. "What has that to do with Miss Violet?"

"It is Miss Violet I speak of. We eloped, not long ago, and I have come to take her home."

Violet felt all the air leave her lungs. All at once, the fear returned. Could he make them believe his story? What if the duke allowed him to take her away? Without thinking on her actions, she rushed into the room, stopping when she reached the center, not wanting to be any closer to Mr. McPhail.

The duke stepped up beside her. She wondered if he knew how much she needed his support. He placed his hand on the small of her back before leaning to the side and whispering in her ear. "I am here. I will not permit him to hurt you again."

Her heart hammered in her chest. She swallowed the lump in her throat. His kindness had eliminated most of her fears, but it left an opening for yearning. If only he would say as much when she was not in danger.

"If this is true, why is Miss Violet here, at my estate; two counties away?"

Mr. McPhail stuttered a little. "You know how women are,

Your Grace. A fickle lot, they are. She ran off before we could even tell her father of the nuptials."

"Miss Violet, is this true?"

She glanced over at him, but his eyes were on Mr. McPhail.

"No, Your Grace. I am not, nor will I ever be, married to this man."

Rose looked on from the couch, her brow creased, while Mr. McPhail glared at them. "Violet, why are you doing this? Come home." He had obviously thought there would be little opposition. He turned to the duke, "We have been friends since we were children. Before I departed for Spain, we pledged our love for each other. And when I returned home a few months ago, we discovered our feelings had not changed." Mr. McPhail's gaze switched to Violet. "Violet..."

"I have asked you not to call me by my Christian name." Violet stomped her foot. How many times must she repeat herself? Her name was the only thing she held control over and she was not about to give it up to Mr. McPhail.

His nose flared, his hands balling at his sides. "She was convinced her father would not grant us permission to wed. So we eloped to Scotland and married over the anvil."

"Miss Violet, do you have anything to add to this imaginative story?"

"Only that it never happened."

"Really Violet?" Rose's voice spoke up from the couch. "You told me yourself you loved him. I do not find it hard to believe his story."

Violet stared at her sister. "That was many years ago. I was young and naive."

Mr. McPhail seemed to change tactics, softening his features and lowering his voice. "I do not understand why you left in the first place. But now to pretend our marriage never took place. It is a mystery to me. I have missed you, sweetling. I just want you to come home."

She cringed at the term of endearment. Even from a distance, she could see there was no love or even kindness in his gaze.

His Grace moved in front of her. "All you need do is show me proof of this marriage and I will allow you to take her."

Violet felt as if she had been slapped. He said he would protect her. He said he would not let Mr. McPhail hurt her again.

Stammering, Mr. McPhail looked to Rose. "I did not bring the papers with me. They are still in Cheshire."

The duke nodded, moving back beside Violet. He swept his hand to the side in a grand gesture. "I bid you a safe journey, then."

Mr. McPhail's eyes darted between her and the duke. "But what about my wife, Your Grace?"

She held her breath until she felt his hand return to the small of her back, his warmth seeping through the fabric of her gown. "Miss Violet will be staying here, under my protection, until the marriage can be verified."

"What?" Rose practically leaping to her feet. "But it is so far. It will take days."

The duke looked at Rose, his head tilted to one side. "Then I suggest he make haste." Turning to the door, he hollered for the butler. "Baker, please see Mr. McPhail out. He must be on his way immediately. He has a very long trip back to Cheshire."

The butler led Mr. McPhail out, accompanied by several large footmen, while His Grace led Violet to the nearby settee. "You may go as well, Miss Allen. You have done quite enough for one day."

As if summoned by the spirits, Lady Rachel walked into the room. "Oh, if I have to look at another serviette today, I believe I shall scream." She glanced at Rose slowly making her way to the door, a muddled expression on her face. "Ah, been indoors too much, Miss Allen? A turn about the park would set you to rights. I am sure Jes would be happy to join you. Not to worry, I shall serve as chaperon here while you are out." She walked over to her favorite chair by the fire and took up her sewing.

Violet sat down on the couch, dropping her head back. The duke sat down next to her, his hand brushing against hers. She looked over at him, but he was looking at the ceiling. Her body slumped back into the couch. It had been an accident.

"I do believe you doubted me for a moment." His voice was scarcely louder than a whisper, but she could hear his disappointment.

Her heart sank. "I confess, I did not know what to believe."

He sighed. "I wish you would believe in me. I told you I would not let him hurt you and I meant it."

Her throat felt tight and her chest ached. She had hurt him. Her hand stayed at her side, should he choose to take it. "What if he comes back with a marriage certificate?"

"Did you sign such a document?"

"No." Did he not believe her still? Her head began to pulse and a deep tiredness draped across her shoulders.

"Then there is nothing to worry about." As he stood to leave, he brushed her hand once more, this time catching her gaze. A storm still churned in his eyes, but this time it was different somehow.

CHAPTER 21

"**W**hy did you not go with him?" Rose stormed into Violet's chambers. "Are you just trifling with the man? And to make him go all the way to Cheshire?" She paced back and forth.

Violet looked at her sister in shock. "Why would I have gone with him? Did you not hear the bouncer he told? How could I have gone to Scotland without you or Papa noticing?"

"Whether the story is true or not, what does it matter? He loves you and wants to marry you. And you love him...or you did. Why should you refuse him?" Rose was practically shouting at Violet.

"He has changed, Rose. He is not the same man who left three years ago." Violet dropped her eyes to her hands. "I could not be married to the kind of man he has become."

Rose spun around, glaring at Violet. "Or is it because you have set your sights higher? You told me you did not love the duke." She narrowed her eyes. "Or are you only trying to earn his affections away from me?"

"Nothing..."

"I expected such treatment from the tabby's of the ton, but I never believed my own sister would be the one to destroy my hopes and dreams." Rose ran from the room, slamming the door behind her.

Violet stared at the closed door. A jerky sigh pushed out. What a mess she had made of things. Her sister hated her now and the duke? Violet was unsure where she stood with him. He had been cold and out of sorts for several days. And it almost seemed as though he was avoiding her. However, he had protected her from Mr. McPhail. He had even appeared to care about her well-being.

A knock sounded on her door and Violet looked up, half expecting Rose to return and lecture Violet. Instead, her father's head poked through the crack.

Violet smiled. "Papa, you are back. How were your travels? Did Mr. Porter's associate prove helpful?"

Her father nodded his head. "Yes, yes, Poppet. It was very informative. I have given Porter his instructions and he will begin the transition." Her father looked at her and she shifted under his penetrating gaze. He had not paid her this much attention in years. She fidgeted, smoothing her skirt and any hair which had fallen loose from her knot.

Finally, she could take it no longer. "What is it, Papa?"

Her father heaved a deep sigh. "I met with His Grace upon my return. He suggested some trouble may have occurred in my absence, although he refrained from giving me details. He hinted you might be able to alleviate my curiosity."

Violet did not know if she was relieved or angry at the duke's presumption. She stood up and walked to the window, looking out over the vast estate.

"Perhaps we should take a turn about the gardens. I am ashamed to admit I have yet to see any of them."

Gathering her things, Violet walked with her father to the

front doors, waiting only for Baker to retrieve her father's hat and walking stick. Holding onto his arm, they strolled down the dusty lane.

"Do you mind if we keep to the lane, Papa?"

He shook his head and the two continued on in silence. The sun hung low in the sky, the pinks and purples just beginning to color the horizon. Violet closed her eyes, committing the sight to memory.

"There are many stones jutting out of this road, Poppet. I should think you would like to pay attention to walking, especially in light of your last tumble."

She tightened her hand on his arm. Oh, how she had longed for his protection over the years.

"Yes, Papa." Violet smiled as she looked ahead of her, spotting a small, old church.

They walked until they reached the churchyard. Her father's jaw clenched and unclenched, but he remained silent. Large trees provided a canopy, encasing the entire area in shade. Headstones in various stages of aging dotted the yard. Many were covered in lichens and moss, making it difficult to make out the names and dates carved there. Others stood unmarred, betraying their more recent arrival. The varying shades of gray and green were broken up by faded hues of purple, orange, and red.

Violet stepped forward, plucking an orange blossom, the dry petals crumbling in her hands. "Honeysuckle. I have not smelled this in ages."

Lord Graystock gently fingered the vine. He closed his eyes. "Your mother loved honeysuckle."

Violet smiled. "I remember. She used to smell of it." Those memories had been hidden away for years. Brushing the petals from her palm, she sat on a bench situated between two large monuments. One stone was covered in moss, with snake-like vines encircling it, hiding the words beneath. The second monument was much newer, making it legible. The marker read His Grace, Henry Beauford Wentworth, 5th Duke of Shearsby. November 12, 1676-May 24, 1724. Violet reached over, running her fingers over the engraving. These were the duke's ancestors and he was Rose's intended. Perhaps if she only thought of him in those terms, she would stop thinking of him in other ways. A moment of jealousy took hold of her insides before she shook the thoughts off.

Her father carefully plucked a delicate flower from the vine, frowning when a petal fell to the ground. He sat down next to Violet and stared at the honeysuckle bloom. "The fragrance was a birthday gift. I had it made for her on one of my trips to London. I cannot smell it without thinking on her."

Violet placed her hand back on his arm, bringing him briefly out of his reverie. "You still miss her." It was not a question.

"Every hour of every day, Poppet. Your mother was my other half. These last ten years I have lived life as half of myself."

She nodded her head. "That is why you had all of the honeysuckle vines removed."

The baron only nodded, sighing as he dragged a hand over his face. "I am afraid I neglected many things. Things that reminded me too much of her." He gave Violet a pained look. "You look so much like her, you know. There were some days I could hardly bear to look on you." Shame joined the pain etched on his face. "I am sorry. You have suffered far greater than the rest of us. You not only lost your mother but oft times, your father as well. I should have been there to protect you."

Violet felt tears forming in her eyes. "You do not need to apologize, Papa. I understand. You were broken, we all were. It is not possible to fix others when you are broken yourself." She brushed an errant tear with the back of her hand. "I have been well. Do not berate yourself. You are here now." Her brow creased. "That is what matters."

Her father turned toward her, taking her hands in his. "Violet, what happened while I was away?" His eyes widened slightly and he leaned closer.

Violet could not count how many times she had wished she could confide in her father. But now that he was before her, watching her, she did not know if she could tell him. He had been absent in her life for so long, she did not know where to begin.

Her father looked anxious and uncomfortable. Violet plunged ahead without plan or organization to her thoughts. She rehearsed her history with Mr. McPhail from the beginning to the charade of this morning. Her face heated as she told of her naive love for him. As she told of their encounter under the willow tree, Violet ran her fingers over her neck, almost able to feel the tender bruises he had left.

She was not sure the reaction she expected from him. Anger and disappointment in her seemed the most logical. But instead, he pulled her to him and hugged her tightly. "Oh, Violet. I have failed you. How can you ever forgive me?" He shook his head.

Violet opened her mouth to speak, but he raised a single finger and cut her off. "Let me see if I understand the situation correctly. He claims to have eloped with you to Scotland? Has he produced the certificate of marriage? Even an anvil priest provides papers."

She looked down at her hands, twisting the button on her spencer and shook her head. "His Grace told Mr. McPhail as much. When he failed to produce it, His Grace advised him to return to Cheshire to retrieve it. I am to be under his protection until the certificate is provided."

Lord Graystock ran a hand over his face. "I forced another man to protect my daughter because of my neglect. I shall speak to His Grace and discuss his plans. Although, I doubt we shall see Mr.

McPhail again. His Grace called the man's bluff. He would make a cake of himself should he return."

He patted her hand, his eyes taking in her whole face. Worry creased his brow, his eyes drawn to her neck. "I should call him out for hurting you as he did."

Violet shook her head. "I am well, Papa." Her eyes closed as she allowed the air to drain from her lungs. The problem was no longer hers to shoulder alone. Although, since her meeting with Mr. McPhail under the willow, someone else *had* shared her burden.

Violet stood up, dusting the leaves and petals from her gown.

"Does this mean you are ready to make our way back, Poppet?" Her father seemed to be in lighter spirits. He leaned upon his walking stick less and his gait was longer.

As they began walking, Violet chanced to put a voice to her feelings. "Papa, what has happened to you?"

His head shook slightly. "What do mean? Nothing has happened to me. I am well, as you can see."

"Why now? It has been years since you paid us any mind." She stopped at the coldness of her words. "Why today did you become interested in my well-being?"

He grunted, his stare focused on the ground. "His Grace possesses the frankness of someone raised to be a duke. He told me I was negligent and I needed to rectify the situation immediately, lest I lose one of my daughters. I confess I was confused by most of the conversation. However, I knew him to be correct about my absence." Her father's gaze flicked up. "I am afraid I have disappointed your sister and you. Not to mention your mother. She would be most unhappy with me."

"His Grace?"

Nodding his head, he patted Violet's hand. "Your sister is very fortunate in her match. I feel His Grace is a man of honor. She should be quite happy, I dare say."

Not that Rose would appreciate him or his honor. Violet shook her head. She must not think such unkind thoughts. Rose deserved to be happy, did she not?

CHAPTER 22

T ad sat at his desk, pouring over the ledgers in front of him. He released a sigh of satisfaction. Everything seemed to be falling into place. The accounts were finally reconciled and up to date, making his plans for the spring possible.

Dawson entered slowly through his adjoining office door. Stopping short of Tad, he raised his chin and clasped his hands in front of him, before dropping his eyes to the floor.

Tad grunted. The overly formal attitude Dawson had assumed must come to an end. Tad wanted—needed his friend back. He could find a new secretary tomorrow, but true friends were harder to come by.

"Here is the correspondence I felt needed your personal attention. There is a letter from Stephens, from Shearsby House, sent a response to your letter. We have not yet discussed your plans for the upcoming season if you would prefer to answer Stephens yourself...or I am happy to pass on any information." Dawson, standing in front of Tad, put the letters on the corner of the desk and clasped his hands behind his back.

Tad looked over the post in silence. He set it to the side. Tossing the remaining envelopes on the desktop, he ran a hand through his hair. "Dawson, please sit down."

Not moving a muscle, Dawson replied rather formally, "I would prefer to stand, Your Grace."

"I wish for you to sit." Frustration infused Tad's voice. He felt like a petulant child.

"Very well, Your Grace. If it be the master's bidding." Dawson moved to a chair opposite.

"If you 'Your Grace' me one more time in private, I shall haul you out to the stables and we will settle this as we did when we were boys. I am still bigger and stronger." He glared at his friend or at least the man who used to be his friend.

Dawson glared right back. "Whatever you desire, *Your Grace*." He drew out the last word, issuing the challenge.

Perhaps this is what they both needed. "I desire to have my friend back. But that does not seem to be within my grasp." He unbuttoned his coat. "But, I did warn you, Dawson. To the stables."

Dawson stood slowly. "You are not serious, Tad."

Tad smirked, extending his hand for Dawson to lead the way. "Oh, but I am."

Dawson shook his head but led the way out of the room. The two walked side by side to the stables, neither one speaking.

As they entered the dim interior, the stable master approached. "Are you both to be riding this morning Your Grace?"

Shaking his head, Tad motioned to the lantern. "Not today, Henderson. But we will need a few more lanterns. Then, if you could please give us some privacy. Mr. Dawson and I have some business to... discuss."

Henderson's brow creased, but he nodded and set about

lighting more lanterns. Escorting all the hands outside, he shut the doors firmly behind them

Tad removed his jacket and began to unbutton his waistcoat. "I know you well enough to see how many times you have wanted to pummel me, now is your chance. And because I am a gentleman, I shall even let you throw the first punch."

Dawson stood silent for a moment, glaring.

Tad placed his tailcoat and waistcoat on the railing behind him, before turning back to face his opponent. "You really should at least remove your coat. It will limit your movements severely." Grinning, he motioned to Dawson. "And as you are already at a disadvantage..."

"You are determined to see this through? You are a duke, Tad, not some common farmer." Dawson studied Tad's face. Shaking his head, Dawson removed his coat and began to work the buttons on his waistcoat.

As Tad finished untying his cravat, he turned to place it with the rest of his outer clothes. Casually twisting back, he was caught off guard by a hard shove. The momentum pushed him backward, sending him sprawling to the floor.

Dawson had not even removed his cravat, yet he stood, his hands balled into fists, raised and ready for a fight. "You are correct, Tad. I have been wanting to thrash something for weeks. I did not, however, think it would be you. But if you insist..." He gestured with his hand for Tad to join him.

Tad regained his feet, moving from side to side. "I give you the first move, and that was all you had? I believed you had more fire in you."

Dawson lunged forward. Tad anticipated the move but was not fast enough. Dawson's fist connected, causing Tad to stumble back several steps, his hand rubbing his burning cheek. "Scarcely better, Dawson." Moving back into place, Tad continued. "Perhaps I was wrong about your discontent?"

Dawson laughed mirthlessly. "You were not wrong, but you already knew that, did you not, Your Grace?" He spit out the title. "You seem to have taken to this new life of yours quite smoothly."

The hurt in Dawson's eyes brought a flood of shame over Tad. He dropped his guard, allowing Dawson to strike out again, catching him squarely in the jaw.

Blood trickled from his lip. Licking it with his tongue, he spit it to the side before moving in and catching Dawson in the eye. "You're so right. What do I have to be dissatisfied with? I have only assumed a title which was never intended to be mine, in a country I hated."

Dawson sprung again, this time Tad dodged the blow. "But it is all in the past for you. I am glad you have forgiven so easily." Tad opened his mouth but Dawson continued on. "You are your own man here, not subjected to a lower status than you were born."

Tad struck, catching Dawson on the jaw. "It was your choice," Tad yelled as he shoved Dawson backward. "I wanted my friend to come—someone I trusted. Someone I could confide in. But you are so blasted proud you would not accept anything less than a paid position." Tad hit him again. "And now this is my fault?"

Dawson flinched. He rushed at Tad, wrapping his arms around him, his head pushing into Tad's gut. They were both carried to the floor, grunting in pain, with Dawson landing on top. He sat up on Tad's chest, his breath heaving. "I did not realize my choices would cause me to lose my best friend. I know I should have, but I did not believe you would ever come to think of me as another servant."

Tad shoved him off. Pushing himself to sitting, he tucked one leg underneath. Slumping forward he rested his arm on his knee. Letting out a sigh he dropped his head to his arm. "I have regretted that remark from the moment it left my lips. I apologize, Dawson. I did not mean it. I have never, nor do I now think of you as a lesser man than I."

Dawson leaned back against the stall post and leveled his gaze at him. "But I am. You are a duke. Even were I not your secretary, you would outrank me in every way."

Tad knew the truth of the statement, but it did not feel right. "But you are a gentleman."

Dawson rubbed a hand over the back of his neck. "A gentleman with no money. I am your secretary and your words only conveyed the truth, Your Grace."

"Gaw, stop calling me that." Tad kicked him in the leg, feeling a moderate amount of satisfaction at Dawson's yelp. "I was angry and let my temper speak for me. I should have rectified this earlier, but I have let my pride get in the way." Tad found it difficult to look Dawson in the eye.

Dawson sat picking apart a piece of hay. "I understood when your foul moods were due in part to Miss Allen and the offer, but I have sensed your displeasure with me as of late. I am at a loss to know what I have done." His gaze never left his hands.

Tad licked at his lip. The bleeding had mostly stopped. "I have a heavy burden to carry now. I guess it has me unsettled." He shrugged his shoulder.

"Balderdash." Dawson threw a handful of straw at him. "You are holding something back. This estate was well run before your uncle's death. We have all but fixed any of the problems that came about after." The Dawson he had known long before they reached these shores, came out. "What is the truth, Tad?"

They locked eyes for a moment before it became too much for Tad. He looked back to the hay shaft in his hands. "I realized something and it disappointed me. I lashed out at the first person I saw. And it happened to be you."

"Not good enough." Dawson got up and dusted the dirt and hay from his pants. "There was a time we were honest with each other." He reached for his clothing. "You see, our relationship has changed."

"We've never shared affections for a lady before." The words rushed out. Tad felt his face heat. When had he become such a dolt?

Dawson walked a short distance before returning. "I have no idea of what you are speaking. What lady?"

Tad grimaced. "Perhaps it is not that we share affections, but rather I have a regard for her and she does not return it."

Dawson shook his head. "Could we quit speaking in generalities and use actual names, please?"

A long, drawn-out sigh was Tad's response. He scrubbed at the back of his neck, his eyes darting about the barn.

After intense scrutiny, Dawson nodded. "Are you speaking of Miss Violet?" He raised a brow. "Please tell me you are not speaking of Miss Allen. I shall have to commit you to Bedlam."

A laugh bubbled out of Tad. "No, I am not speaking of Miss Allen."

"It is Miss Violet, then? You love her?"

A guffaw burst out. "No. No. It is nothing so strong as that. I enjoy her company."

"Enjoy her company?" One brow rose as a chuckle rumbled in Dawson's chest. "I have never seen you resort to fisticuffs because you enjoyed someone's company before."

Tad groaned. He did love her, but to what end? He had never been in love before. There had been a time when he thought himself in love with Becky Shaffer. But in comparison, there were very few similarities in his feeling for Miss Violet and those for Miss Shaffer.

Dawson cleared his throat, gaining Tad's attention once more.

"Then I do not see the problem. She holds the same regard for you."

Confusion wrinkled Tad's brow. How could Dawson think such a thing?

Dawson offered his hand to help Tad up. "Do you not see the way she looks at you?" He shrugged. "Women have always pined for you, but Miss Violet is different. I dare say she is in love with you."

Tad shook his head. "I can assure you that is not the case. She speaks of you often when we are together. Asking about your family and upbringing. I am certain it is you she has cast her eye toward."

Dawson shook his head. "You're a stupe, Wentworth." He handed Tad his coats. "I have scarcely spoken ten words to her. Trust me, old man. It is you she desires."

Tad shoved Dawson lightly. "I saw the blush on her face in the music room. She was embarrassed I had caught the two of you together."

Dawson barked out a laugh. "I caught her leaning over you as you slept. Her blush was because I caught the two of you together."

Tad squinted at Dawson for a long time before he slumped. "What am I to do? How can I marry Miss Allen when I feel as I do for Miss Violet? But what is to become of Miss Allen if I break our contract?"

"I cannot make that decision for you, my friend." Dawson clapped Tad on the shoulder.

Tad hastily put his waistcoat on, followed by his tailcoat. Folding his cravat in half, he draped it around his neck and left it hanging down his front. His valet would no doubt be unhappy when he returned to his rooms.

All the stable hands wandered around the yard, looking

slightly lost. Several mouths dropped open as the two men exited the stable. Henderson's gaze flicked back and forth between them. Tad placed a hand on Dawson's shoulder, squeezing it lightly. "Perhaps we should continue this conversation inside."

Once in the safety of his study, Tad turned back to Dawson. "I am deeply sorry for my thoughtless comments to you, my friend."

Dawson shrugged. "All is forgiven, Your Grace." He moved toward his office door.

"Dawson?" Tad's brow wrinkled, his fingers rubbing up and down a crease on his mother's letter. "Might I ask a favor?" Thinking about what he was going to ask made his stomach churn with unease.

Moving back to the desk, Dawson took the seat opposite him. "Of course. You know I will do everything in my power to help you."

He stared across the desk at his friend. "I am concerned for Miss Violet. I fear she may be in danger."

Dawson steepled his fingers, resting his chin on them. "The fellow that visited yesterday?"

Tad nodded. "Do you remember when we first met her?" His voice softened.

"How could I forget? You have been mooning over her ever since." Dawson gave a wry grin.

"You are a yokel." Tad shook his head, wanting to argue further, but realizing there were more pressing matters. "He is the man who hurt her." His breathing stuttered and his eyes burned.

"Ah." With eyebrows raised high, Dawson slowly nodded.

Tad ran his fingers through his hair. "He came here to take her back to Cheshire. Claims they eloped to Gretna." His voice dropped and his chest tightened. He had never seen someone so scared and yet so determined not to let it show. The admiration he felt for her only increased when he witnessed her strength. "I told him I would not let him take her without proof of the marriage, but I cannot shake the feeling this is not over yet." He stood up and moved to the window. "My head believes he will not return. It makes no sense for him to do so, but..."

Dawson came to his side, content to stare at everything and nothing at the same time. "We need to make the grounds staff aware, Tad. They would be the first to encounter him." He glanced over to Tad. "Perhaps you have the answer to your other problem. It would certainly protect her from him if she was married to you."

"I am not sure he will be so easily deterred." Tad took a deep breath in, staring out at the bleak barren fields.

"We will need to keep our eyes open. I do not trust anyone as much as you. May I ask for your help in protecting her?"

"As if she were my own sister."

"You do not have any sisters." Tad smiled.

"Then as if she were one of your sisters. It is the same thing."

A chuckle escaped Tad's lips. "To me, she is not."

A serious shadow passed over Dawson's features. "I would give my life for Liza and Aisling. And I will do the same for Miss Violet."

Tad put a hand on Dawson's shoulder, his own relaxing. "Thank you, my friend."

CHAPTER 23

Miss Violet entered the breakfast room. Tad glanced up from his paper, folding and putting it aside when he saw her. Her face was drawn and Tad wondered if she had slept at all.

He smiled and when she returned it, his heart picked up speed. Since his discussion with Dawson in the stable, Tad had taken to analyzing every little move and word she said, searching for the truth of Dawson's words. With this new perspective, he could admit that while she may not love him, she did not dislike him. At times he thought she may even welcome his company. "You are up very early this morning. Did you not sleep well?"

She lifted a hand to her mouth, trying unsuccessfully to stifle a yawn.

Chuckling, he stood and pulled out the chair next to him. "Let me get you a plate and we can discuss what is disturbing your sleep."

He dished several items on a plate and placed it on the table in front of her. "I have noticed you seem to enjoy ham at breakfast...."

He had noticed every item she put on her plate. Perhaps he should put something there he knew she did not normally choose, so as not to let her know how much he watched her. But if he intended to speak with her father about changing the contract, maybe it was acceptable for her to know.

"Thank you, Your Grace." She looked over the plate in front of her. "You have picked exactly what I would have picked for myself."

"I know," he muttered, taking his seat. He placed his elbows on the arms of his chair. Bringing his hands together, he rested his chin on top, looking at her intently. He was confident he knew the source of her anxiety, for he felt it also. "I can see you are concerned. Is it Mr. McPhail?"

Violet cast a glance at Lord Mayfield, sitting at the other end with his paper held high. She nodded, pushing the food about without eating any of it. Without looking up she asked, "What if he comes back with a certificate? How can I prove it is not genuine?" Her voice hitched. "What if I have to return to Cheshire with him?" She raised her gaze to his.

"You said yourself, you did not sign such a document. Which means he cannot possibly produce one." He rubbed his chin over his entwined fingers. He hated seeing her so nervous. But even more, he hated that she did not trust him enough to know he would not let anything happen to her.

Her body relaxed a fraction, but not entirely. "How can you be sure? You do not know him, Your Grace. I do not believe he will stop until he has what he wants." Her voice lowered. "I am not even convinced he wants me as much as he wants to win; to get what he has been told he cannot have."

Tad glanced at her hand sitting beside her plate. Reaching out, he placed his hand over hers. She stiffened at first and he almost pulled his back. But then she turned her hand slightly upward, allowing him to curl his fingers around hers. He gave her hand a gentle squeeze. "I have told you I will protect you and I intend to keep that promise."

She looked at their hands, then up at him. What he saw there nearly took his breath away. "I trust you, Your Grace. Indeed, I have not felt so safe since I was a child."

They sat there together for a time. Tad knew he should remove his hand, but holding on to her did not only make her feel safe, it gave him a strength and resolve he had not felt before. He knew he was making the right decision in asking for her hand. Why he had been unsure for so long, he now could not understand. Everything about this was right. It was a feeling he had never felt when he was with Rose.

As if his thoughts had summoned her, Rose walked into the room. Her eyes were immediately drawn to their clasped hands. Tad reluctantly withdrew his hand, wrapping it around the teacup in his other hand. Now both his hands cradled the china cup. Lady Mayfield would surely serve up a mighty lecture on his American manners should she see such a thing. He dipped his head. "Miss Allen."

"Good morning, Your Grace. I trust you slept well?" She did not pause for a response, but hurried to the buffet and began loading a plate before coming to join them at the table.

"Indeed I did. I hope the same for you."

"Oh, yes. I slept very well. Thank you for inquiring." She returned to the table, putting her plate at the place on his other side. Her gaze moved back and forth between the two of them and she scowled slightly whenever she looked at Miss Violet.

Miss Violet pushed her full plate away. Her eyes were cast downward and she swallowed several times. The worry over Mr. McPhail did not appear to be the only thing troubling her.

Tad tried to act as if nothing was amiss. He was not thrilled

Miss Allen had witnessed their moment, but he had more pressing matters to worry about. He could not shake the feeling that Violet was in danger. A knot seemed always present in his stomach.

Using the estate as a distraction, Tad excused himself and went in search of her father. The sooner he had the conversation, the better. He could then ask Miss Violet for her hand and they could be married within the month.

When he could not locate Lord Winslow, Tad asked Baker to locate the gentleman and send him to Tad's study. His aunt was there, sitting in her favorite window seat, embroidery in hand. He shut the door quietly and moved toward his desk. What could she need to speak with him about today?

"You are like your father in so many ways. However, there is one difference between you." She glanced in his direction, an arch in her brow.

He stared at her. "And what is the difference, Aunt?"

"You are a bit of a coward."

Tad's brows rose to his hairline and his mouth dropped open. "I beg your pardon?"

Lady Rachel put down her embroidery, locking gazes with him. "Your father let nothing stand in his way. He wanted a better life for himself, so he moved to a new land. He wanted a feisty Irish lass and he did not relent until she agreed to become his wife." His aunt stood, walking toward him.

Tad nodded. "He was an amazing man. But what has this to do with me?"

"Be the man your father was. If she does not want you, work at it until she does." She smiled.

"Did you not advise me not to allow someone else to make my decisions?" Tad growled.

Lady Rachel shrugged. "That was before I thought you may be

making the wrong one. I don't believe you need work too hard to win this one. I believe she is already yours."

"My father would want me to be a man of honor. A man who did not break a contract just because he thought himself in love."

She cocked her head to one side. "Perhaps you are right. Or perhaps I am."

Tad nodded. He should feel guilty for not telling her of his intentions, but he did not. And bringing up his father now made him question his decision. "I will think on it, Aunt."

Lady Rachel moved back to her embroidery. "That is where you are having the problem. You think too much. It is time to feel."

A restlessness took hold, but when he reached the hallway, he had no idea where to go. He stopped in his tracks when he heard music floating down the corridor.

His legs involuntarily carried him in the direction of the music room. The strains of the pianoforte sounding from behind the closed door surprised him. Miss Violet had spent more time playing the harp since its arrival.

He rested his forehead against the wooden door, listening to the music. Again the feeling of peace and rightness washed over him. He should leave her to her music, but he couldn't get himself to quit the corridor. Pushing the door open, he slipped inside.

Her gaze flicked over to him, but she did not stop playing. The music swelled in tempo and tone. Deep and dark were how he would describe it, as most of the notes were located in the lower ranges.

He moved quietly to a chair on the opposite side of the room. Sinking down, he laid his head back, his eyes closing.

The music she played was unfamiliar, but there was no doubt about the emotions flowing through her fingers into the keys. The longer she played the more turbulent the music became.

Unable to keep his eyes closed any longer, Tad sat watching

her play. Her body moved in response to the music, swaying loosely at some points, while rigid and stiff at others.

Apart from her glance when he walked into the room, she never looked up or even acknowledged his presence. He hoped it was because she had become comfortable with him listening to her play.

She moved from one piece to another, with little space between. Tad did not know how much time had passed before Baker opened the doors and stepped inside. Miss Violet looked up and lifted her fingers off the keys. The pianoforte vibrated with the sound of the music.

"Would you prefer to take tea in the library with your aunts or in your study, Your Grace?"

Tad looked over to Miss Violet. She caught his glance but then looked away. "Perhaps the library, Baker."

The butler bowed and left the room.

Standing, she moved the bench away with a push of her leg.

"Would you please join me for tea?"

She curtsied. "Thank you, Your Grace. That would be lovely."

Extending his arm, she placed her hand on top, curling her hand around it. They made their way out of the music room and down the hall. He tilted his head toward her, speaking loud enough for her to hear, but not so loud it echoed in the corridors. "You played beautifully. I have not heard you play the pianoforte since the harp arrived."

"Thank you, Your Grace. I find the pianoforte is more in line with my mood today."

Was it her concerns about Mr. McPhail or had he done something to upset her? "I am not well versed in my composers. Whom were you playing?"

Miss Violet looked up, vulnerability in her eyes. "No one. I was only playing notes. Sometimes I have to let my feelings play for me."

Tad pulled her to a stop. "That was your own work?" He shook his head. "It was beautiful. Dark, but beautiful. Can you recreate it?"

She shook her head. The rigidness of her posture beginning to relax. "Not in this case. Many times when I play, I will write it down as I go. But today, there was too much coming out too fast."

"Then I shall consider myself fortunate to have heard it when I did."

They entered the library. Both of his aunts, as well as Jes and Miss Allen, were seated with teacups in hand.

Lady Mayfield looked up at their arrival. "Well, it is about time the two of you arrived." She arched a knowing brow.

Miss Violet stiffened and her hand loosened on his arm. Her gaze went to her sister.

He led her over to the couch, seating her next to Jes and Miss Allen.

His aunt continued on unruffled. "We have had a very respectable response for the ball. A great many people are excited to meet the new Duke of Shearsby."

Tad shook his head. "I still contend it is not necessary."

"As if an Amer..." Lady Mayfield flicked her eyes to Miss Violet and Miss Allen. "A man would know what is necessary in regards to a ball."

Tad laughed out loud. It was not often one saw Lady Mayfield flustered. He was tempted to let her flounder a moment longer, but in the end, he decided to come to her rescue. "I am sure you are correct. Thank you both for seeing to the arrangements."

Lady Mayfield opened her mouth, as if she were going to argue with him, but shut it and stared at him. "You are welcome, nephew."

A knock sounded at the door and Baker stepped inside, concern wrinkling his normally smooth face. "Mr. McPhail has returned, Your Grace. I have placed him in the Blue Parlor."

The room fell silent. Even Lady Mayfield seemed at a loss for words, while a smile turned up only the outer most corners of her mouth.

Miss Violet paled noticeably, her teacup beginning to shaking quietly.

Tad stepped over, taking it from her and placing it back on the table. Taking a deep breath, he dropped down to his haunches. Catching her gaze he held it, looking at her, willing his strength into her. "Would you prefer not to see him? I can go it alone." His voice was low, his focus only on her.

She shook her head. "No. I need to be there. I need him to see I am not afraid of him." Her voice caught in her throat.

"Is that what he will see?" It was quite obvious she was scared nearly to death. Tightness squeezed his chest. He wanted to carry her far away, where she would never have to deal with the likes of Mr. McPhail or any of the other people who had hurt her over the years.

"Yes. I only need a moment to compose myself."

Miss Allen stood up, towering over her sister. "Really, Violet. I do not think there is a need for dramatics."

His stomach burned and he glared at Miss Allen.

Turning his attention back to Miss Violet he stood up and extended his arm to her. She clutched her fingers around his upper arm, her knuckles white with pressure. He looked down at her, placing his hand over the top of hers. "Remember my promise."

She nodded. "I will try."

His aunts and Jes stood as well, falling in behind them, with Miss Allen coming last. It seemed they would not be facing Mr.

McPhail alone. They walked down the corridor in silence, lost to their own thoughts.

Tad could not imagine Mr. McPhail had the necessary papers to take Miss Violet away, but his stomach still churned and his breathing became tighter.

Opening the door, he saw the enemy standing by the fireplace.

Tad sighed in relief when he spotted Dawson walking toward them in the corridor.

"He is here, Tad. One of the stable hands just reported seeing him."

Tad motioned with his head into the parlor before pushing into the room.

"Mr. McPhail, I can only assume by your presence, that you have brought necessary papers." Tad was in no mood to trifle with the man.

McPhail patted his coat pocket, sneering at Tad. "I did. Although, I don't know what it will prove. She will just contend she never signed it. It is her word against mine."

Tad grinned a mirthless smile. "Well, if that is all there is to it, you need not have come back. I will accept her word over yours, in every instance."

The man's brows furrowed, his eyes narrowed. "I was unable to locate the witnesses as they were provided by the anvil priest. The only proof I have is the marriage certificate, which clearly has her signature."

With every scowl Mr. McPhail leveled at Miss Violet, Tad moved closer to her, until he was close enough to feel her body shaking beneath her gown. He was impressed with her outward composure. No one observing her from across the room would have any idea how affected she was.

The more McPhail said, the more Tad wanted to land the man a facer, but he knew that would only add to their current trial.

Miss Allen sat on the couch, her gaze darting between Tad, Miss Violet, and Mr. McPhail. She licked her lips several times. Tad squinted at her. Something was off.

Tad motioned Dawson and Miss Violet to the desk.

He held out his hand to Mr. McPhail. "The certificate, please?"

Mr. McPhail scoffed and pushed Tad's hand away. "You will not be touching this paper, Your Grace. I have little faith you'll not try to destroy it."

"I am not a lying snake, Mr. McPhail. I give my word I shall do it no harm. But if it will make you more comfortable, you may keep hold of it."

Mr. McPhail unfolded the paper. He glanced quickly at Miss Allen and she licked her lips again while smoothing her skirt.

Tad looked at the certificate. Miss Violet's name was written clearly on the bottom.

She sucked in a breath next to him and whispered. "That is not my signature, Your Grace."

Mr. McPhail snatched the paper back. "And I say it is. I have provided the certificate as you requested, Your Grace. Now, if you would give me my wife."

Tad snorted in derision. "You are daft if you think I will take your word."

Mr. McPhail sputtered. "Indeed, I have. You demanded the certificate and I have presented it to you. You said you were not a lying snake, but it appears you are."

Miss Violet scooted closer to Tad, the warmth from her body penetrating the fabric of his trousers. He reached down and took her hand in his. Entwining their fingers and squeezing her hand before dropping it again.

He took a step closer to McPhail, forcing the man to take a step back. "I said you were to present proof of the marriage. Until this certificate is authenticated, it cannot be considered proof, sir."

"And how do you plan to prove it?" McPhail's eyes jumped from Tad to Miss Allen and back. His confidence seeming to waiver.

"It should be relatively simple, actually." He glanced over to Miss Violet. "If Miss Violet would sign her name, here in front of us all, we could compare her signature with the document in question. If it is still inconclusive, we will send for a handwriting expert."

"But it could take weeks to get an expert here." Mr. McPhail complained as he shot Miss Allen a look of concern. Her eyes widened as she shrugged and returned her attention to her fingers.

Tad sighed. McPhail and Miss Allen were in this together and suddenly they were not so sure of their scheme. The thought saddened him. Tad could not imagine his brother or sisters betraying him in such a way.

He turned to Miss Violet. "Would you be willing, miss?"

She nodded.

He produced a quill and some paper. With all eyes focused on her, Miss Violet signed her name. He was impressed not so much as a quiver or shake was evident in her hand. The lady had mettle.

She lifted the quill from the paper and pushed it toward Tad.

"We will need your paper, once again, Mr. McPhail."

"You have already seen it. I see no need for you to look at it again." Mr. McPhail reached out a hand, grabbing Miss Violet by the arm. "Now I have had enough of this charade, Violet. You are coming with me." He began to pull her toward him.

Tad stepped between them, trapping her between the desk and himself. "You will not lay a hand on the lady while she is under my protection. I believe it is you who is leaving. Alone."

The scoundrel released her arm, once he realized she was going nowhere.

Tad wanted to take her hand again, but he did not dare move

to the side enough to do so. He held his hand in front of him. "The paper, sir."

McPhail snarled but handed the document over.

Tad turned, making sure he remained between Miss Violet and Mr. McPhail. Dawson had also moved closer to the desk.

Tad laid the marriage certificate next to the parchment Miss Violet had signed. Without even leaning over, he examined them.

A smile curved his lips as he looked at Mr. McPhail. "An expert will not be necessary. The signatures are not the same."

Mr. McPhail growled. "She changed her hand so they would not match. I do not relinquish my claim."

Tad moved his hand out to his side, searching for hers. He felt her soft skin slip between his fingers. There was no way he would allow this man to get hold of her again. He maneuvered her several steps away and out of McPhail's reach.

"You may file a petition with the courts, sir. But I do not believe you stand a chance. They would never rule against someone of my status." He paused, letting his words take root. "Now, I believe you are trespassing on my estate. You had best not do so again."

Tad released Violet's hand and placed his on the small of her back, his thumb rubbing lightly back and forth. He hoped it was giving her as much comfort as it was him. Leading her toward the door, he spoke over his shoulder. "Miss Allen, say your goodbyes to your family friend. You shall not be seeing him until you return to Cheshire. Aunts, Jes. Let us finish our tea in the library."

CHAPTER 24

D awson sat across the desk in his usual chair. He tossed a folded note to Tad. "This arrived in the post this morning. I thought it may be helpful when you speak with Lord Winslow."

Tad unfolded the stack of papers. He scanned the letter from his uncle's solicitor, Mr. Jones. He explained that he was unable to leave Town at present and wondered if they might meet when next Tad traveled to London. He had enclosed papers which he believed may be in need of more immediate attention.

Tad set the letter aside. Scanning the next paper he saw his uncle's signature at the bottom. Inspecting it closer, Tad realized it was a copy of the letter sent to Lord Winslow, requesting the marriage agreement. Tad smiled.

"It does not mention a name. It only says 'the hand of one of your daughters.' What does that mean for me?"

Dawson grinned. "If you look at the next paper, you will see the contract was never sent or signed. No name was ever inserted."

Tad nodded, still studying the papers before him. He could see it would be inferred that the oldest daughter would be the one to accept, but without Miss Allen specifically stated, could Tad convince Lord Winslow to allow him to marry Violet? He paused. When had she ceased to be Miss Violet to him? He thought about holding her hand earlier this morning while they stood together against Mr. McPhail. That was the turning point.

"I don't know how this changes things, but the only thing to do now is to speak with Lord Winslow. Do you know, has he returned from the village yet?"

Dawson shook his head. "I do not believe so. Did you not tell Baker to send the gentleman directly in here?"

Tad sighed. Now that he knew the details of the letter, he wanted to speak with Lord Winslow as soon as possible. "Yes. It appears I am now left to wait." He scowled. "I hate waiting."

Dawson chuckled. "Of that, I am aware."

The two talked until a knock sounded on the door. Baker entered. "Lord Winslow, as you requested, Your Grace."

"Thank you, Baker." Both Tad and Dawson stood as the gentleman entered the room.

"I shall be in my office if you need me, Your Grace." Before he could turn, Tad stopped him.

"I would appreciate it if you stayed, Dawson." Unsure how this meeting would go, Tad was reluctant to let his friend leave.

He turned to Lord Winslow. "Please, sir. Have a seat. There is something I wish to discuss with you." Over the past few days, Tad had rehearsed this speech in his mind a dozen times. But never had it been accompanied by the current waves rolling in his stomach.

"Lord Winslow, I am pleased to have you and your daughters as guests here at Morley Park." That was true enough. One daughter more so than the other. Although, after today, Miss Allen was much less welcome than before.

The older man looked about the room, smiling in satisfaction. "Thank you for your generosity in having us here. And for protecting my daughters. It seems you have done so on numerous occasions." His voice dropped with his head. "I spoke to Violet as you suggested. I had no idea what was happening with my own daughter. While I am embarrassed it took your advice to get me to do so, I must thank you for it. They both deserve better."

Tad cleared his throat, running his hand back and forth along the back of his neck. Perhaps the baron would be open to Tad's proposition. "I am glad to have been of service." He paused. Where did one begin such a conversation? Did he just jump headlong into it? Or start with small talk and work his way up to the real reason for this discussion. The weight pressing down on his shoulders and chest decided for him. "There is no sense making meaningless small talk, my lord. I wish to discuss with you the engagement."

The baron's smile dropped a fraction. His brow creased and his eyes narrowed with every word Tad spoke.

"I will not be marrying Miss Allen."

Winslow leveled a glare at him. "But we have the letter in which your uncle made the offer on your behalf. I realize there was no formal contract, but under the law, the letter is binding enough."

"I understand the law, Lord Winslow. My solicitor has been very thorough on that front."

Lord Winslow sat forward in his seat, looking as though he might pounce at any moment.

Tad leaned back in his chair, straightening to his full height.

"Then why the pretense of bringing us here? Why the ruse? If you never had any intentions of doing right by my daughter, why did you go through the trouble of sending for her?" His eyes bulged and his chair crashed to the floor when he abruptly stood.

Tad rubbed his fingers over his eyebrows, smoothing them

down as he tried to do the same with his emotions. "Baker dispatched the letter shortly after I arrived at the estate, without my knowledge. It was only after I stopped the carriage that I learned the name of my intended. I could not very well send her away at that point, now could I?"

"So what is your intent, Your Grace?" The baron spat out the words.

Tad pulled out the stack of papers from Mr. Jones. "We have a copy of the letter my uncle sent. It does not specify Miss Allen as the intended. It only states one of your daughters."

The baron blustered. "It is only because your uncle was not familiar with my family. He did not know if the eldest was already married. But it is commonplace in situations such as these for the eldest daughter to accept the proposal." He glowered across the desk. Tad raised a brow. In truth, he had not thought the gentleman had it in him. "Either way, it does not release you from the arrangement."

Tad took a deep breath. "Which is why I would like to ask for your consent to marry your other daughter."

Winslow did not look pleased, but the puce color left his face. No words escaped his mouth as he continued to stare at Tad. Finally, he spoke. "Why Violet?"

Tad had known this question was likely, but now as it was before him, he was not completely sure how much to tell the gentleman. His gaze flicked to Dawson who nodded.

"It is simple. I love her. It would be unfair to both Miss Allen and myself if I went through with the original betrothal when my feelings are otherwise engaged." Lord Winslow's eyes widened again. "And I believe Miss Violet feels similarly." As he said the words, his confidence wavered. "Or she could, in time."

Tad glanced at Dawson who was shaking his head and looking heavenward.

"You love my Violet? How could you possibly know that, Your Grace? You barely know her." There was a challenge in the baron's voice, but also a tenderness toward his daughter.

"I know she is brave and strong. I know she has a tender heart. I know she has an amazing wit, especially for someone so mistreated. And I know she plays the harp and the pianoforte beautifully." Tad stared at Lord Winslow. "How well do *you* know your daughter, my lord?"

Winslow's head jerked back before his eyes dropped to the floor.

"I'll love her and protect her, always." Tad rubbed his hands up and down his thighs, under his desk. Could the baron see how nervous he was? His uncle would surely find him lacking at the moment. "I am hoping to make the announcement at the ball."

A rustling in the hallway drew their attention, but when no one entered the conversation resumed.

"Her mother and I were a love match. I cannot deny my Violet the same happiness. If you love her as much as you say, she will be very fortunate."

Tad took a deep breath, his eyes closing on the exhale. But they were quickly jerked open.

"But you shall be the one to inform Rose of your decision."

Tad winced. Could he not just send her home and be done with it? Could she not find out when the banns were read? After realizing her association with Mr. McPhail, Tad felt less concerned about her felicity. "Tell me, sir, what type of response shall I expect?"

With a small smile, Winslow responded. "I would recommend removing anything that could be thrown." At the sight of Tad's wide eyes, Winslow shrugged. "It is only a precaution."

CHAPTER 25

Violet lay abed, looking at the ceiling, but seeing nothing. Her thoughts were a jumble and the duke was at the center of them. The man was infuriating and confusing and sweet, all mixed up in a tangle of emotions.

When the marriage certificate had been proven false, Violet was relieved. But now she did not know what to think. What was she to do? Would her aunt sponsor her for a London season as she had Rose? It was doubtful. Her aunt had never had much use for Violet.

After the way he had held her hand and placed his hand at the small of her back, she had thought...she slammed her hands down into the mattress. "Stop it, Violet." These thoughts were doing her no good. How could she even think of doing such a thing to her sister?

Relenting, she sat up and got out of bed. It was still too early to ring for Becky, so she sat in the window seat and watched the sunrise. It glistened on the river, as the water swirled down its path. The glass was cool, evidence that winter was around the corner.

She sighed. This was a beautiful estate. She could not have dreamed she would ever be the mistress of an estate such as Morley Park. But what would it be like? How would it be to be married to His Grace? She pressed her forehead to the pane, allowing it to cool her warm skin. That was a dream she would never know.

Her eye caught sight of a splash of color peeking out from the wardrobe. She turned to look at the lavender gown she would be wearing to the ball. Violet slumped down in her seat. The day of the ball was almost upon them, thus her time at Morley was almost at an end. And then what?

She would not have the duke to protect her once she returned to Cheshire. She shivered. After what had transpired here, she actually feared Mr. McPhail would kill her if he ever had the chance. Putting her head back against the window, she closed her eyes and tried to push the thoughts of both men out of her mind.

The door opened. "Oh, miss. You are already awake. Give me a moment and I will return with a canister of warm water."

Violet looked up and down their table. Lady Mayfield had suggested a dinner party, as a test for the duke, before the night of the ball. The older woman was convinced he would make a muddle of the evening and wanted to get an idea of how bad it would be in advance. It appeared the entire neighborhood was in attendance. All of the guests seated at the table with the Duke were unknown to her. His aunts and uncle and cousin were the only friendly faces. Rose had scarcely said two words to her since their discussion after Mr. McPhail had left. When she did look at Violet, there was contempt in her eyes.

Violet had been introduced to everyone, along with her father and sister, as friends of the duke's family. But with the sheer number present, she doubted even the duke remembered all of them.

Lord and Lady Mayfield and Lady Rachel sat close to him, with Violet's father and Miss Standish across the table from them. Rose had been assigned to a different table altogether.

A Mr. Prichard was seated opposite Lady Rachel. Violet watched the man interacting with those around him. The wine in his glass never lasted more than two or three large gulps. He looked down his nose at Lady Rachel, which made Violet inclined to dislike him immediately.

She watched him only when she wasn't watching the duke. It was a new experience to see him in the company of so many strangers. He did not appear ill at ease, but his smile seemed forced and artificial.

"I understand that you are a military man, Your Grace." Mr. Prichard leaned back in his chair, his voice too loud for polite dinner conversation. "I confess, I am surprised that your uncle would allow his heir to be placed in that sort of danger."

The duke put his fork back on his plate, smiling stiffly. "I had numerous cousins that stood to inherit long before myself. There was no reason for me not to serve."

"Ah," Mr. Prichard sighed. "I was not aware of your position in the family. My brother's son has purchased a commission in the army, although, he has caught the eye of the Prince Regent. It is quite likely he will become a part of The Blue's before long." A smug look crossed the gentleman's face.

Violet felt her brows raise and her eyes narrowed on the duke's behalf.

"Whom did you serve under?" Prichard asked.

Violet tensed as she waited for his answer. What would he tell Mr. Prichard so as not to give away his secret?

"I served under Captain Maycroft aboard the *HMS Dedication*."

He had seen action? She knew he had served in the war, but they had never discussed what he had done. Violet's brow pulled down. But that was a British ship.

Lord Crunn entered the conversation, admiration in his eyes. "You fought against the Americans."

The duke shrugged.

Mr. Prichard swallowed the remaining liquid in his glass. Motioning to the footman for a refill, he leaned onto the table. "We showed those colonists a thing or two, did we not, Your Grace?" A self-righteous smirk turned the corner of his mouth.

His Grace pushed his plate away and leaned back in his seat. "I do not believe they have been colonists for nearly fifty years. They are called Americans now."

Mr. Prichard sat up a little straighter in his seat, taking a deep gulp from his newly filled glass.

The duke sighed. He sounded tired all of sudden. "I do not believe, in any version of the story, we can claim to have shown them one thing, let alone two. We were the ones limping home." He lifted his claret but stopped short of putting it to his lips. Instead, he looked over the top of it at Mr. Prichard.

Mr. Prichard put his glass shakily on the table. "On whose side did you serve, Your Grace?" His voice slurred.

The duke straightened and leaned forward in his chair. "I believe I have already answered that question, Mr. Prichard." He pulled his plate back to him, pushing the food about but never lifting the fork to his mouth. "The Americans had no option but to declare war. Our dealings with them were no better than Napoleon was with us."

The man next to Lady Mayfield choked on the wine he was drinking and began coughing. Emphasizing the complete silence of the room.

Violet looked across to the next table. Why was Rose not saying anything? Was she not going to come to the duke's defense?

Lady Rachel smiled. "I think that is enough politics for one evening. Lady Billings, what have you heard of the new fashions this season?"

Mr. Prichard's face turned red, his eyes bulging. He slapped his hand down on the table. "Are you actually comparing our actions to those of Boney?" The Frenchman's nickname was practically spat across the table.

The duke leaned forward, a challenging gleam in his eyes. "The Americans declared war because their ships were being seized and their sailors impressed into the Royal Navy. That is akin to kidnapping. I will let you decide how similar we were to Napoleon."

Violet bit her lip, twisting the corner of her napkin under the table, her stomach twisting along with it.

"You condone the actions of Napoleon, then?" Mr. Prichard challenged the duke in return.

"You must be daft. Bonaparte is a madman and had to be stopped. But England would have been better served to stay on our side of the Atlantic. The war with America divided our military by fighting a war on two different continents. In the end, it was an embarrassment."

Violet sucked in a breath, her eyes widening. She looked again to Rose. She appeared completely oblivious to the conversation being shouted across the room.

"How can you say such things after fighting for your country?"

A woman next to Mr. Prichard asked. She added a hasty, "Your Grace."

The duke smiled kindly at the older lady. "Mrs. Bowen, when a man fights for his country, it does not mean he agrees with all the decisions made by his government. We fight because we believe in our country, our traditions and our way of life."

Mr. Prichard frowned slightly. "You're suggesting the Americans can claim the victory?"

Violet spoke up for the first time. "Mr. Prichard, while there were many battles won by our valiant troops, I think in the end, the victory must go the Americans."

Mr. Prichard glared at her. "I do not believe I asked for the feather-brained opinion of a woman." He turned back to the duke. "How can you assert such things? We burned down their Prime Minister's house. It was certainly what they deserved after declaring war on the greatest military in the world." Mr. Prichard gave a hearty laugh. His laughter died on his lips as he looked at the faces around the table.

The duke's eyes widened, his nostrils flared. He opened his mouth, but Violet spoke up first. "I believe, Mr. Prichard, he is called a President, not a Prime Minister. I have read some very good books on the subject. Please, do not hesitate to ask if you would care to borrow them."

Mr. Prichard glared at her from down the table. He sat red-faced and breathing hard. "I have never heard such traitorous nonsense." He stood quickly, swaying on his feet, his chair falling backward with a thud. "And I for one, will not share a table with a traitor."

Lady Rachel stood. "I am sorry you feel you cannot stay longer, sir." A footman stepped forward at the nod of her head.

The duke stood to his full height, leaving Mr. Prichard to stare at the duke's Adam's apple. "Sir. I believe all men are entitled to their opinions, even if I do not share them. But if you ever call me a traitor again, I suggest you have a second on hand. For I will call you out." He leveled a gaze at Mr. Prichard.

The man opened his mouth and then shut it, fists clenching at his side.

The duke returned to his seat, picked up his fork and began to eat.

Lady Mayfield gave the man a withering look. "Mr. Prichard, you are in your cups. I suggest you sober up before you return to offer your apologies."

His jaw twitched but nothing else flowed from his mouth.

From the end of the table, Lady Rachel spoke to the footman. "Thomas, it appears Mr. Prichard will be leaving us early tonight. If you would, please see him out and into his carriage."

The duke turned from the man's retreating form. He resumed his conversation with the lady next to him, signaling for others to do the same. When everyone's focus was elsewhere, he caught Violet's gaze and mouthed, "Thank you."

Violet's breath caught in her throat at the look he gave her. Oh, how she wished it was not Rose who would be marrying this man.

Violet sat near the fire, waiting for the men to return. Quicker than she would have expected, they entered the Long Gallery. Her father caught her eye and smiled, but then proceeded to sit by Rose.

The duke, on the other hand, sought her out and sat down next to her.

"I wanted to thank you, again, for your support at dinner tonight. You were the first to come to my aid. I will never forget your kindness."

The softness in his voice made her stomach flutter. As confused as she was by him, she could not deny the effect he had on her.

She smiled. "I am glad I could be of help, Your Grace." She chewed on her bottom lip, wanting to ask about the details of his military service, but not certain how to do so without causing offense.

He tilted his head to the side. "Is there something on your mind, Miss Violet?"

He admires my courage and forthrightness. Swallowing hard, she pushed the words out.

"Your Captain and the ship you mentioned. Both are part of the British navy. How is that possible?"

His face relaxed into a half smile. "You need not worry I am a liar, Miss Violet. I did serve aboard the *Dedication*. It was not by choice, but it is the truth."

Violet's brow crinkled. Her jaw dropped slightly open, as concern filled her chest. "Those were not merely words at the table. You lived the life of an impressed sailor."

He gave only a shrug. "I fared much better than Dawson because I spoke their same language. After a time, I think they even forgot I was an American."

"What happened after the war?"

He rubbed at the back of his neck, his shoulder twitching slightly. "When word came the war was over, our ship was resupplying in the West Indies." He smiled sullenly. "Dawson and I were left ashore to find our way back. It took us several weeks to find a ship setting out for America. I worked as an Able Bodied Seaman and Dawson as a Rigger, to pay for our passage home."

She did not know what to say. What did one say to such a story? A new perspective was added to this man. It was understandable why Mr. Dawson was unhappy here, but the same was not true of the duke? How did he come to accept and forgive his former enemy which surrounded him daily?

Thankfully, her father arrived, taking away the task of trying to put her feelings into words.

The duke cleared his throat, bringing her attention back to him. "Miss Violet, I have something I wish to discuss with you." He seemed nervous, running his hands up and down his thighs.

"Of course, Your Grace." She was still too shocked by his revelation to begin to analyze what he could possibly need to speak to her about.

"You look thirsty. Let me fetch us some refreshment. Perhaps, take a turn about the orangery. I believe my aunt has placed hundreds of luminaries about the room. Would you care to see it?"

Violet smiled. "Yes, very much, Your Grace."

His body relaxed as he exhaled. "Then I shall return with some drinks. If you will excuse me." He bowed and turned in the direction of the adjoining room.

A moment later Rose sat next to her. "Good evening, sister."

Violet smiled. "Good evening, Rose."

"I was surprised by your conversation at dinner. You are not usually one to be so bold."

Turning slightly, she stared at her sister. "Well, someone had to defend him. I waited for his intended to do so, but she scarce looked in his direction, much less spoke on his behalf."

"His intended was not even seated at his table." Rose snapped. "What was I to do? Yell across the room?"

Violet shrugged. "I suppose you are right, Rose. That would not have been appropriate. I apologize for implying you were wrong."

Rose twitched slightly. "Do not trouble yourself, Violet. I hold no ill will." Her eyes cast downward. "Oh, I almost forgot. I saw the duke in the hallway. He asked me to tell you he wished to meet you in the orangery." Rose paused. "What could he possibly wish to speak to you about?"

"I do not know. We were just speaking of his military service. Perhaps we shall continue that conversation." Violet's brow creased. "He said I was to meet him in the orangery? I thought we were meeting here first."

Rose shook her head. "I am sure he said you were to meet him there. Back by the lime trees." She smiled, but her gaze rested to the side of Violet's earlobe. Rose must not have been totally truthful when she said there was no ill will. Why else could she not look Violet in the eyes?

Violet stood. "Very well. Thank you, Rose. I am sure he will be seeking you out after our walk."

Violet walked to the opposite side of the room and through the large double glass doors which connected the orangery to the Long Gallery and the rest of the house.

The duke was right, the room glowed from hundreds of luminaries placed about the room. Some hung from tree branches, while others stood perched upon a stick. The room was quiet and peaceful.

Violet moved to the far side of the room, stopping next to the lime trees. The duke was not yet here. Staring out through the glass panes, she could see the outlines of the gardens in the darkness.

A noise sounded behind her and she turned, smiling at the duke. The smile fell from her face when she saw Mr. McPhail standing amid the ferns.

Violet stepped back, feeling the branches of the lime tree digging into her back and shoulders. "What are you doing here? You were told to leave and not return."

"I did not get what I came for." He laughed quietly. "You did not expect me to leave without you, did you, Violet?"

She shook her head. "I am not going with you."

In two quick steps, his hand clasped tightly over her mouth as his other arm encircled her waist. He pulled her toward him, placing her back against his chest. "I suggest you keep quiet, my dear. I would hate to hurt you, but I will if you try anything."

CHAPTER 26

The more she struggled, the tighter Mr. McPhail held. He pulled her toward the doors to the terrace. Kicking his foot out behind him, the door swung open. The air of the orangery warmed the outside until Mr. McPhail pushed the door closed with his foot. He dragged her across the terrace and to a horse waiting at the foot of the stairs.

Violet knew he would have to release her, or at least loosen his hold on her when he swung her up into the saddle. If she could slip off the other side, perhaps she could get away before he could capture her again. She relaxed slightly when his grip around her slackened, but his hand stayed firmly over her mouth. She poised herself to escape. But before he hoisted her up onto the horse, a scarf or handkerchief of some sort was shoved into her mouth followed by a burlap bag coming down over her head. Dirt and fibers filled her nose and mouth. The taste of salty sweat burned on her tongue. She coughed and gagged. He leaned in close to her ear. "Perhaps you will think twice about trying to escape if you cannot see where you are going."

Violet tried to cry out, frustration and fear battling for prominence, but all it did was make her gag more. She felt herself being pulled roughly up onto the horse. Her arms felt as if they would be pulled from their sockets.

Before she was even seated, Mr. McPhail dug his heels into the horse's sides and set the horse going. She lay over the horse, her feet dangling over the side. Violet hoped and prayed she would fall off, but he held her firmly in place.

After what seemed forever, the horse slowed and then came to a stop. Mr. McPhail got off the horse and pulled Violet down after him. Her legs crumbled when her feet hit the ground. He hauled her to her feet, practically dragging her beside him. Little pinpricks began to poke at her feet as the blood began to flow through them again, allowing her to run alongside him, instead.

They came to a stop. Violet felt the bag come off her head. Her eyes darted about, trying to see where he had taken her. Before she could get her bearing, she was pushed into a carriage. As she sat up, she turned and looked at him in the doorway. Her eyes widened as she took the handkerchief from her mouth. "It was you."

His face was slack, but it was his eyes that gave him away. She was surprised she had not noticed it sooner. The cold, emotionless stare was what had been so familiar to her when she saw him through their carriage door almost a fortnight ago.

"What was me?"

"You were the highwayman. The one that shot at our driver." A cold fear moved up her spine.

His vile smile stretched his face. "I did not keep everyone away from you for all of those years, just to have you run off as soon as I returned. I had worked too hard." He pulled himself up into the carriage and banged on the roof.

Violet felt the carriage jerk and she realized someone else was with them. "Help me! Help me, please!" she yelled. She banged her fist on the window, but the carriage only picked up more speed.

He laughed loudly. "Bang and holler till you are hoarse, my dear. He is getting plenty of blunt to drive and pay us no mind."

Violet sat up on the bench across from him, curling herself into the corner farthest from him. "You will not get away with this. I will never marry you." Her voice was lacking bravado. "My father will come for me."

She hoped her father would come. He had realized his distance over the years and vowed to make amends. But would he be able to change so quickly? Her breath slowed. The duke would come for her. They were friends. She believed they may even be more, but she would not suggest such a thing to Mr. McPhail.

"Oh, yes. Your father will come." His voice sarcastic. "You always have been slightly delusional, Violet. Your father has not cared about you in ten years. Why would he start now? There is no one who will come for you. *No one.*"

Violet wanted to lurch across the coach and pound her fists on him—scream that he was wrong. But as she sat watching the countryside go by, she could not yell or fight because a small part of her worried he was right.

"And, should someone find you, it will be too late. Your family is already burdened with scandal. This will ensure no one will yoke their names with yours."

Her throat felt tight and her breathing was choppy, but she refused to give him the satisfaction he would surely get by seeing her cry.

"I should rather be an old maid than marry you." She glared at him, hoping he would sense how much she had come to loathe him.

"You will not live long enough to be an old maid. Is death truly better than a life with me?"

Violet shrank back. She did not doubt he would follow through on this threats. "What did you mean, you kept people away from me?"

He grinned at her. "Who do you think told everyone of your mother's unsavory past? I admit it was a risk, as I planned to marry you all along. Such a rumor could taint me by association. But I realized when I came to your rescue and married you in spite of your sorted past, many would see me as the hero. The gentleman who saved his dear friend from spinsterhood." He sighed, his mouth pulled down in a slight frown, his eyes moist. "Once we were married, I could begin to circulate the true story and the fudge would be put to rest."

Violet stared at him. If she did not know him better, she would have thought him sympathetic to her situation. How had she been so deceived? All those years she had believed him a friend and a confidant. The one person she could trust and even love. Violet's stomach burned. There were times she believed Rose had been the one to share their family secret.

A shiver shook her body as the rush of the events subsided. The carriage was cold and she had not been wearing even a shawl. "Why did you not place any bricks in the carriage? It is freezing in here." She rubbed her hands up and down her arms, unable to completely eliminate the gooseflesh.

Mr. McPhail shrugged. "I provide for my wife. When you are such, I shall see the carriage is warmed."

"I'd rather freeze." Violet turned toward the door, calculating if she could wrench it open before he got to her. She glanced over at him. His vile smile told her he wanted her to try to escape. She shuttered again, but this time not because of the cold. "Where are we going?" Violet's voice dropped in tone. She would not allow him the joy he would receive from scaring her.

"Why, to Gretna. I painted such a lovely picture to the duke, I thought we would follow through with it. This time, it will be your signature on the document. I can't believe your sister could not make the last one more convincing."

"Rose?" Bile traveled up Violet's throat. Her sister had helped Mr. McPhail? Why would she do such a thing?

A deep chuckle rumbled from his chest. "I never realized how conniving your sister could be. But when her title was in jeopardy she became quite mercenary."

Violet shook her head. "I don't believe it."

"I do not know the whole of her story. She came to me at the inn in Shearsby the evening last and told me you had changed your mind and wished to marry me. I knew she was shamming it and I told her as much." He smirked. "But what do I care as to her reasons. I am only in it for what I will get and that is you. I have always wanted you or at the very least your dowry. Although, it will be quite the coup if your sister succeeds and the duke becomes my brother."

Closing her eyes, Violet huddled in the corner, closing in on herself as much as she could to keep warm. She did not wish to hear any more. Each statement only brought more despair. And she could not take any more of it. The longer they traveled, the less hope she had of being rescued. Sleep seemed her only escape. Perhaps when she awoke, it would all have been a bad dream.

Violet shifted, the noises arousing her senses. Horses nickering and men shouting to one another sounded in her ears. She cracked an eye open, at first not realizing where she was. All at once the events from last night crowded her brain.

Violet squeezed her eyes shut again. The carriage was no

longer moving. From the noise, she guessed they were changing horses. Her stomach growled loudly.

"I have some bread and cheese if you would care for some. But do not think you are leaving this carriage. I do not want to risk you escaping or worse informing someone of your plight."

Violet opened her eyes fully but stayed tucked in the corner. She wanted to refuse his offer, but the smell of the bread wafted across the carriage and her stomach rumbled again. Her fear of him hurting her, or worse, kept her in her place.

He broke off a hunk and tossed it across the carriage at her. "If I were going to ravage you, I would have done so while you were sleeping."

Her eyes widened as she looked down at the front of her dress.

"I know you do not believe me, but I do have some morality left in me." He looked around the carriage. "And there will be time enough for that once we are man and wife."

She picked up the bread and began to nibble at the crust. She could barely feel her fingers, she was so cold. "You forget that I have no intention of becoming your wife."

He smirked at her. "We shall see how noble and indignant you are in a few days' time."

"My father will have come for me before then."

His eyes flicked to the door and back. "No one is coming for you. The only one who knows where we are going is your sister. And she is too determined to marry the duke to share our secret."

Violet moved back into her corner, afraid that what he said was true and no one would be coming for her. She had trusted Mr. McPhail for all those years and he had only been pretending to be her friend. Even her own sister had betrayed her. How could she believe a man she had only known a few weeks would care enough to come for her if she could be so deceived by those she thought she knew best?

CHAPTER 27

Tad entered the Long Gallery with two cups in his hands. His eyes immediately went to the chair he had left Miss Violet seated in. His smile dropped when he saw it occupied by someone else. He scanned the crowd, looking for her, but could not see her anywhere. The baron sat to the side, speaking with his Aunt Standish. Tad moved over to them, his gaze still searching the room.

"Lord Winslow, I fetched a drink for your daughter, but I cannot seem to locate her. Do you know where she might be?"

The baron squinted into the mass of people. "I'm sorry, Your Grace. I do not see her. Perhaps Rose knows where she is."

Tad spotted Miss Allen speaking with several gentlemen long the wall. When he reached her, both of the men bowed. He nodded to them both before inclining his head toward Miss Allen. "May I steal Miss Allen away for a moment, gentlemen? I shall return her to your sides, shortly." She shook her head lightly, but he ignored her. "Just a quick word, Miss Allen."

When they were out of range of listening ears, Tad leaned in. "Have you seen Miss Violet? No one seems to know where she is."

Frowning, Rose shook her head. "I do not know, Your Grace. I have not seen her since dinner."

Tad smiled politely and led her back to the gentlemen she had been conversing with. "Thank you for your time, Miss Allen." He bowed. "Gentlemen."

Where could Violet be? Would she have retired to her rooms without telling him first? She did not look unwell when he left her. He had only been gone for a few minutes. Ten at the most. His heart picked up its pace and his palms became moist beneath his gloves.

Jes approached him. "Tad, you do not look well. What is the matter?"

"Have you seen Miss Violet, Jes? No one seems to know where she is." Did his voice sound as panicked as he felt?

Jes looked around. "I heard her speaking with Miss Allen a moment ago." Jes turned back to him. "I thought Miss Allen told Violet to meet you in the orangery."

"I never told anyone to have Miss Violet meet me anywhere." Tad turned and walked briskly to the hothouse, paying no mind to the beautifully arranged lanterns hanging about. He moved about the pathway, looking in every niche he passed. After returning to his starting place, Tad started around a second time. This time looking for anything out of place.

He stopped at the doors to the terrace, looking at the blackness outside. He put his hand on the handle, but the door pushed open without turning it. Tad pushed down on the lever, but it did not move. Tad looked at the side and noticed something pushed into the frame, prohibiting the door from latching. He pulled out the sliver of wood, allowing it to close tightly. Looking closer at the door, Tad saw black smudges marring the bottom.

With no evidence of Miss Violet, Tad went back into the gallery.

Jes was waiting by the doorway. "Did you find her? Was she waiting for you?"

Shaking his head, Tad moved farther into the room. "No. Something had been wedged into the door so it would not latch tightly." He spotted Miss Allen, talking with a different group of gentlemen. As if sensing his eyes on her, Miss Allen turned.

"Jes, please ask Miss Allen to join us in my study."

Jes nodded and hurried in Miss Allen's direction.

Tad found his aunts chatting with Lady Crunn, Mrs. Bower and Lady Billings. "Good evening, ladies. I hoped I might have a word with Lady Rachel and Lady Mayfield?" The women excused themselves and moved with Tad into the corridor. "Please meet me in my study. I need to fetch my uncle, Dawson and Lord Winslow." Both women looked at him with creased brows but continued on to the library.

Once they were all gathered, the men stood about the room, while his aunts settled on the couch by the fire.

"Why did you ask us here?" Lord Mayfield grumbled. "I had found myself a perfectly quiet corner."

Tad paced in front of the fireplace. "I'm sorry, Uncle, but I am afraid something is amiss and I thought your wisdom may be needed."

The earl stood a little taller. "Well, in that case. There is no need to apologize, lad." He found a seat close to the low burning fire.

Lady Mayfield sat forward. "What is wrong?"

The door pushed open and Jes entered the room with Miss Allen following behind. Jes looked to Tad and was turning to leave. "You may stay Jes. Miss Allen may find it more comfortable with you here." Jes settled herself in a chair in the alcove opposite the fireplace.

Miss Allen stood alone, looking between the men. Her father patted the seat next to him. "Come, sit here, child. You are not in trouble. His Grace just has some questions." Rose walked slowly to her father, her gaze never leaving Tad's face.

"Miss Allen, do you know where your sister is?"

Rose shook her head. "I already told you, Your Grace. I have not seen my sister since dinner. Perhaps she went to her room with a headache."

Tad resumed his pacing. "I have someone checking her chambers now. Miss Allen, it has come to my attention you were talking with your sister in the gallery." He stopped his pacing and folded his arms across his chest. "Someone is telling Banbury stories and I intend to find out who it is."

Miss Allen stared for a moment. Then she turned to her father. "Papa, are you going to let him imply I am not speaking the truth?"

The baron patted her hand. "Did you speak to your sister in the gallery?"

Before she could speak, Tad interjected. "Before you deny, Miss Allen, I have several witnesses to attest to the fact that you were, indeed, speaking to your sister." He may only have one, but he was sure if he asked everyone in attendance, he could find others who had witnessed the interaction.

Miss Allen's shoulders dropped. "Very well. Yes. I spoke to my sister."

"And what did you speak about?"

Miss Allen's eyes flicked from each man in the room "I do not believe it is any of your concern."

"It became my concern when one of my guests went missing, Miss Allen." The door opened and Baker stepped inside.

"Is she in her chambers?"

"No, Your Grace. Nor is she in any of the public rooms." The butler bowed and left the room.

Tad focused his attention on Miss Allen. "What did you speak about?"

Miss Allen bit her bottom lip, her attention firmly on the lace on her gown. But when she looked up there was no trace of trepidation. "She told me she had changed her mind about Mr. McPhail and had decided to marry him after all. I thought she would wait until morning to seek him out, but she must have decided to leave immediately."

"That is a bag of moonshine, child." Lord Winslow laid a hand on his daughter's arm. "Violet would never go back to the blackguard." He glanced at Tad. "I may not know Violet as well as I once did. But of that I am sure."

The color drained from Miss Allen's face, but she said nothing.

"Thunder an' turf, Rose. Tell us what you know!" The baron shouted.

"Mr. McPhail took her. She was ruining everything. He said if we worked together, we would both get what we desired."

Tad wanted to grab Miss Allen by the arms and shake her. "Where, Miss Allen? Where did he take her?"

Miss Allen stared at him. "If I tell you, you will marry her. I heard you ask Papa. And then what of me? No gentleman will have me after this."

"No gentleman will have you if you don't tell me." Tad thundered.

Lord Mayfield stirred in his seat. "The longer you wait, my dear, the farther away she gets. I think you know your chances here are gone. Now is the time to do right by your sister. Tell him where they are headed."

Miss Allen dropped her head in her hands. "To Gretna. He is taking her to Gretna Green."

Lady Mayfield stood. "We should be getting back to the guests. Speculation will begin soon if it has not already. Rachel and I will see to the guests. The party will be coming to a close soon. We will make your excuses and see them on their way." She walked a few steps before pausing. "Come Rachel. You also, Jes." She eyed her husband. "You may stay here and help. It is not as if people will suspect anything if you are gone."

Lady Rachel stopped in front of Miss Allen. "Come with us. We need as many as we can to return to the party. But I expect a widely publicized headache to drive you to your chambers shortly after we return. You need not speak of anything else." Tad had never heard his aunt speak so harshly.

Once the ladies departed, Tad turned his attention to Lord Winslow and his uncle. "I am in need of assistance as I am unfamiliar with this country. Where do we begin looking for them?"

"We should begin in the village. Perhaps they have not left yet." Lord Mayfield stood.

Lord Winslow stood as well, his head shaking. "I disagree. I believe we should leave for Gretna straight away. They already have at least an hour head start. We do not know if they are on horseback or in a carriage. It will take too much time to stop at every inn along the way" His body slumped. "How could I have allowed this to happen?"

Tad put a hand on the man's back. "We both can shoulder the blame for this, later. For now, we need to make decisions." Tad looked at Dawson. "I am inclined to go with Lord Mayfield."

The baron opened his mouth to protest, but Tad held up his hand to stop him. "I want nothing more than to head out for Gretna immediately. But we have no information. Perhaps we can find someone who saw something. It would give us a very slight advantage." Even as he said the words, his chest was squeezing tighter. What if they were too late because he chose to go into the village? "She is alone with him. What will he do to her?" He could not think on it anymore without going mad.

Dawson stepped forward. "I am inclined to agree with Lord Winslow, Tad. It is late and the chances of us finding a witness seem unlikely. If we went on horseback, straight for Gretna, we could possibly get there first and await their arrival. If we go from town to town searching for them, I am afraid we may miss them altogether."

Tad nodded as the wisdom of Dawson's plan settled on him. "Is everyone agreed?" The men all nodded. The baron looked drawn and worn. Perhaps it would not be wise for the man to go along if he was unwell. "This will be a hard ride. If either of you would rather remain behind...?"

"Nonsense. I will be there for my daughter. Now we are wasting time." Winslow hurried toward the door.

Tad glanced at his uncle.

"Do not even think of leaving me behind. I have very few opportunities to be truly useful. You may be the duke, but you will need me. Or at least my title. You don't yet have the bluster of a duke."

Tad pulled a wooden box from his desk drawer before they all retrieved their greatcoats and gloves. Then they all headed out into the cold night air.

CHAPTER 28

The group rode into Gretna just as the sun was setting on the third day. They had pushed their horses hard, stopping only to get fresh mounts and food. The blacksmith shop sat on the outskirts of town. They inquired if the man had married anyone fitting Mr. McPhail's description.

"Haven't married a soul for a fortnight, at least. The colder weather seems to make couples think twice."

Tad slumped against the wall, rubbing his eyes with the palms of his hands. He believed they had traveled faster than Mr. McPhail, but he had not been able to rid himself of the worry they would be too late. Now, they could find an inn and wait out Mr. McPhail. And Violet. Tad's face heated when he thought of them traveling together. If that man had harmed her in any way, Tad would kill him.

They found the nearest inn and stabled the horses. All of the men looked haggard and worn, but Tad was especially worried about Mayfield. The man hobbled to the chair nearest the fire and sat down. He rubbed at his back. "I have not expended myself like that in..." He paused as he thought. "Never actually. Have not had a reason to do so, until now."

"Uncle, why don't you get some rest? We may not see Violet for several days, yet." He sighed. "And you look exhausted."

"Pon rep, lad. None of us look the pinkest of pinks." He settled into the chair, his brows raised.

Tad chuckled. "Indeed. But the fact remains, we do not know when they will arrive. We will need to take shifts watching the blacksmith."

Dawson stepped forward. "I will take the first shift." He raised his hand to cut off Tad's protests. "I believe we have at least several hours on them if they are on horseback. Go get some sleep so you will be ready for him when they arrive."

Tad nodded reluctantly, as did the other two gentlemen.

"I only need a few hours. Then I will come to relieve you." His eyes burned behind their lids. He moved to his saddlebags he had draped over a nearby chair and removed the wooden box. He opened it and removed a pistol from the velvet lining, handing it to his friend. "We know the kind of man he is. We should be prepared." He then handed him a small pouch containing the powder and balls.

Dawson took the pistol and placed it in his waistband. He placed the pouch in the pocket of his great coat. "Now, go get some rest so one of us will be able to shoot straight."

Tad smiled and moved to the stairway as Dawson vanished through the doorway.

Tad squinted in the darkness at the area surrounding the black-smith shop. A small copse of trees sat off to the side. There were several small buildings scattered around, but none of them offered the view of the comings and goings at the blacksmith's. Tad moved toward the trees, knowing Dawson would be there.

Creeping quietly along the tree line, he peered into the dense foliage, looking for any sign of his friend. He huffed quietly. While it was best Dawson was not easily seen from the road, it was less convenient for Tad. Taking one more step, Tad stopped when he heard the cock of a pistol behind him.

"Turn around with your hands where I can see them," Dawson growled.

Raising his hand slightly, Tad turned around slowly. Dawson took a step forward, peering at Tad. "Drats, man. Perhaps next time you could call out or something. I almost shot you."

"Shall I alert the entire village to my presence? It hardly seems like the best course of action, considering."

Dawson looked terrible. He wore a full beard and his eyes were sunken and drooped. "I was not expecting you back so soon. Are you well rested?"

Tad shrugged. "No, but I got enough."

"You do not look much better than when I left," Dawson growled.

It had only been two hours since he and Dawson separated, but Tad thought he may go mad if he waited any longer. "I wasn't able to sleep. When I think..." he paused. "I am better here, where I know I can help when I am needed." He took the gun from Dawson's hand. "Now it is time for you to go and sleep. I am glad my uncle and Lord Winslow came with us, but I confess I am not confident in their abilities with a pistol."

Dawson chuckled lowly. "I will be back before dawn."

"Thank you, my friend." Tad clasped him on the shoulder.

Once Dawson left, Tad found a tree with a thick, low-hanging branch. Most of the leaves had blown free of the tree, making it unacceptable during the daylight. But in the inky blackness surrounding him, it would be the right spot. Tad wrapped his black greatcoat tighter around his body, both to block out the cold and to better make him invisible on his perch.

He stared up at the sky through the barren branches. It was a clear night and many of the stars were out, bringing on thoughts of his father.

Would he be disappointed in him? His father had taught him honor was all a man had when everything else was gone. Tad had lived by that belief his entire life--even while serving aboard a British ship. But he was not sure if his father would approve of his decision to put aside Miss Allen in favor of her sister. Tad narrowed his eyes at the building in front of him. At least his father would approve of rescuing Violet.

He sat there for hours. No one came or left the blacksmith's shop. As the first hints of pink began to color the sky, Tad dropped from his roost, his legs crumbling when he hit the ground.

Pushing himself up to kneeling, he saw Dawson walking down the road from the village. His hat was pulled low and his collar was up as he hunched against the breeze.

Tad stretched his legs out in front of him, leaning his back against the tree. The low bushes lining the road gave him cover, but they also blocked his view. He shifted his position until he found a hole in the brush. It was a narrow view, but enough to tell them if McPhail arrived. Dawson crawled over next to him. His face was cleanly shaven and his eyes brighter.

"You look much improved this morning."

Dawson grinned. "I cannot say the same for you." He looked toward the shop. "Any activity last night?"

Tad shook his head.

"Why don't you let me keep watch for a while?"

"I will not be able to sleep. Every time I close my eyes I see him, grasping her arm...." He rubbed at his eyes with his palms. "No. I am better here." Tad folded his arms across his chest.

Dawson nudged him over and sat down. "Go eat something, then. And get yourself warmed up before you return."

"I had warmed up that spot you just sat in," Tad grumbled.

"And I am keeping it warm for when you return." Dawson waved his hand toward the village. "Now go."

Darkness settled in on the little village and still there had been no sign of McPhail and Violet. Tad pulled out his pocket watch and check the time, even though it was nearly impossible to read in the darkness.

"Would you stop checking your watch? Nothing has changed since you checked five minutes ago."

Tad grumbled. "It was *seven* minutes, actually."

Dawson released a heavy sigh.

"What if we were wrong? What if Rose was just playing us for fools, again? What if they are halfway to the continent and we have wasted two days by sitting here waiting? I do not know if I can stand it any longer." Tad put his hands against the trunk behind him and pushed himself up. He walked from one tree to the next, rubbing the back of his neck until it burned.

"If you must pace, at least button your coat so your white cravat is not glowing in the moonlight."

Tad yanked his greatcoat around him, mumbling words his mother would not approve. The clap of horse hoofs spun him around as he instinctively ducked below the foliage.

Dawson crouched beside him, both staring as the coach came to a stop in front of the shop. In the darkness, it was difficult to make out the figure, but it was definitely a man. He stood at the carriage door waiting for another person. A woman's head emerged and when she paused the gentleman jerked her down the steps.

When she straightened, Tad breathed out. "It is her."

"Are you sure? I cannot make out their faces in the darkness."

Tad leaned forward even more. "There is no doubt in my mind." The back door of the blacksmith's shop opened and a small boy ran toward town.

"What is our plan?" Dawson put his hand on the pistol grip.

"I will go around front and you come in from the back. We will block his escape."

Dawson nodded his agreement. "I will go for the constable once he is subdued."

"Perhaps," Tad said.

The two men soundlessly left their hiding spot, walking together down the street until they reached the building. Then they each went in a different direction. Tad stopped just short of the door and checked his pistol. Then he lunged, throwing the door open.

McPhail and Violet both turned at his entrance, while the blacksmith did not appear surprised. Violet's face was ashen. From where Tad stood, he could see the knife McPhail held to her back.

"Stop. You cannot marry this couple." Tad glared at Mr. McPhail.

The blacksmith looked from Tad to the couple in front of him. "Why not? Are you her father or brother?"

"No. But he is forcing her to marry against her will. I can see the knife he has pressed to her back from here."

McPhail pulled Violet closer. "This is none of your concern, Your Grace. I suggest you leave now." Violet let out a soft whimper as he pressed the knife to her back.

Just then Dawson appeared behind the blacksmith. Tad shook

his head at his friend, hoping he would understand the unspoken directions.

"I am afraid I can't do that, McPhail. You see, unlike you, I did ask her father for his consent to marry Violet."

Violet's head spun back to look at him. Her eyes were wide and she bit her lip. He smiled at her, even as he wanted to kill the man next to her.

"I asked her first and she chose me. I cannot help it that her father is impressed with your money and title. But Violet chose me." Mr. McPhail growled the last words.

"Is this true, Miss? Do you wish to marry this man?" The blacksmith stared at her.

Tad saw her flinch when McPhail's knife pushed deeper. A small red mark slowly blossomed on her back where the knife rested. The blackguard had pierced her skin.

In four long strides, Tad reached her side, knocking the knife to the ground with the handle of his gun. McPhail gasped and bent to pick it up, and as he rose, Tad leveled the gun at the man's head.

Pulling Violet behind him, he turned slightly to ensure she was unharmed. McPhail lunged with his knife held high over his head.

A shot rang out and Mr. McPhail crumpled to the ground with a moan. Smoke swirled from the barrel of Dawson's gun.

Tad stared at Mr. McPhail as he writhed on the ground, holding his shoulder. "I am not sure I would have just winged him." He flicked a glance at Dawson, who shrugged.

Just then the door opened. Winslow and Mayfield entered with a man and boy following behind. They looked from McPhail to Tad and back to McPhail.

"The man lunged at His Grace with a knife. This other gentleman had no choice but to shoot him, constable." The blacksmith spoke as if people were shot in his shop every day.

The constable bent and grasped McPhail by his uninjured arm, dragging him to his feet. "I will see to him, Your Grace." The constable pulled him out the door.

Tad gave a single nod and Dawson followed the constable out of the shop.

Lord Winslow crossed to Violet, taking her in his arms. "Did he hurt you, Poppet?"

It was the exact question Tad wanted answered but had not had a chance to ask.

"I am well, Papa."

Tad remembered where she had been pierced by the knife. He pointed to it. "He cut you. We should send for a doctor to stitch it up."

She shook her head. "It is not necessary. Please, do not concern yourself."

Violet avoided looking at him. He ran a hand through his hair. Maybe Rose had been right and Violet had wanted to marry Mr. McPhail. Even as he thought it, he discounted it. If that were true, McPhail would not have needed a knife. Then she must be displeased with him.

Her father frowned. "Did he...?"

Violet shook her head fiercely. "We never left the carriage." Her face colored and her voice dropped to a whisper. "Except to use the privy." Dropping her gaze to her hands, a tear slipped down her cheek. "I am so sorry, Papa. I have ruined us yet again."

Her father patted her on the back awkwardly. "There, there. I am sure we can keep this from getting out."

"But, Papa. I was alone with him for days. Who would wish to align with us now?"

Tad stepped forward. "I would. My wishes have not changed."

Violet sniffed. "There is no need for the Canterbury tales now, Your Grace. I am safe."

Her father shook her head. "He is in earnest, Poppet. He asked for your hand almost a week past."

Tad moved toward her. "It is what I wanted to ask you on our turn about the orangery." He had hoped to have this conversation privately, but no one looked to be in a hurry to leave. "I love you, Violet." His eyes flicked to the blacksmith. "If you were to return a married lady, there would be nothing to be ruined."

Violet's eyes grew with every word he spoke. "You cannot mean it."

Tad raised his hand, placing it on her cheek, his thumb rubbing back and forth along her cheekbone. She closed her eyes and leaned into it. He smiled. "Violet? Will you be my wife?"

Keeping her cheek in the palm of his hand, she nodded. New tears pooled in the bottom of her lids. "I love you, too."

"Then let's marry you two." The blacksmith smiled and stepped up to his anvil. "You have the witnesses, I see."

"Well?" Tad pulled his hand from her cheek and instead grabbed both of her hands in his. "I realize it is not what you had imagined for your wedding, but shall we do this?"

Her eyes glittered and a giggle escaped her lips. "I don't care where we get married, just that we get married."

Tad tilted his head to the side. "If we marry here, we could travel back to Shearsby together—as husband and wife." He felt warm as a smile spread across his face.

The door creaked and Dawson walked in. He nodded his head at Tad before moving to stand next to the older gentlemen. He leaned to the side and whispered to Mayfield. "Are they going to do it?"

Violet squeezed Tad's hands. "Yes, I believe we are."

The anvil priest began and before Tad knew it he declared them man and wife. They both signed their names to the paper and it was done. The ceremony was much quicker than he imagined, but in the end, he was married to the woman he loved. Turning, he lifted her up and spun in a circle. He buried his face in her neck, kissing her earlobe then down the slope of her neck to her shoulder. Pulling back slightly, he whispered, "It is official, my love. We are married."

Violet dropped her head back and laughed happily.

Tad's stomach flopped, his chest tightened. Every part of his body jumped and tingled. In a matter of minutes, his entire life had changed and he could not imagine it being any different.

As he set her down, everyone crowded around them, clapping them on the back and offering congratulations. As a group, they walked back to the village.

The lords started up the stairs toward their room. Tad and Dawson had only arranged for one room because they were taking turns watching the blacksmith shop. It had seemed the best plan when they arrived in Gretna nearly a week ago.

Dawson clapped Tad on the back. "If you need me, I will be sleeping in the stables. Rest well, my friend." He inclined his head to Violet. "And to you, Your Grace. I will see you both on the morrow."

Before Tad could object, he walked out the door of the inn and left them standing in the public room.

They stared at each other, neither speaking.

Tomorrow they would need to begin their journey back to Morley Park. His Aunt Mayfield was surely having apoplexy over the ball they had missed. But for now, he intended to enjoy every moment of his time alone with his wife.

Stooping down, he put one arm around her waist and the other under her knees, sweeping her up into his arms.

Her eyes widened and a quiet gasp fled her lips. But then her body relaxed and she wrapped her arms around his neck.

"This time I will not be leaving you at the foot of the stairs, Violet."

He thought his knees might give out when she whispered against his neck. "I would be extremely disappointed if you did, Tad."

EPILOGUE

V iolet sat in her favorite seat near the fireplace in the Red Library, her legs tucked up underneath her. Sleet pelted against the window outside. A rug was tucked about her body and a book lay open in her lap. Turning a page, her eye caught the glimmer of silver from her wedding band.

"May I come in?" Her sister's timid voice broke the silence.

Rose stepped into the room, her eyes never leaving the floor.

"Of course. I had hoped we would be able to talk before you left with Papa." Violet patted the edge of the settee when Rose flicked her gaze to it.

Rose sat down, frowning at her lap. "I'm sorry, Violet. I have not been kind to you of late." She frowned. "But you promised you did not love him. You ruined everything for me. What else was I to do?"

Violet took a shallow breath and fiddled with the pages of her book. "I am sorry, also. It was not my intent to fall in love with him. And I never dreamed he would love me back. What was I to do?"

"Step aside. You should have pushed him away. Did you ever try to sway him toward me?" Her nose flared before she took a long slow breath. "There is nothing for it. I am sorry I wronged you. But you wronged me first. I believe that makes us even." Rose straightened her shoulders, raising her chin a fraction.

Violet swallowed hard, recognizing there would not be a reconciliation at present. "Thank you, Rose. It must have been very difficult for you to say those things."

Rose stood and moved toward the doorway. Before she reached it Violet spoke louder. "Even if I had not been here, he would not have loved you, Rose. Yes, he would have married you, but there would be no love."

Rose stayed with her back to Violet. "At least I would have a title. Now I have nothing, because of you."

"I think you deserve to have someone love you, Rose. I am sorry you don't believe it yourself."

Rose did not reply but continued out the door.

Violet dropped her head into her hands. They had much work to do before their relationship was mended. Violet had an idea, which she hoped her husband would approve and her sister would agree to. But neither seemed very likely.

A kiss on her neck brought a giggle to her lips. "Good morning, my love." He sat down on the couch next to her and pulled her onto his lap, wrapping his arms around her waist. "How are you settling in?"

She traced her finger along the lines on his brow. Her heart racing when he closed his eyes and his breath hissed out between his lips.

"The last time you did that, I did not see you for days. I hope you do not think that is an option this time."

She smiled even though his eyes remained closed. "You could not keep me away for an afternoon, much less several days."

He opened his eyes and grabbed hold of her hand, kissing her open palm. "Let's cancel the ball and send all of our relations on their way." He wiggled his eyebrows at her. "We could spend our last evening here, just the two of us."

She pulled her hand from his and put it on his chest. "Your aunts went to a great deal of trouble to reschedule this ball. They would not be happy if we canceled it a second time."

Tad sighed and fingered one of the curls hanging at her cheek. "Very well. I will concede, but only because I will have you to myself for the next week as we travel to Town."

She leaned in and kissed him before resting her head on his shoulder, running her fingers along his cravat. "What if it was not just the two of us?"

"And why would it be otherwise?" He pushed her gently away from him, catching her gaze with his.

She dropped her eyes, unable to look at him when she told him of her idea. He would not like it, she was certain, but she believed he would agree because he loved her. Violet shuttered at the thought. She would never have guessed such a thing possible.

"I would like to sponsor Rose in London this season." She bit her bottom lip while she waited for his protest. When none came, she glanced up at him through her lashes.

His eyes were wide and his mouth hung open. "But why? After everything...Why can your father not..." He stopped and continued to stare at her.

Placing her finger beneath his chin, she pushed his mouth closed. "It is because of everything. I am not blameless in the events of the past fortnight." His mouth opened and she placed her finger over his lips. "She was your intended. While I did not try to steer you in my direction, I cannot say I did not secretly hope it would happen. I believe I first fell in love with you after you followed me home. I had not felt so much caring in a very long time." She played with a button on his waistcoat. "Regardless, Rose felt I was taking something which was hers."

"I am not some trinket to be fought over. I had a voice in this also." He sounded slightly petulant.

"Yes, you did. I am not implying she should have no punishment, but neither do I wish to constantly be at odds with her. She is my sister. London will be difficult enough for both of us, it would be nice to have an ally there with me."

"But will she be an ally or an enemy?" His brow creased. He was not voicing concerns Violet had not already asked herself.

"I must try. Can you not understand?" Was it even possible for him to understand when she did not wholly understand it herself? When she thought of what Rose had done, her stomach churned and her hands began to shake. But the thought of not forgiving her sister had the same effect.

He nodded. "If it will make you happy, then I will agree. But..." He held her at arm's length. "Only if she travels to London with your father. She may join us once we have settled in Shearsby House."

She wrapped her arms around his neck, snuggling into him. "Thank you, Tad. I knew you would agree." She pulled back and wiped at the errant tears in her eyes.

Settling herself back onto the couch, she picked up her book again. Tad growled and pulled her closer to him. "I just gave you what you wanted and you abandon me? Were you only using me to get what you desired, Your Grace?"

Violet chuckled and snuggled into his side. He brought his arm around her back and rested it on her upper arm, tracing circles on her bare skin with his finger. His chest rose with a long, deep sigh as he dropped his head to the back of the couch.

"I was thinking."

He cracked one eye open and looked at her.

"Perhaps while we are in town, you could introduce Rose to some of your friends."

"You are the devil to pay, are you not, my love?" He chuckled as he placed a kiss on the top of her head. "But your plan has one fatal flaw."

"Oh?" She lifted her head up to look at him.

"It infers I have friends in town. The only friends I will have in London are Lord and Lady Mayfield, your father, Dawson and you. And Dawson already knows Rose. Therein lies the problem."

She swatted him lightly on the chest. "You have met many people here. And you will begin attending Parliament. Besides, I am convinced all of society will adore you. How could they not?" She played with the ends of his cravat. "And once you have gained all those friendships, you can point them in the direction of our sitting room." Her cheek bounced as his chuckle rumbled in his chest.

"If they become my true friends, I could never wish Rose upon them."

"You liked her well enough, before...." Violet sighed. "She is not undesirable. I believe most gentlemen find her very pleasant to look upon. And if you find someone with plenty of gingerbread and a title, she may just forgive us."

Tad laughed. "You win, my love. Please no more scheming."

She patted his chest. Curling back into his side, she opened her book once more.

Pushing her slightly away, he stood up and pulled the book from her hands.

"I was reading." She grabbed for the book, but he placed it on the table out of her reach.

"If you are reading, you will miss my surprise." His eyes twinkled and rubbed his hands together. "I almost forgot about it. Although, I am confident my surprise is much better than yours was."

She tilted her head to the side, narrowing her eyes at him. "My surprise was not so bad." Her eyes widened and she clapped her hands together. "Now tell me. What is it?"

"Wait here. I will be back." He walked to the door and went into the hallway.

Violet sat up on the settee, scooting to the edge of the seat as she craned her neck to watch him return.

When he entered she could not help admiring him. His tall, lean body walked with such elegance and grace. In his hands, he carried a hatbox. It shook ever so slightly as he walked toward her.

"You bought me a new bonnet?" Her brow furrowed. A gentleman had never purchased a bonnet for her. A gentleman had never purchased anything for her. She smiled widely. "Oh, thank you. This is very generous."

As he got closer, he shook his head. "I would not advise you to put this on your head. It will not turn out well."

He set the box on her lap, it bounced and shook almost falling to the floor before Tad caught it and placed it back in her lap.

"What?" She had no notion of what he was giving her. It did not feel like a bonnet.

He laughed. "I think you should open it before it opens itself."

With Tad holding the base, she lifted the top with both hands. A furry black head peeked up over the rim. "It's a puppy." She squealed like a little girl, laughing when it launched itself out of the box and into her arms.

His fur was silky soft with a patch of white over one eye and one surrounding his little tail. She lifted him up to her and he nuzzled into her neck, licking her earlobes and making her laugh again.

Tad reached over and took the box away, scowling. "I thought I was the only one allowed to do such things."

The puppy wagged its tail with such force, its whole body wiggled. It yipped and lunged, covering Violet's face with licks. She looked over at him. "A puppy? But you find them so objectionable."

He scratched the dog between the ears, earning him an excited lick from the imp. Tad shrugged, his face pinking slightly. "You mentioned several times that you liked them. And while I find the little beasts objectionable, I want only to make you happy." He winked at her and her stomach fluttered. "I will concede. He is rather cute. But I can already foresee he will be the devil to tell."

"He makes me very happy. Can he come to London with us?"

"Of course, my dear. Do you have a name for him?"

Violet put her finger to her lips and gazed at the mural on the ceiling above them. A smile slid across her face. "I think I shall call him, Janus."

Tad's brows rose high on his forehead. "The god of beginnings. I approve." He bent down, kissing her cheek and then feathering kisses along her jawbone. "This is just the beginning, my love." He whispered into her neck.

Her whole body tingled as he pulled her closer to him. He pulled back when Janus began to lick at their chins. "Perhaps Até is a better name." He placed the dog on the floor at their feet.

Violet grinned. "Yes, the Goddess of Mischief also seems appropriate."

Tad pulled her back into his arms. "Now, what was I doing before we were interrupted?"

Violet giggled as he slowly leaned forward.

"Oh, yes. Now I remember." He closed the distance, covering her lips with his.

The End

AFTERWORD

Thank you so much for reading!
  Check out my other books-
  Mistaken Identity
  Reforming the Gambler

If you would like to keep up with new releases and current projects, you can follow me at:
  Amazon Author Page
  mindyburbidgestrunk.com
  Goodreads
  BookBub